WHERE SECRETS STAY

CherAnn Wright

Sleuthing Sloth Press

Front Cover Design By : Clarissa Kezen, CK Book Cover Designs

Editor : Sarah Jane Herbener

Contact Info: www.cherannwright.com

ISBN: 979-8-9886557-0-1 (hardcover), 979-8-9886557-1-8 (paperback), 979-8-9886557-2-5(audio), 979-8-9886557-3-2 (ebook)

First edition March 2023

10 9 8 7 6 5 4 3 2 1

———

To my ever-supportive husband, Paul, and my two amazing daughters, Brooklin and Ashley, thank you for your unwavering belief in me.

1962

Dark creeps in as Marge treks through the woods between her house and Dotty's, following a path they used often as teenagers to sneak out of the house. Most nights she has to use a flashlight, but tonight the moon is full. As she walks, the woods hold an eerie brightness. She has no trouble finding her path as a breeze whistles through the trees.

As young girls, Marge and Dotty had been taught that they could do anything a boy could, only better. Each came from a long line of strong-minded women, each of whom made her own way in this world, often without the help of a man. For them, most men had proved to be nothing more than an Achilles' heel, like a piece of candy that starts off sweet in the beginning but turns bitter and sour in the end. Now Marge and Dotty are full-grown women, and life and hard work have proved them to be as strong as their ancestors.

Earlier today, Dotty endured another of Tom's drunken beatings. As the stronger of the two, Marge has pleaded with Dotty on several occasions to get rid of him for good. Seeing her best friend's face and body looking like a used-up punching bag more than once was enough to convince Marge. But Tom's vile final act has sent them both over the edge. There is no way they can allow him to live.

The closer she gets to Dotty's, the more Marge senses a shift in the atmosphere. As she steps out of the woods, she sees a congregation of dark clouds lit by sporadic flashes of lightning—a change will soon come. The faint sound of thunder rumbles in the distance. It's as if the storm is coming to join them.

Marge pauses to watch the brewing storm. Then she takes in a deep breath and closes the rest of the distance to Dotty's house. She enters through the front door and sees Dotty waiting in the kitchen. Two shots of Jack Daniel's stand ready for them on the table.

Her arrival sets their plan in motion.

"Did you find us a rug big enough?" Marge pulls one of the shot glasses close.

"Yep, and it's under the shed waiting for us."

"What about the gun?"

"Right here." Dotty walks to the pantry just off the kitchen and then emerges with a shotgun clutched in both hands. She breaks open the gun and tilts it toward Marge. "I loaded it with the same buckshot Tom uses to kill deer."

"That'll work. You're going to be standing at close range, so it will be sufficient for a slow and painful end."

They look at each other and take deep inhales in unison as they raise their shot glasses, nod their heads to say they are ready, then down the whiskey.

Nerves and anticipation hang in the air as they pour themselves one more. They wait with patience for the man outside to drink himself into his usual coma. Night deepens into the sounds of frogs and crickets, telling them it is time.

They tiptoe out the back door, easing it closed. The humid air that greets them is thick and stale. Their skin turns clammy. By the time tonight's chore is done, their clothes will hug their bodies in displeasing ways; they don't care. The end of something ugly is within their reach.

Dotty's hands are clammy as she clutches Tom's shotgun close to her chest. They tiptoe across the yard as the drizzle mixes with the sweat trickling down Dotty's bruised cheek. They pause and watch the ego-sized toolshed for any signs of movement. Through the window, they see a lantern illuminating the ceiling, shadows dancing up and down the walls. It all seems to invite them to come inside, or perhaps it's warning them to stay away.

Peering in, they decide that the booze-soaked human inside is oblivious to everything. Marge pulls the rug from beneath the shed and rolls it out on the ground. To ensure accuracy, Dotty counts ten quick paces as she walks backward away from the rug, then rests the shotgun on the ground where she stands. She joins Marge, and they ease the side door open. The door creaks but he doesn't stir. They tiptoe inside. The worthless lump lies on a cot in the corner, his mouth gaping open, breathing out a sour stench that has been festering in his stomach from days of drinking. They grab his wrists and ankles and drag his dead weight across the shed and out the door. They have braced themselves for a struggle, but it's more like wrangling a sloth. They let his feet and arms thud onto the ground next to the old rug.

Tom surprises them by beginning to stand up. He teeters but then finds his footing, though his body sways in slow motion as he tries to remain vertical.

"What the fuck?" He slurs the words.

Dotty steps her ten paces backward without removing her eyes from Tom, and her fingers find the twelve-gauge. As she levels it, she's reminded of her swollen eye and busted lip. With a clear focus on what she has to do, her anxious inner chatter shifts; it feels like the calm before a storm. She plants her feet wide and twists her body to support her elbow on her hip. As she looks into her husband's eyes, he stares cruelly back at her.

Marge moves behind Dotty, holding her hands up to catch Dotty when the gun recoils. Feeling the adrenaline pump through her veins before she even pulls the trigger, Dotty hears Marge yell, "Do it!"

A clap of thunder rips through the air at the same time, the sounds joining. The butt of the gun sends Dotty's body backward into Marge, and she feels her heart thump. Immediately following the unison of sounds comes another flash of lightning, and they see that Tom's body has landed right where they'd planned it to be. Scattered across Tom's abdomen are red holes that expand, coloring his midriff.

Dotty and Marge roll him up in the rug, his head and feet protruding from the ends.

Dotty glares at Tom. He has stolen her happiness. Even worse, his evil has spread beyond their marriage and to her best friend, which is unforgivable. She tries for a moment to understand the rapid shifts of emotions flooding her mind as she looks at him. She thinks of the love that once was, but now it is nothing more than lies, bitterness, and hate. There is a pounding in her ears like a bass drum, so loud that she isn't sure if it's an echo of the shotgun blast or if it's her heart continuing to work overtime.

Marge steps around Dotty to walk toward Tom.

"I told you I would kill you," she says to him.

Marge's words seem to echo through the air as Dotty steps beside her. They stare into Tom's eyes. Neither sees repentance there. Just a deep hollowness that someone absent of a soul would possess.

Marge looks at Dotty and asks, "You ready to finish this?"

Dotty finds her voice. "I am." She leans down, her face close to her husband's, to speak her final words to him. "It's time for you to go to hell, Tom."

The AM radio in the filthy work shed behind them belts out the chorus of "Rhythm of the Rain" as they work. The sound effects embedded in the song and the thunder in the distance merge in harmony.

Dotty breathes in sweet victory. With her husband's last breath, her universe has shifted. What she does tonight is personal, yet she is doing the world a favor.

PART ONE

And, when you want something,
all the universe conspires in helping you to achieve it.
—Paulo Coelho, The Alchemist

CHAPTER ONE

Kevan Renee Copeland
Early Summer

"Dollar for your thoughts?"

I snap back into my physical world, naked and coming down from the high following the raw fucking I have just laid on this young man. "I don't need any money. Shhh."

Arms thrown over my head and eyes closed, I enjoy every sensation in my body as my breath slows back to normal. I allow myself to feel the smoothness of the satin sheets against my bare skin and to swim in the tingling sensations of my muscles, down my legs and arms. My whole body is as relaxed and loose as a bowl of Jell-O. I feel Kyle's eyes scan me up and down like he's some lust-struck puppy.

Kyle knows how to please a woman. Of course, a man twenty-three years old has all of his parts working at full throttle. This one is the bad-boy type I seem to find myself drawn to these days. I've found that distracting myself with temporary situations keeps me moving. It helps me avoid the things I don't want to face—relationships—memories.

I've also learned that, regardless of distractions, memories often have their own structures and rules. Regardless of attempts to forget them, escape is only temporary. Our minds behave as they want to. I often wonder why my mind misbehaves like a disobeying child who refuses to play nice. It opens and shuts doors deep within its walls, even though I tell my memories to either stay in or stay out. Some memories are less cruel by nature but are still unpleasant. The forbidden ones are hidden in little crypts far back in my mind, but they still threaten to surface. These keep me alone, not needing anyone. They're also why I welcome easy distractions.

Kyle is the love 'em and leave 'em type, and his witty personality can lighten any mood. He doesn't mind cuddling and having conversations, and he also doesn't require it. It's just part of his charm to keep a girl coming around until he's finished playing with her. Luckily for us both, I don't mind either way. Affection can be like a pair of slippers—it wears out and fades with time. I have never been one to wear slippers, nor have I ever needed them. How can you miss what you've never had? In fact, romantic relationships never make the book's cover in my life.

"Damn, that was good. What other tricks are you hiding?" Kyle rubs his hand up the inside of my thigh.

I grin. "I'll show you next time. I have to go."

"Okaaay." He drags out the word with pretended disgust, followed by a perfect pouty frown. "See you at school on Monday?"

"Only as my student. If the college finds out, it's my job."

"Grad student! I am a grown man. Fuck 'em if they can't handle it," he says, shrugging one shoulder.

"It would be very serious if they discovered it."

I bounce twice on my bottom to the end of the bed, in search of my clothes on the floor. I bend forward to retrieve my garments, ease back to standing with a straight spine, and end it with a hair toss, channeling my inner stripper. I feel sexier when I'm with Kyle.

As I slip my sundress over my head, he comes up from behind, wrapping his arms around me, pressing his naked body into mine. I breathe in his scent as I press my shoulders back into his chest muscles. I fumble with my panties and roll them upward as he leans down to kiss the side of my neck. After I pull away to grab my phone and keys from the nightstand, I give him a quick kiss on the cheek and dart toward the front door of his tiny apartment.

"Oh, come on! Look at him! He's standing at attention for you," Kyle jokes behind me.

I pause and turn. Kyle swings his hips from side to side, letting his penis swing back and forth. It thuds against his hip bones while making the sound a seal makes in an aquarium act. "Ow, ow, ow. Your little friend and I will be right here."

I laugh. "Hardly a *little* friend."

I step outside and a gentle breeze tickles my face. The horizon is swallowing the sun as dusk takes its turn. The start of summer is always my favorite time of year. Classes at the college are minimal, allowing me to focus on myself. I stroll down the front walk of the apartment building to my car.

Treating myself to a fuck-and-run is easier than worrying where things will go next. I'm fine with being alone most of the time; in fact, I bask in it. Isolation has a way of soothing something inside me. In fact, the quiet is my favorite orchestra. When silence becomes too loud, I hang out with Kyle, which is just fun, easy, and convenient.

At one point in my life, I convinced myself that I needed someone. That only led to an unsuccessful, boring marriage. It's a mistake I'll never make again. The entire marriage, from legal beginning to legal end, spanned two years, three months, and two days. It only lasted that long because divorce is slow torture. I kept the last name Copeland, because I had no desire to go back to living my life as a Mays. It isn't a last name I want to associate myself with.

I plunged myself into wedlock for the sake of escape and convenience. Where I grew up, getting married at seventeen, even without the consent of your parents, was legal. I did it to escape the home that had me trapped. However, it granted me a start toward a college degree—so it wasn't entirely useless.

Our marriage was as exciting as a pair of nun's undies—practical, predictable, and sexless. In its last year, I could count on my fingers how many times my ex-husband and I had sex. On the rare occasions that we did, intercourse lasted, from start to finish, a grand total of about twenty seconds. Combined, that's three minutes and thirty-three seconds of wedded bliss. Eventually I found that he wasn't living a nearly sexless life after all, and in the end, neither was I.

My thoughts flutter around in no particular direction. Still wearing the elated smile from my evening, I enjoy a pleasant drive down the quiet streets of Vinbrooke toward home. I grew up in the small town of Bitterton just to the north but have lived in this small town outside Savannah for almost ten years. As in Savannah, towering trees graced with garlands of Spanish moss line the streets. Something about the way the moss clings to the trees gives them an elegant yet haunting appearance—as if they have their own stories of sorrow.

As a girl, I struggled to fit in and was never treated as an equal. In the eyes of my father and three brothers, being a girl meant you were weak and stupid. My ambition in life was to become anyone other than the person I had been while I was growing up. Even more, I didn't want to be the person my mother was, or is. We women all become either exact copies of our mothers or the complete opposites. I strive to be the opposite. However, I haven't always made myself known in the politest ways. I learned to fight hard and dirty. My Gammie taught me that.

In the town's heart is a beautiful historic cemetery—loved by the living and, I suppose, the dead. Tourists travel for miles to see the massive oaks and willows and the intricate floral gardens. Savannah is a beautiful city, but it's burdened with too many tourists and trans-planted residents. What I love about Vinbrooke is that it's tucked away from the city, protected from the clutter of overcrowding. The only outsiders here are a few tourists passing through and the college students who come to study art. The students move away with their memories, and new students temporarily move in. The town starts over every year.

I drive past the archway of the cemetery, and something under a streetlamp catches my attention. As I strain to focus on who or what is standing there, I blink rapidly, trying to determine whether it is a trick of the light. It creeps into view and I slow my car to a crawl. A boy stands alone in the streetlamp's shadow, one hand resting against the pole. He raises the other hand in an attempt to wave but then drops it to his side. He looks familiar. His hair is light, his skin pale. Khaki shorts hang loose around his legs, and he wears a striped shirt and brown Jesus-like sandals. He is similar to my little brother, Tommy, as a boy. I scan the surrounding area, then turn my eyes back to him. He continues to stand there, motionless. I roll down my passenger window and stop my car in front of him.

"Are you okay? Do you need some help?"

The boy nods his head and turns to walk toward the entryway of the cemetery. I put my car in reverse and back up several feet, keeping him in view. He stops and turns toward me once more, face solemn, eyes dismal, then disappears under the stone archway. I'm not sure if I should follow him or drive like hell. Had I seen him, or had I imagined him? I hear the quick toot of a horn behind me and see headlights in my rearview mirror; I am blocking the road. I drive on.

Dazed, I pull into the parking lot of my weekend spirit store to pick up a bottle of Shiraz. Wine is definitely what I need right now, and lots of it. I take a moment to compose myself before I get out of my car. As I prepare to open the door, my phone vibrates inside my purse. It isn't Kyle as I expected, and I don't recognize the number. I look at the screen as something in the pit of my stomach stirs with a familiar burn that tells me I shouldn't answer it. Shaking myself loose from the dread, I answer anyway.

"Hello?" I muster, and before he even speaks, I know who it is.

"Kev-ree?" comes the lazy pronunciation of my name on the other end. The caller is Matthew Shawn, my oldest brother, who only calls when he is drunk and wants to reminisce down what I only remember as nightmare lane. He has changed his phone number again, always avoiding the law or bill collectors. I'm quick to hang up. The phone immediately vibrates again. I toss it into the glove box. Conversations with my brother accomplish only one thing: digging up a forgotten past I wish to keep buried. Tearing open old scars is not on my to-do list.

A dark cloud has quashed my earlier mood as I walk into the store. Behind the counter, the owner sits on his usual pub chair, smoking a cigar and watching a baseball game on the television in the corner. The lights on the ceiling are blurred by the cloud of smoke. Another man stands at the end of the checkout counter, engrossed in the TV. He turns away, glances at me, and then turns his body as if to get a better look, making me self-conscious.

"Hey, Ms. Kevan. How are you?" says the store owner in his Italian accent, raising his cigar. He bears the same name I do, only spelled differently.

The other gentleman gives Kevin a look when he speaks my name —the name that usually belongs to a man.

"Hey, Mr. Kevin. I'm doing fine. How are you?" I say.

The other man doesn't attempt to hide his persistent observation of me. He is standing tall but relaxed, leaning with his hip propped against the counter, one hand relaxed to the knuckles in his jeans pocket, the other gripping a beer. His navy blue T-shirt is tucked into the belted waist of his pants. The pleasing way he wears this attire shows off a nice V-shape from his shoulders to his lower torso. When our eyes meet, his are a deep blue that could strike anyone's interest. I look away despite my curiosity, and I feel my face shade with an involuntary flush. *I wish he would stop looking at me.*

I turn away and walk down an aisle of assorted red wines, feeling the man's eyes still fixated on me.

"Hey, Mr. Kev," I call, "are you out of my usual?"

Kevin makes his suggestion for an alternate red wine. As I search, heat continues to rise in my face, and I fear it will show. My heart thuds so hard that I can hear the blood in my ears make a swooshing sound with every beat. I haven't experienced this adolescent sensation since early high school, when a crush gave me my first smile. Frantic, I search for the wine Kevin has suggested, pick the bottle up by the neck, then send my gaze down to the floor. As I walk toward the counter, I want nothing more than to forget the bottle of wine and leave the store. Why is one stranger having such an effect on me? Reluctantly, I approach the front of the store, my eyes directed toward Kevin, and place the bottle with a gentle tap on the counter.

"You will like this Renzo, Ms. Kevan," Kevin says as he looks down at the bottle and gives it a nod of approval.

I feel my confidence shrink to the size of a needle hole when I make eye contact with the other gentleman again. I flash him a fake, sheepish smile and shove my money over the counter. "Keep the change, Mr. Kevin," I blurt and bolt for the door. Flustered, I push the wrong side of the door, scramble to correct my error, and finally exit the store. I stub my toe on the edge of the concrete bump at the end of a parking spot, nearly falling, as I race to the safety of my car. *What the hell is wrong with you, Kev?* Something about that man addled me, and I have no idea why.

I take a moment to gather myself. As I back my car out, I steal one final look at the man through the store window. Driving away, I feel myself calming to normal, but I can't help thinking that I am losing my mind. There was something about his eyes. I swear I have seen them before.

The drive home ends with no recollection of the trip itself as I pull into my driveway and exhale a sigh of relief. I reach into the glove box to retrieve my phone, tapping the screen to see ten missed calls and three voicemails. I'm not surprised.

In my kitchen, I set the bottle of wine on the counter alongside my vibrating phone.

Eleanor meows and slides the side of her body against my leg, back and forth.

"Hello, Miss Eleanor. Come here."

I hug my overweight, gray-striped cat to my chest. She purrs and then meows, only a partial sound this time.

Eleanor is the sort of cat who takes her eating seriously. I rescued her from a shelter not long after I bought this house. Life before that must have been traumatic for her. She eats her food like it's going to be her final meal. I set her down and walk over to give her some food. Turning back to the bottle of wine, I pour myself a large glass and take a soothing gulp. With reluctance, I retrieve my phone and retire to the study, sinking into my favorite chaise lounge, delaying the inevitable. After one long exhale, I tap my phone to listen to the past.

Message one: silence. *Delete.* Message two: the sound of a disgusted exhale, then silence. *Delete.* With an aggravated sigh, I tap the third one. There he is, malice driving his voice. "Kev-ree, it's Matthew. You've left me no choice but to tell you this on voicemail. Gammie Frances is dead!"

———

I stand waist-deep near the edge of a pond—the surface of the water reflects a smudged image of the gray sky above and hides what lies below. The cold water drains the heat from my body and the wind stings my face. My reflection resembles a woman, yet it appears much, much younger. My eyes are blackened and smudged as if I have been crying. I am wearing a white sundress that feels too snug around my chest and waist—small enough to fit a little girl.

Everything around me is dead. The tall weeds are dry, and they droop as if only standing against their will. Deadened trees reach their branches outward as if pleading for the life they once embraced. To my right is a wooden dock, only a few feet above the water, looking as if it could descend and disappear forever. Straight in front of me is an abandoned house, aged and alone. Its tall roof sags in the middle. It has two eyes as windows along the front. Honeysuckle vines, with only a few blooms—so few that their scent can't escape—have taken over the wall.

This place isn't all that strange to me. I wonder if it was more inviting when it was new.

A small splash brings my attention back to the pond. A bright green frog with a humped back creates tiny waves as it swims toward me. Its legs sprawl out from side to side as it kicks itself forward, separating a tiny path through the duckweed and algae. The small creature pulls a long, slender object along the surface of the water with its mouth. More dull than shiny, the object is a silver necklace with something dangling from it.

I bend forward to see. Frightened, the frog dives, pulling the necklace under the water with it. "Wait," I say, reaching out to grab it, but the frog and its gift disappear into the darkness. Frantic, I reach below the surface with both hands, moving my arms as quickly as the water will allow. Nothing but cold water slides between my fingers.

You need to grab it, *something inside my head warns.*

I take in a deep breath, hold it, and immerse myself, eyes open, as I flip my body in different directions. Through the murky water, I see the frog kick away from me. I paddle harder. Fixated on the frog and its baggage, I see a key attached to the necklace. I swim faster and deeper, eyes ahead and focused. Some-

thing solid slams into my left side. Instinct and adrenaline take over. I jerk away as my heart pounds.

Two black, hollow eyes stare into mine as a hand reaches toward me. Horror rushes in. I try to move away, but the faster I paddle, the more immobile I become.

I am looking at a dead woman.

Her hair is brown, knotted, and caked with mud. She reaches toward me with dirty fingernails as my eyes dart from her hand to the rest of her body. She is swollen and blue.

The woman moves her lips in an attempt to speak, but in the water, I cannot hear. She raises her other hand. Drifting from her fingertips are the necklace and key.

I hesitate, afraid to move, but I understand this must be important. Despite my fear that she will grab me, I reach for it anyway.

I cup my hand around the key as the woman pulls her own hand away. Her empty eyes stay locked on to mine as she sinks deeper and darkness swallows her.

CHAPTER TWO

Nathan Thomas Hill

Damn! The word draws out in my mind the second I lay eyes on her. As she walks in, a breeze flows across the room, carrying her sweet scent with it. I unscrew the top from my bottle of beer and turn away, taking on a casual posture. This woman has grabbed my attention as quickly as if I were a kid spotting a colorful candy store. Despite my efforts to seem aloof, I realize I am staring at her like some creepy old man as she speaks to Kevin and walks toward the back of the store.

"Hey, Mr. Kev, are you out of my usual?"

"Sorry, Ms. Kevan. Try the Renzo Masi. It's close to what you like," Kevin suggests from behind the counter.

God, even her voice is intoxicating. She is quite small—not much over five feet tall—and her floral summer dress hugs her perfect curves. Her auburn hair cascades across her shoulders, ending in the middle of her back.

As the woman approaches the counter, she glances at me briefly with coffee-colored eyes, but her head remains tilted toward the floor. When I realize I'm staring, I gulp a large swig of beer, which goes down hard and makes my eyes water. I look away. Now she looks at me again, and like a moth unable to avoid the light, my eyes find their way back to hers. I find their color crazily fascinating. I swing my head back to the TV, and when I look back, she is gone. I examine my behavior as my mind scolds me: *Well, that was pathetic, Nate. Since when do you allow a good-looking woman to intimidate you?*

I turn back to my friend behind the counter. "Hey, Kevin, who was that lady?"

"She pays me a visit sometimes on the weekends." Kevin's eyes remain glued to the game on TV. "She's a photography professor at the art college." Turning to me, he asks, "Why?"

"No reason." I shrug, nonchalant. "Just looked familiar, that's all."

She hadn't looked familiar, but there was something about her that sparked my curiosity. I slide my fingers through my hair, trying to tame the wild, windblown look from my drive earlier. Often I don't care what I look like, but now I acknowledge I am a little disheveled as I run my fingertips over three days' worth of stubble.

I've always enjoyed getting to know new people—especially women. Conversation with anyone has always been easy for me. This woman made my confidence teeter just a bit.

"She caught your eye, didn't she, Signor Nathan?" Kevin asks with his slight accent, eyes devilish.

Kevin is somewhere in his mid to upper forties. He came to America with his parents when he was a boy. His accent is slight but has a distinct difference to the local Southern twang. His parents wanted him to be a true-blooded American, so they gave him a basic American name when they arrived; I don't know his original name. Kevin draws you to him right away—it's not unusual for people to hang around the store and drink a cold beer with him—but I've never really asked him much about his personal life. During one of our conversations he told me his parents left Italy because of some family feud. He hinted that it wasn't your typical family rivalry.

"There's something about her that makes her stand out. Who wouldn't give her a second glance?"

"Aww, you should have said something. I would have introduced you," Kevin offers with a wry smile. "Why are you single, signore?

Good-looking man like you. You should have women falling all over you."

I laugh. Most men my age are married, have two kids calling them Daddy, and are already thinking about retirement. I have none of these things. Sometimes I like it this way. Then there are times I wouldn't mind coming home to a how-was-your-day kiss and a couple of youngsters swinging from my arm.

I finish my beer, then stroll to the back of the store to retrieve two bottles of Chardonnay. The wine is for my landlord and godmother, Dorothy Ivymond. She insists that the wine in Vinbrooke is better than the wine close to home, so I buy some for her each week when I drive here to visit family graves in the local cemetery.

I say goodbye to Kevin and start heading home. The stretch of road from Vinbrooke to Bitterton is an endless display of plantations and farms with marshland in between. I've lived here most of my life, with the exception of college and a yearlong job in upstate New York. Moving somewhere else has crossed my mind occasionally, but this is the only home I know. When the roots of your whole life are planted in one place, it's hard to dig them up and transplant yourself somewhere unfamiliar and strange.

My godmother is the only family I have left. Even though I'm grown, she takes her role very seriously. Dorothy June Ivymond is a woman to be reckoned with. She is nosy, crabby, demanding, and stubborn—but I love her. She knows what she wants, and she gets it. She speaks her mind—even when you don't want to hear what she has to say. To this day, Dorothy reminds me of the character Ouiser from *Steel Magnolias*, as played by Shirley MacLaine. As with Ouiser, a permanent frown has made itself at home on Dorothy's face. It's deceiving, because she has a heart bigger than anyone's, but her big heart doesn't stop her from being stern.

I press in the code that opens the massive iron gate at the entryway of the property. When I was a child, there were no fancy codes to open this gate—you just pushed or pulled it—but after my mother's death, Dorothy had one installed. The Ivymond plantation, which has been in Dorothy's family for generations, is one of the largest and grandest in the area, making it the envy of many.

I pull my truck through the gate, pause at the entrance, and look down the beautiful, tree-lined lane toward the faint lights of the main house in the distance. The massive oak trees that line both sides of the front drive are awe-inspiring. As a young boy, I often ran down this private drive, mesmerized by the moss hanging from the trees. My mother and I took many walks through here too, stopping before one tree and then another, finding imaginary creatures in the shapes of the hanging moss as if finding shapes in the clouds. The most distinctive shapes were massive dinosaurs that appeared to be roaring. I can still see them today. The beauty of this place, and the memories, have both played a role in my staying.

I was just a little boy when my pregnant mother and I moved onto the plantation. My memories are vague before that. Childhood memories are like puzzle pieces that are spread apart in the mind and don't always fit together to complete a clear picture. Some fragments, you aren't sure if you imagined them or if they're real. When I moved here, I remember thinking that we had somehow struck it rich. I later came to learn that Dorothy was the one who was rich, and that we worked for her to cover rent for the house we were living in. Of course, Dorothy owns the house—she owns several similar houses on the plantation. She let my mother and me live in the largest of the homes aside from hers.

I pull in front of the old Victorian manor house and walk up the steps. Dusk hands itself over to darkness as the songs of night creatures become the dominant ones. The sweet scent of honeysuckle wafts from the edges of the veranda. The wraparound railings embrace the front of the house in a circle, rather than your typical rectangle shape. It seems a lifetime since I first walked on to this porch, though age hasn't discriminated against the details that mold and shape the entire house. It must have taken years to carve the many spindles lining the porch. I stop and look at the huge wooden front door, with its intricate, raised carvings of a massive oak. Its details are so vivid that it could make a person wonder if the leaves come to life sometimes and flutter in the breeze. I grab the cast-iron knocker and tap it on the door three times. Even after all these years, I always knock before I enter.

Dorothy opens the door with her usual half smile, half scowl. Regardless of the time of day, her lips are always shaded in red lipstick and her cheeks blushed a shade lighter. She reminds me of the sophisticated version of a grandmother, only without the grandchildren. Two things you never see Dorothy without: makeup and shoes.

"Evening, pretty lady," I say as I hand her the canvas bag holding the two bottles of wine.

"Took you long enough," she gripes as she takes the bag. "My damn pantry door is squeaking again."

"I'll take care of it first thing in the morning."

"I'll have to listen to it in the morning. What's wrong with right now?" She turns to walk toward the kitchen. Dorothy gets around quick for someone her age and is far stronger than most older women. Age and time have been kind to her. I fall in behind her as she scurries through the house. She walks over and opens the pantry door wide, then swings it back and forth, forcing a barely detectable sound. "Do you think I want to hear this before my morning coffee?"

For someone who claims to be losing her hearing, Dorothy doesn't miss a thing.

"It's okay for the doors that lead outside the house to squeak," she says. "Lets me know if I'm being intruded on. It's not okay for the inside doors to be heard. I'll be in the sitting room when you finish."

As I turn, I give her an eye roll like an annoyed teenager not getting his way. I go out to my truck and retrieve my toolbox. I'm not sure why I don't just bring it in. Every time I come inside, I either have to fix, tweak, or inspect something before I can leave.

The task doesn't take very long, but I hang in the kitchen for a bit, not giving Dorothy the chance to complain that I did a poor job since I finished so quickly. Before entering the room, I tap on the sitting-room doorframe. Dorothy is sitting in her favorite chair, in the corner, holding a leather-bound book that resembles a journal or sketchbook. I see another one just like it on the table next to her.

"Door is good as new," I announce.

When visiting, I don't frequent this room often. Dorothy has always been private about her personal life. I know little about her past or what she does in her spare time. Regardless, she can be a busybody to those around her. She knows everything about everyone. If she doesn't know it, she finds it out. She keeps a close eye on me and on her workhands. She employs them to do specific jobs and trusts that they will keep the knowledge they acquire private. She keeps everyone in place. If they get out of line, I hear about it—then I take care of it.

Dorothy looks up from her book, and I am certain that she has been crying. For Dorothy, crying isn't normal in any situation.

"Are you all right?" I ask.

"I'm fine," she says, making a swift wipe of her face. "Come in. Please. Sit. I'm just looking through some old journals and reminiscing."

"Yours?" I ask as I step into the cozy room. The furniture consists of a small floral couch and two matching high-backed chairs, in one of which Dorothy is seated. Beside each chair is a table with a lamp, each of them lit. They are the only lighting being used at the moment, and the room has a warm feel, kind of like visiting your favorite grandmother.

"No, no. These belonged to a very dear friend of mine," she says, motioning for me to sit in the other chair. "I guess the old hag had enough and checked out."

"I'm sorry. Did I know her?"

"Nah. You might have met her once or twice. She's the girl in the picture with me here." Dorothy picks up a silver frame from the table next to her and hands it to me. "Of course, she was much younger there—we all were."

The frame contains an old photograph taken when color film was new. As I glance at the picture, I see three young ladies wearing trousers and riding boots—each with a horse at her side. All the young ladies are beautiful in their own ways. Each of them stands with a sassy posture, and all are wearing mischievous grins that spell trouble. I pick Dorothy out right away. Age hasn't changed her as roughly as it does most people. The girl to her right is petite, with curly brown hair. The girl on her left appears smaller, and her hair is long and red. She reminds me of the woman in the spirit store. Maybe it's the hair or the way she is standing. My thoughts wander off to the way the woman walked, her hips swaying. Her walk reminded me of the sass of Scarlett

O'Hara, with just a hint of tomboy hidden underneath. She walked with confidence, but there was something about her that seemed . . . lost.

"The brunette on the right was timid and a follower, unless what we were doing was wrong," Dorothy is saying. "Then she was only a rule follower. The girl in the center is me. I was sometimes a follower, but I could also be stubborn, which got me into trouble. The red-headed girl on the left—she was a mean, tough bitch." Dorothy chuckles. "I guess you could say that she was the ringleader. Rarely ever followed the rules. At least when we got into trouble, she bailed us out. I once saw her take a young man twice her size to the ground."

Dorothy's gaze is aimed at the picture, but it's obvious her mind is somewhere else.

Shaking the effect the mystery woman still seems to have on me, I say, "She sounds interesting."

"She was." Dorothy looks down at the journal, rubbing her hands over the cover. "I acquired her diaries years ago. She knew they were safe with me. A lot of our history is in these books. Most of it would make your hair curl."

"What can I do to help, Miss Dorothy?"

Dorothy looks down at the journal for another moment and then brings it up to her chest, hugging it close to her heart. "I need a ride into town tomorrow. Can you take me?"

"Me? Of course." I agree, but I'm confused, since she usually doesn't ask me to chauffeur her around. I look from Dorothy's face to the journal she holds. Engraved on the front cover are the words *Frances M. Mays.*

CHAPTER THREE

Kevan Renee Mays
1994

Kevan awakes to the sound of a fly buzzing close to her ear, a window fan humming, and her heart pounding in competition. The effects of the dream linger as images replay. The faceless man pins her mother to the ground, one knee pressing into her chest, his hands on her throat. Kevan attempts to drag him off her, screaming and begging for him to stop, but to no avail. His words sound cold and harsh but are unrecognizable as the loud cries of cicadas ring in her ears.

She sits up in bed, ready for the images to leave. Closing her eyes, she chants a favorite nursery rhyme to push them out of her mind. *One, two, buckle my shoe. Three, four, shut the door. Five, six, pick up sticks. Seven, eight, lay them straight. Nine, ten, a big fat hen.*

It doesn't make the images from the dream go away, so she repeats it, only this time she changes the words in hopes of distracting herself more. *One, two, where are you? Three, four, behind the door. Five, six, stop playing tricks. Seven, eight, it's not too late. Nine, ten, to start again.*

This version seems to work better, so she repeats it.

She hates dreams like this. Gammie Frances tells her she should listen to her dreams and that, for her, they mean something. In Kevan's case, something terrible tends to follow one of her dreams. The intensity of this dream seems particularly threatening.

She repeats her newly made rhyme one last time. Kevan is very good at morphing the words of happy nursery rhymes to whatever she wants. Something about it distracts her when she feels scared or upset. When she finally shakes off the dream, she kicks back the sheet, walks over to greet her pet rabbit, Whiskers, through its cage, then goes straight to work on her chores. Afterward, she finds her mother.

"Mom, can I please go out and play?" Kevan pleads. "I finished cleaning up the kitchen and my room."

Her mother looks around and sighs. "Yeah. I guess I'll let you this time, since your father isn't home."

Kevan often has to spend her entire day indoors, doing chores, because she is a girl and that is what's expected. Being a girl in the Mays household means you are stupid and useless, other than cooking, cleaning, and being a man's servant. A woman's place is at home, according to Clyde Mays. This means Kevan as well. Her father believes he is "king of his castle" and that females are beneath him. Kevan assumes that he gave her a boy's name because he wanted another son instead of a daughter. Her middle name, Renee, came from Kevan's mother. The statement *You're a girl, you can't do that*, is something Kevan hears from her father almost daily. She's glad he isn't home to say it today.

She runs down the hall into her brother's bedroom, flips on the light, and shakes the bed. "Come on!"

"What do you want, Kev-ree?" Matthew groans, squints, and throws an arm over his face.

"Come on! Let's go out and play." Not waiting for him, she squeals as she runs back through the house. Her two other brothers are already outside on their bicycles, dodging junk in the front yard. It's early morning and already hot outside, but Kevan doesn't mind. She runs behind the rickety, two-room shack her parents use as a workshop, where they fix things they've bought secondhand and then sell them—sometimes—at a small profit. To an outsider, items exchanged from the shack usually just look like junk. Most of it belongs to Kevan's father and clutters the whole yard—back and front.

Parked behind the shop is an old car Clyde claims to be restoring. Not much work has been done, since it has remained parked in the same spot for as long as Kevan can remember. She climbs into the old car and pretends to drive while making motor-revving sounds deep in her throat. Her brothers James and Tommy hop in and pretend to go along for the ride. They lean to one side and then the other, speeding around curves, and they make their own revving sounds.

They bounce from one pretend game to another as the morning wears on.

Kevan's oldest brother, Matthew Shawn, is eight. James Dustin is seven, less than a year older than Kevan, who just turned seven. Tommy Dale is six. Barely eleven months separates any of them from the next in age. The four of them are close, but they often have little sibling duo cliques. Their cliques change when a conflict arises and one of them uses the other to get what they want. Kevan uses this tactic often, which could be the reason her brothers call her the evil, red-headed stepsister.

When Matthew comes outside to join them, they sit in a circle, making mud pies and fake beans for their pretend dinner. The sun beats down on their heads as sweat beads trickle down Kevan's scalp. It feels like bugs are crawling in her hair. As she packs mud into a rusty pie-pan, Tommy lets out a frightened murmur: "No."

A sound registers with each of them after Tommy says the word, and they look at each other in fear. A car stops in front of the house, and then its engine dies. As the car door creaks open, it sounds as if it might fall from its hinges. A boot stomps onto the dirt. Another sound carries on the sultry breeze, darkening the surrounding air: their father's drunken voice. Clyde has been on one of those three-day binges to Whiskeyville that always brings him home wanting to pick a fight. With one glance around the sibling circle, each of them knows what's coming. The tone of his voice tells them they are in for another of his damned rampages.

"Where are they at, Edith? Tell them to get their sorry little asses out here!" Clyde slurs as his other boot stomps the ground. Kevan

wonders what they've done wrong now. She hears the car door pop
from the weight of his body as he leans on it to stand.

"Clyde, don't come home and start this! We'll talk about it when
you're sober."

Kevan hears fear and pleading in her mother's voice. The siblings
exchange long looks. Kevan immediately wishes she could send herself
somewhere else. After a long silence, they begin to whisper.

"Go look," Matthew says.

"No, you!" James and Tommy say in unison.

"No! Why do I have to?" Matthew asks.

"I'll go." Kevan wants to get it over with.

She swallows hard and squeezes her eyes shut for a moment,
making a wish that this is just another of her stupid dreams. She
crawls as quietly as she can to the other end of her parents' shop
and peeks around to locate her father. There he is, still by the car.
He sways and struggles to hold his body upright as if his upper
body is too heavy to balance on his bony legs. He's wearing the
same shirt and the same pair of droopy blue jeans from three days
ago, dirty and sweat-stained. Kevan smells his body odor, sour skin,
and foul breath from where she lies. He stands with only one pant
leg stuffed inside his black biker boots, while his shirt is only
partially tucked into his jeans. He has never ridden a motorcycle in
his life. A thick chain is hooked to his front belt loop; it circles
around his hip and connects to a wallet in his back pocket. Kevan
doesn't recall seeing her father without it. She's always thought it
was stupid.

Edith has moved herself closer to the front steps of the house, and
Clyde staggers along with her. His swollen, purplish face means he's
been drinking the hard stuff. Kevan notices movement in her peripheral vision, and to her relief, she sees her grandmother stomping
toward her parents, calm but with the same hateful frown etched on
her face that only appears when Clyde is around.

"What the hell is your problem this time, Clyde?" Gammie Frances
barks. The wind blows her straight ponytail around in a circular
motion as the sun shows just a tiny amount of gray in it. She might as
well be invisible, though, because Clyde continues to swerve on his

ranting path. Gammie steps in front of Clyde. She will not be ignored —especially by her own son.

"You get on out of here, Clyde!" Gammie throws her hand forward as if she's trying to shoo away an unwanted animal.

Gammie has never backed down from him or from anyone. That's why she is known as "that mean-ass, swearing granny." She steps between Edith and Clyde, placing her palm on her son's chest. "Clyde, you better get the hell out of here before I shove my foot up your ass!"

"Get back to your house, Ma! This is none of your business!" Clyde barks in a sour tone that stinks just as bad as his breath.

Gammie doesn't budge.

Clyde is often violent, but Kevan has never seen him raise a hand to her grandmother.

"Clyde, please, let's go in the house." Kevan sees fear on her mother's face as she steps forward beside Gammie.

"Did they do their chores? What about Kevan—where's she at? Is she in the house where she belongs?" Even though he has no reason to be upset, his rant continues. Kevan has learned that a drunken rant is never reasonable. She closes her eyes, hoping the moment will disappear. She clenches them so tight that when she opens them, she sees white spots like fireflies that bounce every time she blinks.

Gammie glances in Kevan's direction and shakes her head, warning Kevan to stay put. As she looks from her grandmother to her father, Kevan's dream flashes through her mind and she feels panic grow larger inside her chest. She knows what is coming. Taking in a deep breath of courage, she runs blindly toward her parents, just wanting her father to stop before it gets worse. Her brothers follow close behind.

"I'm right here!" Kevan steps forward, her chest puffed out and her chin tilted up in defiance.

Clyde turns to look at her and she sees his eyes fill with the look of the devil. The same look as in her dream. He turns his dark eyes back to Edith, reaching around Gammie, pushing her aside. He grabs Edith by the forearm and bends it outward in a direction that an arm shouldn't bend. Kevan and her brothers break into a run, screaming.

"Dad, please stop!"

"Clyde, please, I beg you, let's just go in the house," Edith pleads.

But now there is no defensive tone in her voice. Her plea sounds like pain and fear.

Without turning his head, Clyde slurs, "You little shits get your asses in the house where you belong!" He looks back at Edith. Her arm is becoming discolored, growing redder under his grip. "You're turning my kids against me now?" He squints with a new fix of anger and purpose.

Matthew yells, "Dad, leave Mom alone! Go back to where you came from!"

Everything plays like a slow-motion film with no pause, rewind, or fast forward. Matthew rushes toward Clyde like a bull charging a matador. Before Matthew can cover much ground, Clyde removes his hand from Edith's arm and brings both hands to her throat. His whole body stiffens. In that moment, Kevan fears she is going to watch her mother die.

"Get your damn hands off of her, Clyde, or I swear I will kill you!" Gammie Frances shouts as she grips two handfuls of his shirt, trying to pull him off Edith. She pounds his back with her fists, but he doesn't seem to notice. She steps back and looks frantically around the yard.

His hands clamp down harder. Crying, Kevan screams, "Stop! Dad, stop!"

Gammie takes several steps back toward the house and picks up a wooden baseball bat from the yard. Sensing what is coming, everyone steps aside as Gammie grips the bat with both hands. Her eyes displaying a rage that matches Clyde's, she swings hard, and a hollow thud echoes as she makes contact across Clyde's back. The impact forces him to release Edith and he staggers backward. Gammie hits him so hard that she knocks the breath out of his lungs, and he gasps. Not giving him a chance to fight back, she pounds him one more time, forcing him to his knees. She steps back and braces just in case she needs to hit him again. Extending her arm and pointing the bat at his head, she says, "Clyde, get your ass off somewhere and sleep it off! You show your face again before you've sobered up, I'll aim for the head."

Clyde crawls a few feet, still gasping for air, then manages to stand up and stagger across the yard and up the front steps of the house. He disappears through the screen door, and it slams closed behind him.

Kevan looks at her Gammie in shock as relief takes over fear. Gammie steps toward Kevan and takes her hand.

"Come with me. It's over." She pulls Kevan close to her side and walks her from the yard, carrying the bat with her. Whispering softly, she says, "Don't worry, honey. Gammie will take care of you—always."

As they approach the house, Kevan hears her grandmother mumble something almost inaudible, something Kevan doesn't understand.

"Karma is coming. I promise."

CHAPTER FOUR

Kevan
Early Summer

Despite the room temperature being normal, I wrap a small blanket around my legs and curl my body close. The room is getting dark, so I turn on the lamp next to me. I replay the message, hoping I heard my brother wrong. His words, drifting in from somewhere far away, create a heavy sense of despair in my heart, and I cry for the first time over Gammie's death. The person I loved more than anything is gone. As sobs consume me, I curl more tightly inside my small blanket as if to swaddle myself.

Gammie Frances was the one who comforted me through everything. She pushed me forward in life and gave me the courage and strength to become the person I am today. She always made me feel I could survive anything. Now I feel lost, like an orphaned child, and I question what will become of me.

I open a drawer in the side table and pull out a box of old photographs taken throughout my childhood and young adult years. They tell the story of my life with Gammie. She could have given birth to me herself, we were so much alike—red hair and determination. My mother would say, "You are just like your Gammie—pigheaded and stubborn!" That always enraged her, but I was proud of it. I still am.

I take a large sip of wine and set the glass on the table.

In the first picture, I am seven years old and Gammie and I are sitting on the top step of her front porch. She took the picture with a disposable camera by turning it backward and snapping the button. She would always say that she invented selfies long before there were cell phones. I think back to the small camera that took only twenty-four photos, remembering how Gammie would then hand the entire camera over to a cashier to be developed. I miss the excitement of opening the package of finished pictures.

My gaze travels deep into the photo and I become lost in the events of that day.

My father is preparing to take my brothers on an overnight hiking and camping trip. Of course that means that they camp and he gets soused. Following them around as they pack, I am stooped over and heavy-footed, begging to go with them. After several pleas, my father says, "You're a girl, you can't do this. You're not tough enough."

Angered by his words, I bolt toward the road and in the direction of Gammie's house. Tears streaming down my face, I scream, "Gammie! Gammie!"

Gammie is sitting on the porch with a book and a glass of lemonade. Placing them on the table next to her, she comes forward to meet me. "Come here, Renee. What's wrong?"

I run onto the porch as fast as I can and sink my whole body into the cushion of her embrace, sobbing. "Why am I a girl? I hate being a girl!"

"Aww, honey, being a girl isn't so bad." Squatting down, Gammie takes my face in her hands, looks into my eyes, and says, "Girls make the world swirl, and you, my dear, are special in your own way. To hell with that mean-ass daddy and those brothers of yours!"

It isn't the first time I have run to Gammie's to escape the males of my house.

Gammie guides me across the porch with one arm wrapped around my shoulder and the other hand holding mine. I lean into her side, listen to her voice, and smell her perfume. I stop sobbing and just cry silently. We sit on the porch swing and Gammie hands me her glass of lemonade.

"Do you know why I'm always telling you that you are special?" Gammie asks.

I wipe my face with the back of my hand and try to control my crying by taking quick breaths. I shake my head, gulping lemonade.

Gammie pushes her glasses high up on her nose. "I want to tell you a story. Would you like to hear one?"

I nod.

She pats me on the leg, then says, "Okay, you sit back and get comfortable."

I inch my bottom back into the swing, holding the lemonade high so that I don't spill it. Gammie waits until I'm settled before she begins.

"The day you were born and I first held you in my arms, I knew you were special. You and I had this instant bond like no other from the very beginning."

"What's a bond, Gammie?"

"It's when two things are attached to each other and can't be pulled apart. I believe that bond is partly because you and I both have special gifts. Different kinds of gifts, but similar. We can sense things that others can't. I knew that the very first time you told me about one of your dreams."

"I hate my dreams, Gammie. They scare me, and sometimes they come true."

"I know. But that is a gift. They're not always going to be bad. But I don't think your dreams are your actual gift, or your only gift. I believe your abilities go far beyond that."

Still fixated on dreams, I say, "I wish I would have good dreams that would come true."

"It's possible that you already do, but people tend to only remember the bad stuff. I think it's our brain's way of protecting us from the same bad thing happening twice." Gammie pauses for a moment and smiles at me. "We'll save that for another day. Do you remember that time when you were five years old and stepped on a nail, and it went completely through your foot?"

I nod again, my eyes growing wide. "It hurt so bad."

"Yes. Your father was gone, your brothers were off somewhere else, and your mother—well, who knows? You were outside by yourself."

"I don't think I dreamed about that, though."

"No, but what I'm trying to tell you is that I was at home, and I heard this voice say to me that you were hurt."

My mouth drops open. Then I ask, "Whose voice?"

"Well, it sounded just like a little girl's voice—almost like yours, but it couldn't have been yours. Maybe my brain heard it that way. But anyway, the voice told me you were hurt and needed my help, so I ran to your house."

"I remember, Gammie. You didn't have shoes on." I giggle.

Gammie laughs. "Yes, you're right. But somehow, I knew you needed me. I always know when you need me. That is my gift. But I think your gifts go far beyond my own, and far beyond dreams."

I scrunch my face, take a gulp of lemonade, and wait for Gammie to tell me more.

"My grandmother always said that people who dream things that then come true have all sorts of abilities that others don't have. She believed that their brains were wired differently. Something to do with the frontal cortex and how they perceive things."

I scrunch my face even more, and Gammie laughs.

"That's a little over your head for now, but anyway, I think you are one of those people. And I think my grandmother was right when she said those people can see and do things that others can't. Possibly they can see ghosts or spirits—maybe even talk to them."

My eyes expand as wide as they'll go. "I don't want to do that, Gammie."

She laughs. "My grandmother also said those people could be stronger than other people, tougher."

I lift my elbow, curl my arm, and show off my tiny bicep. "Like this."

"Yes," Gammie chuckles. "Like that. She said that they could run longer, jump higher, and hold their breath forever, even making it impossible for them to drown."

"I can hold my breath for a long, long time, Gammie, and I can swim really well," I say, all excited.

"Yes, I know," Gammie says. "But some of these ideas may be nothing more than make believe, so don't go jumping into some pond by yourself, understand?"

"Yes, ma'am."

"I'm not sure how much of it is real, but I do know that you are special. And I believe our connection will keep us attached to each other—always."

"Promise?"

"I promise."

I grin and lean into Gammie, and she wraps her arms around me. "Renee, *remember, one day you will be strong, independent, and most of all, proud to be a woman. People will admire and look up to you."*

I take a deep breath, give the picture another long look, and set it aside. Gammie always took time to explain things. She always made me feel better. I pick up my glass of wine, take another drink, and wonder, *Who's going to do that now?*

———

Disoriented, I frantically swim to the surface and fill my lungs with cold air. As I cough and try to restore my body with adequate oxygen, I stare at the necklace and key in my hand. Looking back at the pond, I shudder.

I turn toward the shallow edge of the pond and stagger out of the water. Legs heavy with every step, I walk in the direction of the house. Something makes a sound over my shoulder. When I turn to look, I feel my body turn cold as if I am immersed in the pond once more.

A man walks away from me down the overgrown road. His outline stirs a frightening emotion in my core, like when I used to imagine that the boogeyman was after me. This man's frame is familiar—and not a good familiar.

I place my fingertips on my eyes and rub as if it will change what I am seeing. It doesn't work. I squat down in the tall, dead grass to hide. Uneasiness turns to panic, burning in the pit of my stomach.

The man peers around as if afraid of detection. He carries something large and bulky over his shoulder—it's humanlike. Something tells me I shouldn't be seeing this, but I watch anyway. I must be looking at a ghost, because this man has been dead for years. I must be dreaming. I want to wake up!

My wet sundress plasters itself to the skin on my back, stomach, and thighs as the cold air stiffens the material, making it even more uncomfortable. I shiver from seeing him as much as from the cold.

The man looks around again, then stops. He tosses the large object from his shoulder onto the ground, and the thud echoes from the trees to my ears. I close my eyes and hold them shut, breathing in deeply, then holding it. I open my eyes and the scary man is gone.

CHAPTER FIVE

Kevan
1995

"One, two, buckle my shoe. Three, four, behind the door. Five, six, not making sense. Seven, eight—"

"What are you doing out here all by yourself, Renee?" Gammie asks.

Hunched over and chanting, Kevan raises her face from her hands. Tears streak down her cheeks.

Gammie takes a seat next to her on the fallen tree log and brushes aside the hair that sticks to Kevan's wet cheeks. Gammie's glasses are missing from her face and her hair is lying around her shoulders. Her charcoal-colored eyes look deep into Kevan's. Kevan believes that her grandmother is the most beautiful woman she knows.

"What is wrong, my girl?" Gammie asks.

"I can't tell you, Gammie, or I'll get into trouble." Kevan looks down at the ground, shoulders slumped like a camel's back.

"Can you tell me what you're doing in the woods?"

"I just wanted to get away from *him*."

"Is your father home?"

"Yes, that's who I'm talking about."

"But you can't tell me why you want to get away?"

"No!" Kevan sobs. "One, two, buckle my shoe—"

"Okay, okay." Gammie holds up both hands. "We should go for a walk. What do you think?"

"I'm not supposed to go out of hearing distance from the house."

"Oh, it'll be okay. You're with me. I'll just tell your father that I kidnapped you and you had no choice. Or he might not even notice. What do you think?"

"Maybe. He's just playing cards and drinking with the neighbors."

"Then I say, let's go. But first I have to ask: can you keep a secret?"

Kevan perks up and nods vigorously. "Yes!"

Gammie reaches out her hand and urges Kevan to stand. "Come, then. I want to show you something, but it has to be our little secret."

The woods, a chorus of greens and browns and a variety of trees in all sizes, is easy to maneuver through, since there is little undergrowth. As they walk side by side and hand in hand, last year's leaves crunch under their feet. A short distance into their walk, Gammie stops to stand in front of a large tree. She pulls a pocketknife from her jeans and uses it to carve a small X on the trunk. As they turn one way, then another, Gammie continues to mark X's on several large trees along their path.

"This is so you can find your way in the future," she says.

"Find my way where?" Kevan asks.

"You'll see."

After Kevan asks "Are we there yet?" several times, they clear the woods and step into an open meadow. To Kevan, it feels like stepping into another era encircled by a wall of trees. Although it isn't far into the woods, the meadow seems secluded. In the middle is a huge pond with a small dock. Behind the pond is an abandoned farmhouse, and even farther behind is a tall stone building with vines growing up the walls; the property must have been forgotten long ago. Next to that building, Kevan sees half a door hidden below ground level.

"Come. Let me show you around," Gammie says.

Gammie walks Kevan around the pond and toward the dock. They take a seat on the edge of the dock and Gammie removes her shoes. Kevan does the same. Gammie dips her feet into the water, but Kevan's feet won't reach. Placing her hands into Kevan's armpits, Gammie picks her up and sets her on the dock between her knees. Wrapping both arms around Kevan's chest, she lowers her just enough to allow her to put her feet into the water, letting her splash for a bit, then sets her back on the dock.

Sitting in the sunshine, they swing their feet and gaze across the pond.

"Look, Renee. It's an eastern spadefoot. The cute kind." Gammie points to tiny ripples in the water.

"What's an eastern spadefoot?"

"That frog. See it?"

Kevan squints her eyes. Then they grow wide as she spots the frog swimming toward the dock, its tiny legs sprawling out to the side. "I see it."

They watch the frog as it swims closer; then Kevan lets out a squeal. The frog darts underwater.

After a few moments of silence, Gammie looks around carefully and then looks back at Kevan. "Do you want to tell me why you're upset?"

Kevan lets a rapid breath escape her nostrils as her face shifts into fear. "I'm afraid to tell you."

"Why, honey?"

"Dad said if I told anyone, he was going to beat me." A tear slips down from the corner of Kevan's eye. She rubs at it, creating a dirty smear across her cheek.

"You can tell me, Renee. It will never pass my lips. I can hold a secret better than Victoria herself." Gammie brings her hand to her mouth, turns it in front of her lips as if locking a box with a key, then pretends to throw the key into the pond.

"Who's Victoria?"

"A smart lady who has a secret no one has figured out. Doesn't matter."

"Promise you won't tell?" Kevan asks, looking up at her.

"I promise."

Kevan's words fall over each other as she retells her story. "Mom and Dad and our neighbors, Ron and Jackie, from down the street, are at the house playing cards. Dad and Jackie were playing as a team—Ron and Mom were too. They were sitting at the kitchen table and I was sitting in a chair beside Mom. I dropped my baby doll on the floor and when I bent down to pick it up, I saw Jackie rubbing her foot between Dad's legs. I raised up and Jackie gave me a mean look. Dad snapped at me and made me go outside to play. He said I had no business being inside with the adults. I just went and sat on the porch."

Kevan pauses and gazes into the pond, sighing deeply. "Dad said he was going to the shop to get another beer. Then Jackie said she was going to her car to get a cigarette. She didn't go to her car—she followed Dad. I peeked behind the workshop to see if they were there."

Kevan stops talking, debating whether to finish her story.

"Then what? You can tell me."

"Dad had Jackie pushed against the wall. He was kissing her and she was making funny noises. I tried to run before he could see me, but he saw me anyway. He grabbed me and said if I told Mom or anyone, he would beat me black and blue." Kevan wipes a stray tear from her cheek.

"That piece of—"

"Please, Gammie, don't tell."

"I won't, my dear. Karma will take care of him. It's a vengeful thing, and he will get his share when it's due." Gammie looks away, eyes squinted, as she takes a deep breath. "You shouldn't see such things at your age."

"Does this mean Mommy and Daddy will get a divorce?"

"Don't worry about stuff like that."

"Can I tell you another secret, Gammie?"

"You can tell me anything, my dear."

"I wish they *would* get a divorce."

Gammie smiles. "Don't worry about big-people things. If anything ever happens, you will always have me—always."

Gammie kisses Kevan on the top of the head and hugs her close as they sit on the dock, talking about everything from the sky to the earth.

CHAPTER SIX

Kevan

Early Summer

As I sit slouched in my chair, I thumb through the pictures one last time and dissolve into my grief. I hold back the flood of tears for fear that if I weep, her passing will become a reality. I don't want to believe she is gone. I loved my Gammie so much.

When the tears come anyway, I fear I can't stop crying. I jump up, grab my empty glass, and head to the kitchen. I pour myself more wine and slump over the counter. "You're going to be okay," I tell myself aloud. I swallow a large mouthful of wine and walk, heavy-hearted, back to the study.

In an attempt to remove the dark cloud around me, I bypass the stack of pictures sitting on the end table and move over to the area rug between the sofa and fireplace. In the center of the rug is a large collage in progress. This piece of art comprises many photographs, ephemera, and other materials that form a cluster of images of unique houses. I have collected each piece: newspaper and magazine clippings, photographs I've taken, and drawings I've made of specific structures

I've seen in vivid dreams. Scattered throughout are letters of the alphabet and word fragments.

My favorite thing to photograph is houses—especially old and abandoned ones. I try to capture the stories they have to tell. I sense a positive aura around some, while others pulse with a darkness that seems to lurk in the photos after I've developed them. The houses that make it into my collage have drawn me to them in ways I can't explain. The collage's story is a mystery to me; I must finish it to figure out the ending.

This piece of art, among several others, will be on display at the Museum of Modern Art in New York sometime next summer. The exhibit will be my second such accomplishment and the one I'm prouder of. The thought of Gammie not being there sits on my chest like a heavy weight. Closing my eyes, I breathe deep and exhale long, counting backward from five.

I open my eyes and look over details of the collage. Most might view it as chaotic or childlike in organization, but I know its patterns have purpose. This is how all of my art begins and develops into maturity. Picking up one side of the collage, which is feeling quite heavy, I drag it over to the unused fireplace. I stand it up and lean it against the stone wall, then step back to take in the piece as a whole.

Swallowing more of my wine, I move my eyes over each piece, remembering when and why I chose them. Each smaller house of the collage is meticulously placed to form one larger house, and its obscure complexity reveals a story through all the smaller pieces it contains. As I look at it, a weird tingling sensation travels down the backs of my neck and arms. Suddenly, something about it feels real and familiar. It tugs at something in my mind, but like a shadow that doesn't come fully into view no matter how it turns, it remains unclear. I look hard at it but decide it isn't going to come to me yet.

My study has become my personal museum of accomplishments. My art and photographs, some of which have earned prestigious awards, decorate the walls. I have spent countless hours doing what I love and being rewarded for it. It's a dream come true, made possible by encouragement from Gammie and hard work. Gammie believed I was proof that one can survive the worst of childhoods and still become a woman of importance.

Several in my family have various artistic talents, but I am the only one who has followed this gift and made it into an actual, successful career. Gammie spent many of her days painting as a hobby or pastime. She sold a few paintings through local art shows, but she never cared about making money from it. Each of my brothers showed great promise in artistic abilities with drawings and cartoons. Matthew liked to illustrate his life as a child, but my father discovered his drawings and destroyed them. That was the end of his art career. James dabbled in landscapes as a young adult but never took it seriously. They say even my father had some artistic abilities. I don't care what those were.

The side door creaking open in the kitchen detours me from my thoughts.

"Kev, you home?"

"In the study," I call back.

Beth walks in with a bottle of white wine in hand. "You start without me, bitch?" She turns and walks back to the kitchen, chatting as she does so.

Beth has a unique style only she can pull off. Today she wears white shorts covered in glitter and a bubblegum-pink tank top, her blond hair pulled back with a bright yellow bow. She is at least four inches taller than I am, with the long, tan legs that every woman dreams of having. Her eyes are the color of blue that people buy contacts to achieve. Beth doesn't have to work hard to be beautiful—it comes naturally to her. Her beauty sometimes makes me envious, even though I try not to be. Beth's ability to speak her mind is what I love about her. She can make a grown man blush just with her personality.

I force a smile. "Guess you better catch up," I say as she disappears around the corner. Eleanor jumps down from the sofa and crouches under the table next to it. I hear her low growl as she looks toward the kitchen. Eleanor has never liked Beth.

"The bottle opener should be out already," I call out.

Beth and I met when we were approaching eight years old. She went to a different elementary school, so I didn't know her until she discovered the secret spot with the pond and old house by accident one day. That day, I was sitting on the dock, using pieces of limestone as chalk to draw on the boards. I heard a sound behind me, and there was Beth walking across the field. I asked her how she had come to find my secret place. Beth pointed to the woods, opposite the direction I usually traveled, and said that her mother allowed her to explore the woods behind their house as long as she came home before dark.

From then on, we met and played together when we could, usually whenever I could sneak out of my house. I never told my family about Beth, because if I had, they would have found out that I was sneaking away. The secret spot in the woods then became hers, mine, and Gammie's.

Beth and I have been friends ever since. She is the only friend I have a genuine connection with these days, and she's the only person in my life now who knows about my troubled past. Sometimes Beth stays here with me, but she comes and goes, living her life to the fullest. My focus has always been more on school and career, whereas she is a fly-by-the-seat-of-her-pants kind of gal. I'm glad she's here tonight.

Beth enters the room with her wineglass in hand. "I came as soon as I could. How are you doing?" she asks, walking over to the stack of pictures on the table. "Never mind, I can see." Beth takes a large sip of wine as she flops down on the chaise. Eleanor hisses and runs around the corner toward the stairs. Beth tries to coax and even bribe the fat cat, but Eleanor only growls and flees the room. If Beth doesn't pay attention to her, she stares at her from afar, tail flipping, with a displeased expression on her face. No one else ever visits me, so I'm not sure how she would act around anyone else.

"I love you, but I hate your fat cat," Beth says jokingly. Then her face turns serious. "What can I do to help?"

"You're helping just by being here."

"Good God! I haven't seen this picture in ages." She picks up the picture of two little girls sitting on a dock. "What were we? Seven? Eight?"

That year Beth had gotten a Polaroid camera for her birthday and brought it with her. We had taken two selfies, one for me and one for herself. Beth's camera was one of those fancy ones that had a timer on it. After placing the camera on a dock-post, we smiled for the camera, our arms draped across each other's shoulders, heads together.

"We were so young here! I can't believe you still have this."

We talk through most of the night as I share my fondest memories of Gammie and myself. As I unload a multitude of stories, my mood shifts to the lighter side and I feel myself smiling.

"Well, before you found out about your Gammie, did you get laid?"

"Absolutely!"

"Ooo. Spill it, girl." She flops over onto her stomach and props up on her elbows.

"Just what I needed! Everyone should have a younger toy." As I take a sip of wine, I remember the man from the spirit store. "But . . ." I say, drawing out the word. "After I left Kyle's, I stopped to buy some wine and saw this guy. He was, for sure, every bit the tall, dark, and handsome type. You know, long hair just past his shoulders, blue eyes, and very tall. I mean, his eyes! I'm so drawn to beautiful eyes."

"And asses!"

"Of course, that too!" I giggle.

"Did you get his name? Say hi or grab his ass? Something?" Beth teases.

"No! I bolted like an idiot schoolgirl. I've never let anyone fluster me like that. God, he was gorgeous."

"Sounds like your type. Hell, he sounds like *my* type. Maybe we can look him up somehow."

"Maybe. Or maybe I should stick to my boy toy."

"Ah, yes! Boy toys are nice."

I wait, remaining crouched until I'm sure the man won't return. Then, cautiously, I stand and walk toward the house. The tall weeds scrape against my damp legs, irritating my skin. My feet are bare and the dead earth feels prickly and sharp. I step one foot, then the other, onto the old stone steps. The wooden boards on the porch show discolor from age. Weeds grow up through the cracks. On each end of the porch are remnants of broken furniture; only pieces of porch swings remain.

A few boards still hang on the exterior walls. They have aged into a blackish-gray, showing that time didn't pass this place by. Can a house feel pain? This house screams isolation—as if its people have left it behind against its will. It seems restless and troubled.

An intense tightness forms deep in my throat, and I dread what awaits inside the house. I fear that what made me cry earlier is waiting on the other side of the door. I take the key in my fingers, ready to unlock the door. When I reach for the doorknob, the door creaks open wide. The dark house swells before me, wafting the smell of damp air.

I step inside and, with caution, walk toward a bookshelf against the far wall. At eye level is one lonely book lying on its side. The cover—which has no writing on it—resembles leather, and the pages are trimmed in gold.

To the right of the bookshelf is a door that stands half open. The sense of loneliness from the house feels much stronger here. The room is cluttered with debris and fallen pieces of ceiling. A closet door stands open in the corner. Only a section of a wooden ladder hangs from the ceiling, too dangerous to climb.

In another room, only parts of a kitchen remain. Most of the cupboard doors are missing, and those that remain are standing open. Except for one. I attempt to open it, with no success. One small cupboard that hangs close to the ceiling contains something yellow sitting toward the back. I jump to see what it is. I feel apprehensive, but something tells me I'm supposed to find it. I retrieve the bottom half of a chair from a corner of the room and slide it in front of the cabinet, then step up and reach for what's inside. It looks like a vase, but when I pull it down, I realize it isn't. It's an urn, bright yellow, etched with blue honeysuckle vines circling and trimming the vessel. Blue hummingbirds fly above the vines and sample the nectar.

I rotate the urn in my hands and wish that I could stop the dream now before I see any more, but I see a name. I slam the urn down and try to back away, but I'm stuck in place. Engraved on the side, in a zigzag pattern, is one name: Beth.

CHAPTER SEVEN

Nathan

I decide to call it a night and allow Dorothy—who is still clutching her friend's journal close to her chest—to tend to her grief alone. Dorothy believes that being alone is food for the soul and that you can't fear loneliness if you've welcomed it most of your life. As long as I can remember, she has lived alone on this big plantation. Her husband ran off years before my mother and I came, and she never took interest in finding another.

I climb behind the wheel of my pickup truck and drive toward the back of Dorothy's property to my residence. The tree-lined lane hasn't changed much since the day my mother and I came here, except for the size of the trees. As I cross under their high, curved branches, I flash back to my first time here.

The evening my mother and I pulled up to the front of the house, I couldn't contain my excitement as I bounced in the back seat. I was moving into a mansion. I had never seen the inside of a two-story house before, but this one would be ours. I took in every detail—its brick walls, its massive shutters, its large windows.

As we pulled around to the back of the house, I had my door open before the car even stopped. With my dog, Donatello, at my heels, I ran across the back porch and into the biggest kitchen I'd ever seen— bigger than the entire house we'd been living in. As I sprinted through the dining room and the already furnished living room, I was in awe. There were *two* couches—one large and one small. I flopped down on the smaller one and bounced. Then I spotted what I'd been looking for: stairs. I climbed them two at a time and ran from one upstairs room to the next, settling in the room I chose for myself. Donatello must have sensed that it was our room now, because he lay down in the center of the floor, trying it out. I'd been an only child for almost eight years, and my dog was my closest friend.

Tonight, I step through the back door and into the same kitchen, and a different dog waddles toward me, folds into a downward-dog stretch, then loudly yawns before making his way over. Jake is a chocolate lab, the only breed of dog I've ever owned. His name is a common one, as opposed to the Teenage Mutant Ninja Turtle names I chose when I was young. I scratch him behind the ear.

"Hey, boy. You ready to go outside?"

I grab a beer from the fridge, open it, and step through the squeaky front door to sit on the porch. Crickets chirp all around as if they are talking back and forth.

I sit down in the old chair that was my mother's favorite. Now it's mine. Its wood is slick in places from years of use. I tilt the chair toward the wall, the back legs holding my weight as I rock back and forth, looking at the same scene she always looked at. As I sit, my mind wanders backward again. I think about how my mother loved it here, spending many hours on this front porch. Now I find myself doing the same.

Most of my childhood memories began here. When we moved here, I was only seven years old. My mother had been working as a waitress, but the tips were poor. The job still allowed her to put food on the table. There weren't many men around, and I only remember her having one boyfriend. When he found out he'd gotten her pregnant, he split.

I met Dorothy one day after school in the diner. I sat in a corner booth, where the manager treated me to a milkshake for good behavior. Dorothy came in and requested that my mother be her waitress. She claimed that no one else knew how to make her tea correctly and that Mom's service was better than anyone else's. On this day, Dorothy sat down next to me in the booth. Confused, I looked at my mother, seeking her approval to talk to a stranger. My mother nodded, and I gave the lady a half smile and continued drinking my milkshake.

"Would you be interested in making money to put in your piggy bank? I assume you have a piggy bank?" Dorothy asked.

I looked at the woman and thought her face looked crabby. Wide-eyed, I glanced back at my mother again, and she nodded for me to answer the question.

"Yeah, but it ain't got much in it."

"Well, then, it sounds like your little ass needs a job. You can't make any money sitting around here stuffing your face with ice cream."

My mother came and took a seat next to me, wrapping an arm around my shoulder. "Nate, this gracious lady has offered us a place to live and a job. What are your thoughts on moving out into the country?"

I shrugged. "I guess so."

I was unsure whether I would like this woman, but I knew the decision had already been made. When I looked up at Mom, she smiled down at me with so much love and reassurance that I felt everything would be all right.

I smile at this sweet memory of my mother, but then my thoughts shift to a much darker time. These thoughts usually stay tucked away like a book on a shelf, but every now and then, the book opens. Some stories of the past have deep, painful chapters. Like the night I found out that my mother was going to die.

I was away, attending my first year of college, when I got the news. Dorothy called, saying I needed to come home as soon as possible. My mother had been involved in an accident and was in critical condition. When I got to the hospital, she was unrecognizable. The broken bones, bruises, and wounds had misshaped her into someone who wasn't my mother. And then she was gone.

Devastated and feeling lost, I took the next year off from school and stayed around to help Dorothy. Dorothy had always encouraged me to spend time with the workhands, and I'd learned enough to be of help. With Dorothy's encouragement and support, I then went back to college and worked to finish my degree. I knew that my mother had sacrificed a lot for me to attend college. I finished school and achieved what she had pushed me so hard to do.

Somber memories push back even further than the death of my mother. Four years before her death was the mysterious disappearance of my little sister. Gracie wandered off to play as she often did, but this time she didn't return. To this day, there are no leads, and her body was never found, though we spent two years searching. Despite our efforts and those of the police, my mother and I succumbed to the idea that we would never know what had happened to her. My mother did the best she could to piece her life back together, pushing me to get through the rest of high school, although she was never the same. She was only an empty shell of a woman.

My mother made decisions that weren't always rational and that became more reckless over time. When I left for college, she was frequenting pubs and bars, staying out until the early hours of the morning. Her nurturing side had disappeared. Rumor had it that my mother was under the influence when she had her accident, but the sheriff didn't pursue it. He thought finding this information would cause more harm than good. I had lost my mother—I didn't need to be punished with useless knowledge.

Skrreee-skrrrt. A sound similar to sharp nails on a chalkboard interrupts my thoughts. Jake jumps to his feet and barks. Giving a lazy moan, he lies down again, dismissing it. I do too, but then a tree branch sliding across an upstairs window jerks me from my thoughts. A gusty breeze carries the sound of the tree branch again, and I bring myself fully back to the current sounds and smells. Deciding to close the book of memories, I drink down the last of my beer and retire.

As I'm drifting off to sleep, I hear a voice.

Here, Nate. I made this for you. Hold out your hand so I can put it on.

I feel a light tap on my wrist, and I spring from my pillow. I look at my wrist and rub it with my other hand. I can still feel the lingering sensation where someone touched me, but there's no one here to have done so. I sit up and look around the room. The voice I heard was my little sister's. It seemed very real, but it was not possible. She's been missing for a long time. Besides, she would be fully grown now. The voice I heard was the voice of a little girl.

I sit, stunned, as I try to remember if I had been dreaming, but I can't recall anything else. I am pretty sure I wasn't. *I had to be.*

I shiver from the whole event. Gracie's voice was so vivid. I hadn't experienced an episode like this in years. In the first couple of years after she disappeared, I seemed to hear her voice often, in a similar manner. Not in dreams, but upon waking or just before falling asleep. At one point, it began to happen when I was fully awake. I would hear her down the hall in her room. I thought I was losing my mind.

It happened so often that first year. As time passed and the search for my sister slowed to nothing, it stopped. This is the first time it's happened in a long time. I ponder on it a bit longer, staring at my wrist, then shake it off and go downstairs.

With a big yawn, I pour myself a cup of black coffee to combat a restless night of sleep, then grab my laptop and take a seat at the kitchen table. I open the laptop to search for the woman I saw yesterday. Kevin at the spirit store had said she was an art professor, specializing in photography, at the college in Vinbrooke.

I google the words *Vinbrooke College of the Arts* and locate the college's official website. Clicking on a drop-down menu under *Faculty*, I scan the list of professors, searching for her first name, since I don't know the last. When I see it, I click the mouse and her dark eyes look back at me. They are bright and beautiful, and I am immediately lost in them. What is it about this woman? I read her entire name, *Kevan Renee Copeland*, then search further, hoping to learn more about her.

She holds a doctorate and teaches an array of art classes. Her position has given her the opportunity to travel the world—France, in particular, where she teaches young, aspiring artists. The background of her webpage displays several interactive thumbnails of her artwork and photographs. I click on one icon and a larger photo appears.

In the picture, a girl seems to be falling from a second-story window, but on a longer look she seems to be levitating, frozen in midair. Dolls and toys hover around her. The atmosphere is stormy and gray. The girl is falling toward a body of water, and the surface of the water shows her reflection. Her eyes and skin are a different color in the reflection: the girl frozen in midair appears alive, with blue eyes, but the girl in the water has dark, haunting eyes and her skin is a bluish color.

The picture floods me with an overwhelming sadness. Something about the falling girl makes me think of my little sister.

Below the photo is a title and caption:

Secrets

Winner of the International Photography Award, 2017

I wonder what makes someone create a piece of art such as this. Was it inspired by some tragedy?

I click on a few more photos, lingering on each. With the hope of seeing a glimpse into the artist, I click on the photo of her to enlarge it. I stare at her eyes a while longer, then bookmark the page for later. I then close the computer and head to the back door. Out of habit, I retrieve a toothpick to chew on, trying to kill the craving for a cigarette—a habit I kicked two years ago. During my short drive to the main house, I plot a few ideas on finding a way to meet this woman.

CHAPTER EIGHT

Kevan
Early Summer

The moment my eyes open, I bolt upright, then try to identify where I am and catch my breath. I'm not sure which woke me first, the end of the terrible dream or the thumping of my heart. Flashes of the dream continue. *The frog. The necklace and key. The dead woman. The horrible man.* I press the palms of my hands over my eyelids in an attempt to erase the images.

I have no desire to revisit the nightmare by allowing myself to go back to sleep. I've had unwanted dreams most of my life, and I know from experience that if I go back to sleep, they pick up where they left off. During the past few months, my dreams have become more aggressive, and I'm afraid of returning to this one, though I'm tired from having stayed up late chatting with Beth and drinking wine.

I grab my phone from the nightstand and make my way downstairs to the kitchen to make some coffee. It is almost 6:00 a.m., and dawn peeks through the window. When my coffee finishes perking, I carry it to the study and take a seat in the corner at my drawing table.

What is it about dreams? Mine appear like ghosts that hide themselves away; I can't predict when they will make an entrance. Some seem to come only to cause my mind harm and stress, and it's impossible to stop them. Chaotic or organized, they are always a mystery, but no matter the order or nature of events, I know they have to mean something. I used to try to understand them, but now I often choose not to. Like unwanted guests, they have worn out their welcome.

I open the drawing pad to a blank page and begin to draw the house from my dream. I draw with a sense of urgency, including every detail before it leaves my mind's eye. Something about the house makes me feel as if I owe it the respect of helping it live outside my dream. As I transfer the images to the page, I get a sense of déjà vu. I draw the outside of the house, with two windows and a steep roof. In the background of one window, I draw the countertop with the urn sitting on top of it. I neglect to put Beth's name on the urn as it was in my dream, because I don't want that part to seem real—or maybe it is fear that doing so will cause something to happen. Next I draw the pond, careful to add every detail of its contents below, including the outlines of a woman and a frog. I draw the back view of the evil man walking down the overgrown road. As I sketch his outline, I shudder.

As I finish the drawing, Beth walks into the room, coffee in hand. I look at the clock—8:00 a.m.

"It looks like you've been up a while." She plops down on the chaise, eyelids still droopy.

"Had another of my infamous dreams. This one sucked!" I say.

"Don't they all?" She walks to the drawing table to see what I've been working on. "Another house for your collage?"

"It's from my dream. Something about the place freaked me out. This was the first time I dreamed of a dead person, too. The woman was trapped in the pond, and she gave me a key."

"Good God! You and your screwed-up dreams!" Beth tilts her head, looking at my drawing. "Any idea what the key is for?"

"Nope. Why on earth do I dream stuff like this?"

"Well, you know what I think? Staggering down memory lane last night wasn't a good idea."

"Maybe."

The woman in my dream seems significant. Even more, I wonder why Beth's name was on an urn—it scares me. Afraid of freaking her out, I keep this to myself.

Burying the disturbance of it for now, I ask, "More coffee?"

We walk to the kitchen and I make a quick bite to eat.

"So, what's the plan for today?" Beth asks.

"As much as I despise the idea, I know I have to go to Bitterton, which means seeing my mother and brothers." The words invoke a deep and brooding dread in the pit of my stomach. "There's no way I'm going to let my brothers handle Gammie's arrangements. Knowing them, they'll bury her in a box made from wooden pallets or cardboard."

"I wouldn't put it past that second bastard brother of yours," Beth says, adding, "I'm not letting you go alone."

"You don't have to go. I don't think I can plan more than one funeral today," I say as a joke.

"Why on earth would I miss out on all the fun? I can make myself scarce when you need me to. I can also pop back in just as easy."

My cell phone bleeps, and a message appears on the screen from a sender identified as *K. B.* Beth glances at it, eyes brightening. "Oh, it's your young toy."

I slide right, and the message opens to a pic of Kyle holding a cup of coffee. The text reads, "Good morning, beautiful." I smile and turn the phone toward Beth.

"I see why you picked this toy. Handsome young devil."

As quickly as a teenager might respond, I text a reply, then take my cup of coffee with me as I head upstairs to the shower. Kyle's teasing message makes me smile again as I sit on the edge of the bed for a moment. I think about what Gammie would have said about my little fling. Probably something like, "There's nothing wrong with a girl having a little fun. Especially when you have a sexy thing like that to play with." My smile fades as quickly as it came. I had planned to tell her about Kyle, but I'd never gotten the chance.

I turn the shower knob an inch or so from the hottest setting possible, wanting to feel the sting of the hot water on my skin. Allowing myself one last moment to feel grief, I succumb to it as tears merge with the water from the showerhead. I give them time to pass, then push myself to move on with my day. I get dressed and go back downstairs. There I find Beth ready for the day, holding my recent drawing in her hand, staring at it.

"Hey, Red? Did you pay close attention to what you drew this morning?" Beth asks.

"Of course."

"No, really! Look at your drawing and then look at your collage." Beth turns the sketch paper to face me.

"It looks the same as it did in my dream." I walk over and stand next to Beth, rotating my body toward the collage. My mood shifts to confusion, then realization. "The drawing *is* my collage." I look at the two of them several times, noting the comparisons.

"Do you remember dreaming of this house before now?" Beth asks.

"No, but I must have."

Then, like an immediate slap to my brain, I realize I *have* seen the house—in real life. Picking up the photo of Gammie and me seated on the dock, I focus on the house in the background. "It's this house. I hadn't realized that my collage is this house. It makes me wonder why I'm focusing on this place. Why now?"

"I hadn't realized it either, but you're right. I remember it now, from all the times we played nearby," Beth says. "How long ago did you start working on the collage?"

"A year ago—give or take. I can't believe I didn't notice this. I hadn't thought about that property in years—at least not consciously." After turning the photo in Beth's direction and then back toward myself, I look at it longer. "Maybe the photo made me dream about it."

"Maybe. But it still doesn't explain why you began making a huge-ass collage about it over a year ago. At some point, you were thinking about it."

We both look closely at the large piece of art, neither of us sure what to say.

Beth breaks our silence. "Here's what I think—I think you shouldn't drink and dream," she says with a nervous laugh. "Makes me wonder what else goes on in that fucked-up head of yours. Never mind!

Don't tell me." Beth holds up a hand and turns her head away in a teasing manner.

Beth and I walk outside to the car. A white piece of paper is pinned underneath my windshield wiper. Confused, I look toward the road in both directions, then turn my eyes back to the car. Something about this is unnerving. I lift the wiper and pluck the piece of textured paper from underneath. It's the same type of paper I use for drawings and sketches. I turn it over and suddenly feel a tingling sensation move over the surface of my arms, like tiny bugs crawling, as my hair stands at attention.

"What is it?" Beth asks.

I turn the drawing toward her. Her expression turns cold, mirroring my own. "What the fuck?"

CHAPTER NINE

Kevan
1995

Kevan sits on her bed and strokes her pet rabbit as she tries to tune out her father, who is in the living room taunting her mother. Whenever she closes her eyes, it seems to prompt her father to rant louder, his words becoming even more hateful. She knows that closing her eyes doesn't cause this to happen—still, she fears leaving her room.

She and her brothers hide in their rooms all day. She feels like a coward but doesn't know what else to do. She preoccupies herself with reading, drawing, and listening to music. It does little to soothe her anxiety.

"Why do you have to be a goody-two-shoes bitch, Edith?" Clyde's words carry through the walls. "You think you're better than me because you go to church every Sunday. If I have to be boring and miserable to make it into your heaven, then forget it." His voice takes on a fake whiny tone as he speaks to the dog. "Ain't that right, Bo? Look at her, she's all fat and ugly." It snaps back to a tone that is sharp and hateful. "Why can't you keep yourself in better shape? Your sister does. Our neighbor Jackie does."

Our golden retriever whimpers as if he knows something bad is about to happen. Bo rarely gets to enter the house, and when he does, it's only because Clyde has been gone for several days. When Clyde does return home, smelling like a soured whiskey barrel, Bo often becomes one brunt of Clyde's drunken rampages, which can result in a boot to the rib cage for shits and giggles. When Clyde gets in these moods, Bo shifts from a protective canine to a clinging, sad puppy.

"Clyde, you're drunk. Please just go somewhere else until you sober up," Edith pleads gently. Kevan's anger brews as she hears her mother speak as if to coax a scared child. She can't understand why her mother is so nice to her father.

"I am not drunk! Why do you always accuse me of being drunk?" Even as he says it, Kevan hears him slur his words. "I know why! You're too saintly to drink with me. Maybe we wouldn't have such a shitty marriage if you'd have a shot with me once in a while. Maybe you would stop being such a lame-ass, boring bitch. I could go down the street and drink with Ron and Jackie. *She'll* drink with her husband."

"Well, why don't you?" Edith's tone shifts from calm to aggravation. "You think being there is better than here, then go for it."

Kevan waits for Edith's words to anger her father.

Bo's whimpers turn into a desperate whine, and Kevan senses what will come next. She jumps out of bed, crawls into the closet, closes the door behind her, and begins to rock and chant. *One, two, buckle my shoe. Three, four, shut the door . . .*

She finishes the rhyme, but it does nothing. She starts again.

One, two, the sky is blue. Three, four, sing some more. Five, six, stop playing tricks. Seven, eight, it's getting late. Nine, ten, I'll start again. One, two, the sky is blue . . .

This small rectangular space has shielded her many times. She feels safer in the closet. The trauma her father inflicts doesn't seem to follow her here. She squeezes her eyes shut even though it is dark in the small space.

Someone gently taps the other side of the wall she's leaning against, and a small voice says, "It's going to be okay, Kev-ree." Her brothers have climbed into their closet, which is right next to hers. Her little brother Tommy sobs as he repeats over and over, "Make him stop. Please make him stop."

Kevan doesn't know what she would do without her brothers. They help her through so many moments like this.

"It'll be over soon, you two. He'll pass out on the couch and we can all go to sleep," James reassures.

"I'm sick of this shit!" Matthew says. "I want to hit him."

James shushes him. "Matthew—don't," he pleads.

Kevan plugs her ears to block out her father's rant, but some of his words still pierce through. "Edith—stupid cunt—should be kissing my ass—sorry lay—" Kevan plugs her ears harder. "Fucking dog! I'll teach you to get in my face!"

"Stop it, Dad!" Matthew yells from somewhere down the hall.

Panic and adrenaline take over, and despite her fear, Kevan finds the courage to burst out of the closet, fists clenched. She runs into the living room to face another of her father's horror scenes. Bo lies on the floor, and her father is stomping his foot over and over on the dog's chest, hip, and head.

"You fucking dog! I'll teach you to disobey me. No one gets in my face!"

"Dad, please stop!" Tommy cries.

"Stop, Dad! You're killing him!" Kevan screams. Tears blur her vision as she sees that Bo is no longer moving. Her father's boot crunches Bo's ribs with an audible sound. Her mother and Matthew grab her father's arms and attempt to pull him off the dog. Tommy slumps in place, wraps his arms around his knees, and sobs.

Rage fills Kevan as she stiffens her arms and her hands squeeze into tighter fists. Her grip is so tight, her fingernails dig into her palms. She launches herself at her father and pounds those tight fists into his lower back. On the fourth blow, her father steps back, out of breath, and slings his body from side to side, breaking free from the grips on his arms. He turns to Kevan as she continues to punch him anywhere she can. She inflicts two more blows to his stomach, which makes him wince, but only a little.

"You fucking twat!" Clyde backhands Kevan across the cheek,

which sends her to her knees. "Yeah, that's where you belong, you little bitch—on your knees. That's where all women belong—on their knees in front of a man. That's all you're good for." Clyde hocks up phlegm from deep in his throat and spits it at Kevan.

"Clyde, stop it!"

Gammie Frances has sneaked into the house, unbeknownst to anyone. She somehow always knows when something is wrong here. She steps in and shoves Clyde. He staggers backward, loses his footing, and lands on the floor with an unbraced thud. His sit bones pound the hard surface first, and then he rolls the rest of the way onto his back.

Tears of anger turn back to tears of fear as Kevan crawls over to Bo and strokes his face. She kisses him on the nose and pleads with him to open his eyes. His chest rises and falls, but not enough to fill his lungs with the air he needs.

"Get the hell out of here, Dad!" Matthew yells.

Clyde laughs as if the entire episode has been funny. Kevan glares at her father and imagines herself standing over him as she presses her foot down on his throat until his face turns purple. She wants to see him gasp for air as his body becomes lifeless—wants to beat him like he's beaten her dog. She wants him to die.

"I mean it, Dad, go somewhere and sleep it off!" Matthew stands over his father, just beyond kicking range.

"And what'll you do if I don't, son? You think you're big enough? Then bring it." Clyde belts out a patronizing laugh and attempts to get up, but falls back on his drunken ass again. "You little bastard. Get your ass back to your bedroom—all of you, take your asses to your rooms!"

Gammie exclaims, "Matthew's right. Why don't *you* go somewhere else?"

Clyde laughs again—only this time it's a deep, smoker's laugh—and then he coughs. "You should see all of your faces," he slurs. "Lighten up. I was just having fun." He rolls to his side, pushes himself off the floor, and staggers to the couch. There he flops onto his back, throws his arm over his head. A cheap picture frame bounces from the wall, slides down, and lands behind the couch. "You should learn how to have fun."

The dog tries to raise his head with help from Matthew. Gammie joins in and lifts the dog up into her arms, cradling him.

"Come with me," Gammie says to Kevan. "Matthew, you boys stay here with your mother in case your father wakes up."

Kevan follows Gammie out of the house and into the woods. "Where are we going, Gammie?"

"Somewhere Bo can be at peace. We'll take him to our secret place."

Kevan follows behind her, crying for her dog. She mumbles under her breath, "I hate Dad. I hate him. I want him to die."

"It's coming, my dear. One day."

CHAPTER TEN

Nathan

I drive with Dorothy across town and listen to her talk about her friend Frances and the fond memories they shared. Her stories paint a nostalgic picture of two interesting women who, to the curious eye, appeared staid and innocent, but behind that perception, they embodied Thelma and Louise—it was them against the world.

"Frances could be as friendly as a letter from home, or she could be as mean as a coiled snake. But her heart was bigger than anyone's. You always knew where you stood with her. There was no in-between. She either liked you or she didn't, and you didn't have to guess which one."

Dorothy's description sounds as if she's describing herself. I wonder why I never met this woman, Dorothy's best friend. Maybe I did when I was younger, but if so, I don't remember.

Dorothy instructs me to park in front of her friend's house.

"Do you need help to get inside, Miss Dorothy?" I ask.

"You know better than that, young man. Since when do I need help walking?" Dorothy's eyebrows shift together, intensifying her usual scowl, but her brightly colored lips manage to form a smile. She hooks her square purse over her forearm and shimmies out of the truck with ease.

I raise my hands in surrender. "Just being a gentleman. When would you like me to return?"

"You don't have to. My driver will come get me. I have plenty to attend to today."

After I leave Dorothy on the doorstep, I decide to take a drive to Vinbrooke, swing by the college, then stop at the cemetery. For some reason, Mom and Gracie have been on my mind a great deal lately.

I complete the trip to Vinbrooke on autopilot and then drive across the college campus. I pause in front of the art building in hopes that I will catch a glimpse of Kevan Renee Copeland. Other than a few students walking past, though, campus is fairly deserted. A casually dressed gentleman steps from the front of the building and shoots me a puzzled look. Suddenly feeling like a stalker, I shake my head and move on. How can I find a way to meet this woman?

Near the college, I approach the massive, ancient stone archway that leads into the cemetery. The archway resembles the entrance to a medieval castle. At the base of each of the supporting pillars is a giant stone paw. Two massive gargoyles perch above as if guarding the entrance. Once inside the cemetery, I roll down my window to inhale the fragrance that radiates from this place, with its flowers and greenery. Although these grounds entomb the dead, they are beautiful. Tourism brochures describe this as an outdoor museum of the dead. The headstones, with their elaborate carvings and poetic epitaphs, are historic and beyond ordinary. This cemetery attracts visitors from around the world.

My mother and sister's graves are in the newer, west section, farther back, but I park my car near the entrance and set out first across the east grounds. Walking these stone paths, which are named after trees and flowers, is like walking through history, past centuries-old headstones. Each time I come here, I feel a sense of peace as I listen to the sounds of birds, smell the flowering trees, and watch birds and squirrels play. Today, a mockingbird overpowers them all, boasting its stolen songs.

I come to the two familiar headstones. As always, I read the engravings in a whisper: "Mary Grace Hill. Born July 10, 1964. Died September 12, 2000. Loving Mother." I move my eyes to my sister's headstone. "Grace Elizabeth Hill. Born October 1, 1988. Missing August 27, 1996."

I perform my ritual of placing my hand on my mother's headstone as if it were her shoulder; then I sit at the foot of her grave. The spot is worn and bare from my many visits here. I pluck a handful of grass, let it fall from my hand, and watch as the wind blows it about.

"Good morning, my beautiful mom. Sure is a pretty day." I look up at the cloudless sky and wonder what I should talk about. "I had to bring Miss Dorothy into town, and since I have the day free, I thought I'd come say hello. She lost a close friend and is having a hard time. Our tough old Miss Dorothy. As usual, my life is boring. Same old, same old."

Though orphaned as an adult, I often feel like an abandoned child, desperate to hear my mother's voice. I have forgotten the details of her face, the details that made up who she was.

"I saw a beautiful woman yesterday, and something about her caught my eye. Do you think I should I try to meet her? I know you would say, 'Go for it, son.' I even looked up where she works." I pause as if I may get some sort of response. "She's a college professor here in Vinbrooke." I gaze at Mom's tombstone and struggle to find words.

Then I turn to my sister's headstone. In my imagination, my sister's face has faded too, and what I can remember of her is still frozen in time—she is still a little girl, never growing older or changing. When she was alive, I was a teenager and found her annoying. It's funny how time and the absence of a person changes the way you think of them. Their nonexistence has a way of altering your memories.

"Hey, li'l sis." Gracie was eight years younger than I, so long conversations never happened. Our relationship consisted of events where she would bug me and I would tell her to go away, or I would bug her and she would stomp off to tell our mother. On rare occasions, we would do a craft together.

"If you were here," I say, "we could make a bracelet."

I pluck three tall clover flowers, braid the stems together, then bend them around and tie the ends into a bracelet. "Here, this is for you." I lay it on my sister's grave.

From the moment Mom taught Gracie how to make a braid, Gracie made bracelets from anything she could: grass, paper, candy wrappers, anything that was flexible enough. Sitting at the kitchen table one day, she made me a bracelet from a wrapper of my favorite candy bar.

"Here's a Snickers bracelet, Nate," she said as she slid it onto my wrist.

I think I might still have it somewhere.

Gracie's disappearance remains a mystery. On the terrible day she disappeared, she had gone to play in the woods behind our property, carrying a backpack full of dolls. Living in the country, my mother wasn't afraid to let her walk alone in the woods behind our house as long as she made it home before dark. The last morning I saw her, I rode my bike to a friend's house and got back home just at dusk. Gracie had always come home before dark—except for this day. The later it got, the more frantic my mother became.

The police told my mother they would begin searching immediately but that there wasn't a need to worry until it had been twenty-four hours. Gracie had more than likely just gotten lost, but they would find her. I felt helpless and pleaded with my mother to let me search for Gracie, and finally she agreed. Dorothy came to sit with her while I went out to search. I'm not sure how long I roamed, but I came up empty, and there was no word when I returned.

When twenty-four hours had passed with no sign of her, a county-wide search began. Volunteers came from everywhere. They found her backpack near a country road that led to an abandoned property. This was the only trace found anywhere. The police believed that someone had seen her there and grabbed her.

During the next two years, volunteers showed up to search. Gracie even made it onto an episode of *Unsolved Mysteries*. Mom hung a ton of posters, but over time, the posters took on a ghostly hue as the sun faded my sister's image. Election signs and advertisements took their place. For the longest time, we spent our Sundays replacing signs that had been covered or removed. As the years passed, people lost interest or gave up on finding her. My mother slowed down on replacing posters and eventually also gave up.

After that, Mom became someone I didn't recognize anymore. I lost both my sister and my mother the day that Gracie disappeared.

At a rustling behind me, I startle and turn from Gracie's tombstone. It's only two squirrels chasing each other around a tree. A tingling and numbness in my knees suggests that I've been sitting far too long. Standing to stretch, I look around the cemetery.

In the distance, I see a little blond girl walking hand in hand with a woman. I squeeze my eyes shut, then look again, because for a moment, I see Gracie. The little girl looks at me and smiles. I feel a lump swell in my throat as I stare, unable to move. Her little hand raises, waves at me, and her smile widens. The breeze carries a giggle to my ears. This time, I hold my eyes shut and rub them with my knuckles. Then I look again. The woman and child are facing away from me now, continuing down the walk.

I'm losing my mind. I watch the little girl until she has left my sight, and then I stare at nothing. *Why is this happening now? I haven't had this experience in years.*

My gaze moves back to the headstones, and I'm speechless for a moment. I clear my throat.

"I sure miss you two. I guess I'll see you next time."

As I make my way back across the beautiful grounds, pondering what's just happened, something nags at me. Like a deep itch I can't scratch. I find myself thinking about the past, my mind following an old path I haven't been down very often in many years. I start to replay the day of Gracie's disappearance from start to finish. As usual, I don't establish anything new, but the nagging questions are back, louder than ever. I'm not sure if it's caused by my recent episodes of hearing my sister, or if the questions are prompting the episodes. Either way, I'm back to that old unsettled feeling.

I leave the cemetery and drive back to Bitterton. I can't seem to stop these thoughts of my sister. My mind as attentive as a fluttering bird, I find myself on the country road where volunteers found Gracie's backpack. *Why am I here again after all these years? Something is telling me I need to do this.*

I pull my truck off the road at the entrance of an overgrown path and step out into waist-high weeds—to search again.

CHAPTER ELEVEN

Kevan
Early Summer

My mouth still gapes in confusion, and I search the road as if I might see the person who put the paper on my car. It's a drawing of a house and pond surrounded by a copse of trees. Though the drawing of the house lacks detail, somehow I know it's the same one I remember from our special place in the woods. My mind spins with thoughts. *I had forgotten about this place, but someone else hasn't. Whoever drew this picture has been there.* I pore over the drawing as if it might reveal the answers to my questions. How did someone else know about that house, and why would they leave me a drawing of it? Why is the drawing on the same unusual type of paper I use for my sketches? Did they come into my house and take it?

Most of all, I wonder about the words written at the bottom corner of the page:

FORGET THIS PLACE.

I look up at Beth. "What the hell? Why is someone warning me to stay away from an abandoned property? I'm not even sure it still exists."

"Do you think someone's watching you—or has seen your art? This can't be a coincidence."

"Who would connect me to this place, and why would they care?"

"Perhaps the house meant more to your Gammie than she told."

"I just assumed it was somewhere she went as a kid—I didn't ask. I'm sure other people knew about it."

"Yeah, but why leave this on your car, and why now?"

I check the time and toss the drawing into the back seat. "Come on—we have to go." I plop down behind the wheel, determined to focus on the day ahead. Beth climbs in next to me.

This visit to Bitterton is planting dread in the pit of my stomach, and there's still a long drive ahead of me. With each attempt to calm myself, the anxiety rises in waves and nausea settles in my throat. I have felt this way before. When I was a teen and young adult, it plagued me every time I stepped foot on my parents' property. Even though that house was technically my home, the dread wrapped around me like a dark, impenetrable cloud every time I returned from school or from Gammie's. Today, I knew, would be no exception.

"You look like you're going to your *own* funeral," Beth says.

"It's been more than five years since I visited, and I still don't want to see my mother or my brothers. In fact, I dread seeing them as much as I dread walking into that house."

"Don't let them get to you. Take care of business, and to hell with them!"

"Much easier said than done. My family is notorious for digging up buried bones."

"Then don't give them the chance to find the shovel!"

Feeling flushed, I turn up the car's air conditioning and try to cool my face and my nerves.

"Tell me again: why are we going to your mother's?" Beth asks.

"My dream last night made me remember a necklace Gammie gave me a long time ago. If I remember correctly, it had a key on it."

"The mysterious key. What's it for?"

"I don't remember. I hid the necklace from my parents because I knew they would take it. It's still in the house."

"How do you know they haven't found it already?"

"I had a secret hiding spot only Gammie and I knew about. It's hidden very well."

After driving for more than an hour, mostly in silence, I pull into a space just off the road in front of my mother's house. Even though it's been several years since I last visited, nothing has changed. I suppose I should feel guilty for the time that has passed since I've been here, but I don't. I know this visit won't be any different from all the others. I fear the house could suck me in forever just by looking at it. Leaning forward, I drape my hands over the steering wheel and force myself to take a closer look.

The house itself looks the same. Its ranch-style siding is dingy, the paint peeling like a horrible sunburn. Small windows add to the gloom. On each side of the windows, faded green shutters hang, some missing. The front door is pathetic and rusted at the bottom.

This is a house where children were raised by hate and hurt instead of love. Painful memories are in every room, trapped inside the material things. The house reflects the wounds of those who have lived here.

My father was in his thirties when he ran off. Once he had been missing for more than seven years, he was declared dead. The sheriff didn't pursue it, given my father's track record for binge drinking and raising hell. All I know is, my father made life a living hell for us. Gammie would say, "There are two creatures that don't survive long on this earth. That's hogs and wicked men." My father certainly fit her description of one of these two, maybe both. His mental and physical abuse left scars that may not be visible to others but are impossible to shed.

My mother didn't inflict physical harm, but the emotional harm was worse. Part of that was her denial of the truth. Part of it was her doing nothing to save us. People who do nothing about abuse are as dangerous as the abusers. Their denial forces others to live with the abuse for a lifetime.

I spot my oldest brother, Matthew, crouched under the hood of a truck, so engrossed in what he's doing that he doesn't notice me. He and my brother James both live nearby but spend a lot of their time here. He looks more like our father than ever. Matthew is the kind of person who only speaks the truth about our past when he has ingested a fifth of his whiskey truth serum. Even then, it's only partial truth, an altered tale he weaves for himself.

My second-oldest brother, James, lives in complete denial and cuts anyone off at the pass if they try to visit memory lane. He thinks our mother did what was necessary to raise us. My brothers choose not to see our parents in a realistic light. Some say that we are merely echoes of our parents. I became the only echo that didn't carry back; nor will I ever.

Taking one last deep breath, I stare at the house a bit longer, as if it will become more inviting. Visiting a crypt would be less bleak.

Beth breaks the silence. "Tell me where it is, and I'll get it."

"It's hidden pretty well." I pause, then say, "I got this. Right?"

"Piece of fucking cake!" Beth says, smacking me on the arm. "You sure you don't want me to come in with you?"

"Nah." I shrug with little confidence. "Alone, I can get in and out quicker."

I step clear of the car. The yard has an unpleasant smell that immediately makes my stomach roil. Broken lawn furniture, rusted barrels, and various engine parts are strewn about. Years of junk that my father collected and my mother won't part with. It looks like a garage sale that exploded. The only thing changed is that there's even more junk now, brought in by my brothers—carrying on my father's legacy.

Matthew rises from his stooped position and wipes his hands on a blackened rag. Looking surprised, he says, "Hey, sis! I was wondering if we would see you."

"Oh, yeah? I figured I should stop by since I was in town."

He walks toward me, one arm outstretched to give me a half hug. Hugging in this family happens as a formality. He makes the effort, wrapping one arm around my shoulders, but there's no energy behind it. I notice he has turned his head away, probably to keep me from smelling his boozy breath.

The front door opens and James comes outside. He shoots me a look of disgust. "Well, look who it is. Doctor Copeland coming to grace us with her presence." He stresses *doctor* with a mocking tone. "What the hell do you want?"

"Good to see you too, brother," I say with obvious sarcasm and a fake smile.

James stomps past me. He and I no longer speak. Our relationship fell apart years ago, and even more when I became Doctor Copeland. I'm not sure if it stems from jealousy or intimidation. Regardless, he behaves more like our father than anyone. Matthew may be the drinker, but James sucks at being a decent human being. Or at least that's how I see it.

"So, where is Mom?" I ask reluctantly.

"What do you care?" James blurts. His face twists into a deeper scowl as he walks toward his truck to leave.

"She's in the kitchen," Matthew says. "She may not be happy to see you. It's been a while, and I think she's pretty much written you off."

I shrug. "What's new? I got over that long ago." I continue my walk of doom, not allowing my mind to drift back to the apprehension I've felt all day. Trying to calm my nerves, I pause at the top of the steps and glance back at the car. I'm unable to see Beth through distorted reflections on the window.

I open the squeaky screen door, taking only one step inside, careful not to let it slam closed behind me. I look across the couch and loveseat to the kitchen. My mother is standing at the kitchen window with her back to me, resting one elbow on her hip as she takes a cigarette away from her mouth. There's already a lingering stench of countless cigarettes here, and they've left a yellow stickiness on everything. Smoke escapes into the air above her as she lets out a long, unhappy exhale. "Look who finally remembered she has a mother."

I continue to stand just inside the door. "May I come in?"

"Suit yourself. You'll do whatever you want to anyway." My mother says the words without turning around.

Sighing under my breath, I walk across the living room to the kitchen's edge. As I pass, I look at the walls of the living room. They have fewer pictures than I remember. Patches of less faded paint mark the places where the pictures once hung. Of course, the missing ones are of me. It isn't the first time that my mother has drastically written me off.

"So, how have you been?" I ask, forcing sincerity. "Have you been feeling okay?"

"I'm old and alone. What do you think?"

Why doesn't this response surprise me? My mother has always been a Negative Nancy. She takes another puff of her cigarette and blows the smoke into the air; it forms a cloud around her as she turns her head partially in my direction. She looks at me for a half second, then turns back to the window, stamping her cigarette into an ashtray crowded with butts.

"What do you want, Kevan?"

"I came to arrange Gammie's funeral, and I figured I would stop by."

"Why? You never cared before." Idly, she pushes dishes around in a sink full of water. "And Frances had nothing here."

Not long after my father disappeared, Gammie had sold her house and moved closer to town. My mother wouldn't let me see her as much after that. I got to spend more time with her after I left home.

"I just came to visit."

This time my mother turns to face me fully, and she doesn't hide her expression of loathing. "You have never cared about me or your father. We worked hard to give you everything you needed. We loved you, and all you did was turn your back on us." She picks up her pack of cigarettes and stares me down as she lights another, taking several puffs in quick succession, creating a fog between us.

Who is she kidding? I scream inside my head, trying to hold my composure. My father only worked hard when it suited him. As far as loving his family, he had a twisted way of showing it, and my mother had a twisted way of believing it. Depending on who you ask, my father had many reputations. Few knew his true colors. He wasn't an angel in anyone's eyes, but some people saw good in him. He would offer free repairs sometimes, for instance, although usually he had an eye on getting something in return. Then there was the devil Clyde Mays. If you knew that person, you knew it wasn't wise to turn your back on him. That's the side I remember.

"Mom, I didn't come here to fight."

"Who's fighting?" My mother barks, cutting me off. "You didn't know everything about our lives, and you didn't know everything about your father. You don't know what I went through to protect you."

My voice betrays my attempt to remain calm. "If you'd left him and taken us with you, you wouldn't have had to protect us." I feel myself regressing to the person I used to be, and I have to force my brain to stop.

Without missing a beat, my mother continues. "I loved your father, but even without that, I still had to stay. A marriage is sacred in the eyes of God, and if you break it, you go straight to hell. Even though I loved him, I was also terrified of him. It can be deadly when you're stuck in that situation." My mother stops abruptly and turns to put out her cigarette.

I breathe deep, push down the rise of anger and frustration toward her. I realize there are years of it bottled up inside me. She continues to look away.

Time has not been kind to my mother. She has aged tremendously since I last saw her. Her hair has more streaks of gray, and her skin has turned to an aged leather. Decades of smoking have drawn a roadmap of lines across her face and neck. Years of mental and physical abuse inflicted by my father, and by herself, have aged her beyond her years. If there was still love between us, I might feel sad. When bridges are destroyed far beyond repair, though, one must find a different route entirely—never returning to the place the bridge gave passage to.

"Mom, you didn't have to go through anything. You chose to stay here and with him."

She turns abruptly. "I stayed with the man I love! Is that so wrong? Family don't run out on one another. They stick together. It would have been wrong for me to leave your father."

"That's what you believe. Mom, I don't!"

"God puts us in these lives, based on whether we are worthy or unworthy."

"So, what are you saying? You're worthy or unworthy? Which is it? I don't think God intended for anyone to live like you lived. Like we lived!"

"You have no idea what you're talking about!" My mother grabs a dish towel from the counter and kneads it across her hands. "I don't know why you even bothered coming here." She throws the towel on the counter, stomps to the screen door and kicks it open. She hobbles down the steps and across the yard, not turning back.

Why do I let her drag me into the same old arguments? I breathe in through my nose and let it escape my mouth.

This room is where my father carried out his retributions. Kitchens are supposed to be the heart of a home. Not this one. My eyes move over the room and pause on a muddy foot track on the floor. Shaking my head at the sight of it, I survey the dirty dishes on the table and the spilled milk on the counter. The sight of it shifts my mind back to being eight years old and having to scrub all the cracks in the linoleum with a toothbrush. It was my punishment for giving my father a cross look. My eyes were filled with tears, and my back and knees throbbed with pain. I worked quickly, because I knew he would soon be back to inspect my work. I didn't want to think what would happen if I didn't finish in time.

The memory creates a lump in my throat, so I force myself to snap out of it to focus on what I came here for. I walk down the narrow hallway that leads to my old bedroom. The wall at the far end of the hallway is covered by a large mirror that's been hanging there since I was a small child. I always felt like something in it was watching me. I kept my eyes on the floor when entering this hallway, especially at night.

My mind still struggling to stay out of the past, I see a glimpse of my childhood self in the mirror. My hair is a light shade of red, almost blond, and my face is covered in freckles. My dirty pink shirt, with red trim around the sleeves, has the face of Strawberry Shortcake on the front. I smile for a brief moment as I remember my favorite shirt. The smile doesn't last long when the memory begins to turn to an unpleasant feeling. I seem to be a ghost in this house.

My old room looks smaller than before. It's bare except for a bed and a chest of drawers—no trace of me. I look at the bed and see myself once more as that little girl, kneeling, my mother bowing next to me. My hands would be palm to palm as I recited the bedtime prayer she had taught me. We did this every night. As a child, I didn't mind it. It was the rare occasion that I got to spend time with her alone and feel like she was all mine. We would say the words in unison:

Now I lay me down to sleep,
I pray the Lord my soul to keep.
If I should die before I wake,
I pray the Lord my soul to take.

As I got older, it felt more like I was being forced to chant the words of a cult. It became just another manipulation forced by my mother. I remember twisting the words inside my head to say something much different, directed toward my father:

Now I lay me down to rest,
I pray to Satan and all his guests.
Come take my father while I sleep,
To your home in hell and forever keep.

"It's all in the past," I whisper to myself. "It doesn't matter anymore."

I rotate to look around the rest of the room. Dread overwhelms me as my eyes rest on the closed closet door. I open it and gaze at the space that seems so much tinier now. I step in and squat down to look at the wall that stands between my closet and my brothers' closet. It smells musty in here—a combination of stale smoke and wood paneling. Tapping on the wall, I feel a knot ball up inside my stomach as memories of hiding in here flood my mind. I spring back out and close the door.

I squeeze my eyes closed, force away unwanted emotion, and pause. Then I move toward the headboard of the bed. I place my hands underneath the bed frame and inch the bed away from the wall as quietly as I can. When I was a child, Gammie cut a long slit in the carpet at the edge of the baseboard and chipped out a spot in the wood, making a small hole through the subfloor. When she finished, we could see dirt underneath.

She told me this would be our hiding spot for the things I didn't want my parents to see. That meant anything Gammie gave to me. They would take anything that was precious to me, just for the pure joy of punishment.

I peel back the carpet, reach my hand in, and retrieve a Prince Albert box. I brush my hand over it, removing years of dust. I remember putting a tooth inside. The tooth fairy never came to visit, so I thought I might as well keep it.

At the risk of my mother walking in, I shove the box into the waistband of my jeans and pull my T-shirt over it. I move the carpet and bed back in place and leave the room. On my way out, I avoid the mirror.

Something makes a sound behind me. I jerk my head around, look straight into the mirror, and see a little boy with strawberry-blond hair staring at me. His skin is pale and his eyes are sunken and dark. I feel my head recoil, but I continue to stare. The boy is wearing khaki shorts, a striped shirt, and brown leather sandals. I throw myself back into my room, my heart pounding in my ears.

"Tommy?" I whisper to myself.

When my heart calms, I peek around the door. This time, it's only a mirror. I'm still unable to make myself step into the hall.

My mind digs up a memory of Tommy before his death. He had taken ill, and his stomach and bowels were refusing to function. His body weight dwindled to less than thirty pounds; his bones protruded just under his skin. I squeeze my eyes shut, hesitate, and then bolt for the front door. Thankful that my mother still hasn't returned, I scurry into the yard, my heart moving faster than I.

Matthew is still attending to something under the hood of his truck. He looks in my direction and then back to what he's doing. "You're leaving already?"

"Yeah, you were right. She wasn't happy to see me. Nothing has changed."

"It never will, Kev-ree. You should answer your phone sometime. Some of us would still like to talk to you."

"You know I'm not much for talking on the phone," I say. "I see James hasn't changed a bit. Still the same stubborn asshole."

"Cut him some slack. He's going through a tough time. He lost his job, and his only income right now is whatever Mom hires him to do."

"That explains it. He's hanging around our mother and absorbing an excessive amount of her brainwashing."

"It's not as bad as you make it out to be, Kev-ree. Mom doesn't know how to be any other way. She put up with our asshole father for twenty years. The woman is just tired."

"Like I told her, she didn't have to put up with it!" I've allowed myself to be drawn in again; I shake it off. "I'd better go. There are a few things I need to do for Gammie's ceremony."

"Good to see you, sis. Keep me posted on the arrangements, will ya?" My brother gives me a half-hearted smile and stretches out one arm again for a hug. At the first step in his direction, I can smell his foul breath. That smell and this place seem to go together like migraines and pain. There are no memories of this place without that smell. It only makes me want to run faster, putting as much space between myself and my past as possible. I back away from the hug, giving him a one-armed pat instead, then dart to my car and shut the door.

I realize that every muscle in my body is as tight as a stretched rubber band.

"Well, I see you made it out without blood on your hands," Beth jokes.

"This time!" I pull the tin box out of my waistband and place it in the cup holder next to the center console. All I want to do is get as far away from this house as possible, and leave the memories with it.

CHAPTER TWELVE

Kevan
1996

Kevan is in the living room when Tommy, looking panicked, runs into the house, grabs her by the arm, and drags her toward his bedroom.

"What are you doing?" Kevan fusses, but she goes with him.

"Shhh." They reach Tommy's room and he eases the door closed behind them. Kevan looks at Tommy's clenched teeth, her eyes focusing on the two holes where his top front teeth should be. Then she sees his eyes fill with tears.

"I broke the antenna on Dad's radio," Tommy says. "I didn't mean to. Dad told me to sweep the floor in the workshop, and I wanted to listen to some music, and . . ." He begins to cry in earnest.

Kevan understands. She's broken that rule herself more than once, turning the AM/FM radio to a local pop station. Edith forbids this kind of music, believing it is the music of the devil, but if they play it in the workshop, she can't hear it from the house.

"And the station wasn't coming in right, so I tried to move the antenna, and it broke in two. Please, Kevan, you have to fix it." Tommy cries harder and sinks his teeth into his fist.

"Okay, okay, just stay here. I'll be right back."

Kevan tiptoes out of the house and runs to the workshop. She locates the broken antenna and searches for tape to piece it back together. Her skin prickles as she searches, terrified she'll get caught before she has a chance to fix it. She comes across several rolls of gray duct tape but figures this tape will be noticed. Then, in a drawer, she finds some clear packaging tape. She pieces the antenna back together as neatly as she can. She changes the radio station back to the whiny bluegrass music her parents like to listen to. Seeing that Tommy didn't finish the sweeping, she finishes it for him and returns to the house.

Tommy has gone into hiding.

She hears a faint sob and walks straight to the kitchen, knowing where to look. She opens the cabinet door and sees her little brother curled in a fetal position. This has become a regular occurrence for him. Even though Tommy rarely does anything wrong, he seems to stay in trouble with their father and gets punished for no reason. Now he stays suspended in his own anxiety and fear to the point that he either clings to Kevan like a fly on a sticky trap or hides himself away in the kitchen cabinet. Tommy has always been timid, but lately it's gotten much worse.

Easing out of the small door, his face still wet with tears, Tommy asks, "Did you fix it, Kevan?"

She knows she didn't fix it well enough for their father not to notice, but she says, "Yes. It's going to be okay, Bubbie." She knows better than to promise this—their father is sure to notice damage to any of his possessions, and he gets pissed off if the wind is blowing the wrong way—but she promises anyway, if only to give Tommy a brief calm before the storm.

Several days pass, and Kevan and Tommy think that maybe, just this once, they have dodged their father's wrath. Late one evening, though, Kevan and her three brothers are sprawled out in the living room watching television when they hear their father yell from the front porch.

"Get out here, you little fuckers!"

"Shit!" Matthew exclaims. They stare at each other, their hearts kicking into the same rapid rhythm.

"I'll give you to the count of three."

"Come on, we better go." Matthew stands and urges the others to follow.

Matthew walks through the doorway first, followed by James and then Kevan as she takes Tommy's hand. One by one, they see their father holding the AM/FM radio in one hand and the broken antenna in the other. Kevan feels Tommy squeeze her hand as he moves to stand behind her.

"Who did it?"

No one says a word. Suddenly they all feel like marble statues, stiff and cold.

"I'll punish each of you if you don't tell me who did it."

"I did it, Dad," Matthew says, his chin tipped upward in defiance.

"Well, that's mighty brave of you, but now it's gonna be an ass-kicking for lying. I know it wasn't you. It was either James or Tommy, because it was their job to sweep the floor of the shop this week. So, which of you broke it?"

Kevan lets go of Tommy's hand, steps forward, and says, "I did it by accident."

"Kevan, stop. No, I did it, Dad," James confesses.

"You three are digging a hole you can't get out of. What about you, you little shit?" Their father looks at Tommy and he shrinks, curling in on himself, not saying a word.

"Well, since I can't get a straight truth, then I guess it'll be all of you."

Tommy stands close to Kevan, and she can feel him trembling. Looking down, she sees that he has wet his pants. She moves to stand in front of him, trying to keep her father from seeing the stain.

"March your asses in the house," Clyde demands as he climbs the steps. They look at each other in fear.

Clyde's punishments come in two forms. The first is when he takes off his belt and uses it to hit them across their backs and backsides. The second is when he makes them drink a nasty-tasting liquid that punishes them for hours afterward.

He isn't removing his belt.

The children move into the living room, one by one, saying nothing. Lining up military style, they wait for their sanction. Voice shaky but bold, Matthew says, "I'll go first."

"You think you're a big tough man, don't you, boy? We'll see just how tough you are when you're shitting your brains out later."

There it is—our punishment. Swallowing castor oil. The color leaves Matthew's cheeks at the thought of swallowing the foul liquid.

Kevan takes a deep breath and swallows hard. She hates this form of punishment. She knows that people used to take castor oil as a laxative or as a scurvy remedy. When taken as directed, symptoms are mild, and a gentle clean-out will follow. The amount of the foul liquid their father will force down them, though, will disrupt their intestines for hours. It will make their insides feel as if they want to make their way outside, the result being burning liquid pouring out of their assholes. This idea of retribution stems from Clyde's military days, when they forced him to take castor oil as a brainwashing technique.

He steps into the bathroom and Matthew follows.

Matthew turns to look at the others, who are standing motionless in the hallway, dreading their turns. Then the door slams, closing him inside the small bathroom. They hear Matthew gag as he's forced to swallow a tablespoon of the oil.

"You better not spit it out," their father commands.

A second gag comes even louder after swallowing another tablespoon, then a third. Matthew walks out of the bathroom, his face shaded a tint lighter as if he could puke at any moment.

"Who's next?" their father asks, sounding as if he's enjoying himself. James volunteers with a slow hand raise. His back curves in defeat as he steps into the bathroom. A deep burping gag carries through the closed door, followed by another warning—and then it repeats.

The door opens, and Kevan doesn't wait for her father to command her to step into the bathroom. She moves in, holding her breath, just wanting it to be finished. She looks back into Tommy's frightened eyes as the door closes. Kevan watches as her father fills the kitchen tablespoon to the rim. The substance is so thick that it mounds up rather than spilling over the edge. She opens her mouth reluctantly, and he shoves the entire spoon in, reaching the back of her throat, causing her to gag before her taste buds even register. Then comes the pungent flavor, with a nauseating aftertaste. It's like tasting one of her brothers' dirty socks.

She forces herself to close her mouth over the spoon, trying to keep it from spilling. If any of it escapes her mouth, he will multiply her punishment. Forcing herself to swallow, she feels the oil sliding down the inner walls of her throat, causing her gag reflex to spasm, but she forces her lips to stay closed even as a portion of the oil makes its way back up and into her mouth. She opens her mouth to show him it's all gone, and he pours another and then another. She almost hurls at the sight of it. Three times she gags, feeling the liquid come back up, and three times she forces herself to swallow it again. She powers through the torment.

Kevan walks out of the bathroom, and immediately her father summons Tommy. "Get your ass in here, Tommy. Since you were the only one who didn't open your mouth before, you get more."

"Dad, no," Kevan says as she steps back into the doorway.

Her father shoves her hard enough to make her fall backward, landing on her bottom. "You want another?"

Tommy eases into the bathroom, holding both hands over the front of his pants.

"You pissed yourself, boy?" their father growls. "Well, maybe I should give you half the damn bottle. You'll be too busy shitting to piss."

Tommy's wide, dark eyes plead for help as the door closes. Kevan bites her tongue to keep from saying what she really wants to say—that Tommy wouldn't piss himself if their father wasn't such an evil asshole. She bites so hard that she tastes blood. Through the door she hears the kitchen spoon ping against Tommy's teeth as their father shoves the spoon into his mouth, and then the sound of Tommy's gag. A gross amount of liquid hits the toilet—more than the contents of the spoon. It is impossible for Tommy to avoid throwing up any time their father forces this kind of punishment.

"You little pussy." Her father's taunting echoes. "Just for that, you win another spoonful." Tommy's sobs come louder, but it doesn't help the situation. "Dry it up, boy. Crying like a girl won't get you out of it. Drink it! You drink until I tell you to stop."

Although Kevan can't see what's happening, she knows her father has shoved the entire bottle into Tommy's hand. She gives her brother James a pleading look. His face is as drawn and white as hers. Matthew leaves the hallway.

"I didn't tell you to stop, boy. Take another one!"

Tommy's crying turns to a defeated whimper, followed by more gags.

Kevan hears the screeching of the screen door, then footsteps stomping through the house. Gammie moves around her, not saying a word. She slings the bathroom door open, steps in, and grabs the bottle from Tommy's hand.

"How much of this did you make him drink, you asshole?" Gammie holds the bottle to look at its contents. "Too much of this shit will poison his system. You'll kill him!"

"A little shit medicine isn't gonna hurt him. It didn't hurt me. He'll learn to keep his paws off my stuff and do as he's told. Besides, it's none of your business. I will punish my kids however I see fit."

"Not while I'm around." Gammie wraps one arm around Tommy and rotates him around her body, urging him to walk out of the bathroom. Her eyes never leave my father's, and I see his defiant expression waver as his eyes dart away for a second.

As if he realizes he has allowed her to overpower him, his eyes turn to a dark, daring gaze as he says, "Get the hell out of my house!"

Gammie stands her ground. "Not until you get out of here."

"Oh, I'm finished now. They'll need the bathroom, anyway." He smirks at Gammie as he walks past her, thumping her shoulder with his as he passes.

Gammie stares him down until he disappears out of sight. She squats down in front of Tommy and Kevan and strokes their cheeks. "I promise you, one day that man will get what he deserves. I'll make sure of it. In the meantime, you'll come stay with me until your mother gets home."

CHAPTER THIRTEEN

Nathan

I bend my elbows and hold my arms higher to prevent the weeds from irritating my skin. I swing my legs to the side with each step to flatten the weeds as I try to pinpoint the general area where my sister's backpack was found. I know it was near the overgrown lane ahead. I'm pretty sure this lane leads to the abandoned property that can also be accessed from behind my house. If memory serves, it's a shorter distance from this direction.

Back when my sister disappeared, police speculated that she must have been taken from this property, that her kidnapper had snatched her and then ditched her backpack here before heading to the main highway.

The overgrowth of briars and fallen trees makes it difficult to recognize much. Curious as to whether the old house still even exists, I decide to try to find it.

A large tree blocks the path, so I hoist myself up and jump to the ground on the other side. As I climb over the tree, I begin to wonder what I'm doing here. Just what is it I hope to find? Doubt seems bent on discouraging me, so I push forward.

I can't determine exactly where I am, but I continue until the path opens into an untamed field. I recognize the abandoned farmhouse and the oval pond that's surrounded by marshy grass and cattails. Time and Mother Nature haven't been kind to the water, as algae have grotesquely colored the pond. I continue to flatten the weeds with swipes of my feet as I walk toward the farmhouse. I look at the woods to determine which direction leads to the back side of the plantation. As I gain my bearings, I'm pretty sure I can find my way to the plantation from here. The path my sister walked.

Police believed she had been here, but there was no evidence in or around the house. Everything was searched, including the stone structure out back.

The once-lively farmhouse is tall, with a porch that spreads across its front. The stone porch steps have become uneven from years of settling; the porch itself is missing many of its boards and sags in the middle. Vines cover the front wall; a few honeysuckle vines still remain. The front door lies on the floor just inside the entrance. The windows on each side contribute their own harm to the house, broken, their frames warped.

I place a cautious foot on the door and step inside. It smells musty and moldy. Several small swallows burst from hiding and fly toward absent windows, and I duck my head. It also quickens my heart a beat or two. I assume the space to my right was once a living room, with its far wall lined with a few ineptly installed shelves. The center of the room gives way to rot, and I see dirt underneath. I imagine that the space was cozy and inviting years ago. I wonder what the people who lived here were like. Were they happy? I turn and look back toward the pond. I think, *I could see myself loving it here. Fishing in my own personal pond.*

As I look farther into the house, I see faded yellow cabinets along the left wall, empty, their doors open or absent. The bottom row is more dilapidated, with only one door remaining. That door proves to be corroded shut, and it moves only an inch or so, with a metallic thud. I try to open it again and throw myself off balance and backward. It's probably been like this since before the place was abandoned, but I am determined to open it. I search for anything to pry it open with. In the corner, a few metal kitchen chairs in various conditions lie about. I manage to remove a leg from one. After trying it on the cabinet door several times, I think to myself that if the police couldn't get it open during the search for my sister, then why should I be any different? Or maybe they did get it open but didn't find anything. This only makes me more determined to see what's inside.

For more than ten minutes, I bang, wedge, and pry on the door. Just as I'm on the verge of giving up, the door pops loose and I open its tight hinges.

The smell of rust and metal invades the air as I look into the dingy white interior. Fragments of rusty metal and chips of paint lie on the floor. Visible through the debris is something lying on the bottom of the cabinet. As I brush shards of metal and paint around with my fingertips, I find half-buried strips of paper. I pull them out and rotate them in my hand. The three folded pieces of paper are braided together into one long strand. I feel my heart pick up its pace as I look at it. The strips of paper are a faded black, with red lettering folded into the braids. Rotating the plait around in my fingertips, I make out the word *Pop* on one strip. As I rotate it more, separating the strips only a little without disturbing them too much, I read the word *Rocks*.

"Pop Rocks!" I say aloud. "Candy wrappers!"

If police did find this, they must have viewed it as nothing more than trash. I wrap the strands of paper around my wrist, the tips not quite touching. *Maybe my sister was here.* Pop Rocks were one of her favorite candies, so why wouldn't she make a bracelet out of the wrappers? My heart pounds like a giant bass drum.

Determinedly, I crouch down and peer further into the cabinet. I wipe the bottom of it with my bare hands and then tap the wood. It sounds hollow. One of the boards moves when I tap on it. I reach in and find a space between the board and the wall. I pick up a second board and then a third. Reaching into the hole, I feel something on the floor below. I pull out an old Barbie doll dressed in a faded yellow dress with pink flowers. The doll's hair is a blondish-yellow and is sticking out in all directions in a matted mess. My hand reaches in to search for more, and I retrieve another doll. This one is a Ken doll, with similar-colored hair and blue clothing. I hold them in my hands and my mind swims with questions. *Could these have belonged to my sister? Was this her hiding spot?* I sit back on the floor, staring at the bracelet and the two dolls.

A memory flashes through my mind: My sister sitting in the grass, asking, "Can you play with me, Nate?" and my response that boys didn't play with dolls. She had a couple of dolls that looked similar to this Barbie doll, but I don't think she had one like this Ken doll. Of course, I'm not sure I would have noticed the difference between one and another that much. The memory fades and I am left still staring at the items in my hand.

Eventually, the shock subsides and I stand and explore the rest of the house. I grip both dolls by the legs and slide them and the braid down into my back pocket so that I can take them to the sheriff later.

The next room I explore has a closed door in the corner that grabs my attention. When I open it, I find a long, rectangular closet. It looks empty. I pull my phone from my pocket and shine its flashlight around the dark space. A partial ladder hangs from the ceiling; its bottom section lies on the floor. Due to the deterioration of the rest of the house, after a short debate about whether to search the attic, I decide that falling through the ceiling isn't something I want to do today. Especially since no one knows I am here. I pass it up and move on to explore the rest of the house.

My tour through the skeletal rooms raises questions about the life that once lived here. Did this place harbor happy memories? Was it a home to a loving family, with both a mother and father? It's hard for me to picture, having been raised by a single mother. It looks like the sort of place that, if it were in good repair, one might find on the front of a Hallmark card. I find it a shame that it stands abandoned and alone.

I come up empty in the rest of the house and go outside through the absent back door. The grass reaches my knees as I make my way to a tall stone building. The rough, stacked stone has stood the test of time. The door open, I step into a tall room. Wooden beams cross the width of the ceiling. Attached to one is an old light fixture, minus the bulb. On another hangs an old pulley. I look upward in all directions as I admire the old structure. The worn stone floor is stained dark brown. My eyes follow the pulley system and the huge stain on the floor, and I assume the building's purpose was to process and cure meat. Something about the space gives me the willies. I imagine that the whole setup could be used for lots of unpleasant things. I shut the thought down.

Outside, I walk along the wall and then down a set of stone steps to what appears to be a cellar. As a full-grown man, I would have to duck to enter through the wide wooden door. My sister could easily have walked through it without ducking. I turn the metal handle and push on the door. Having no luck the first time, I pound my shoulder into the door and jar it loose from the long-held seal. The door drags across a wooden floor, which surprises me; I'd expected to find a stone or even dirt floor. I step into the dank, cool room, and the smell of old wood, earth, and time moistens my nostrils. Illuminating the room with the light on my phone, I feel a chill that goes beyond physical. The chill sends a dark shiver down my spine. The space feels more like a crypt.

CHAPTER FOURTEEN

Kevan
Early Summer

"What's in the box, Red?" Beth picks up the rusty Prince Albert can.

"I didn't open it—I just got the hell out. It's been so long since I looked, but I remember the necklace and key. When Gammie gave me the key, she said she would tell me what it was for when I was older. I guess we both forgot."

I wonder if she forgot or if she wanted to keep it a secret. You never knew with Gammie, because she had her fair share of secrets. She believed girls had to keep secrets in order to survive.

"This is a blast from the past. You ever sneak and try to roll one of these?"

"Once. Coughed until I almost puked. I never smoked cigarettes, but I was good at rolling a joint in my college days."

Beth laughs in agreement. "Shit! If we had some good weed, I'd roll us one right now. I bet a nice fat one would do you just fine."

"Hell, yeah!"

"How did it go with your mom?"

"Oh, the usual. I'm an ungrateful, horrible person. And she's the saint, and our lives were picture perfect. Speaking of pictures, there wasn't a picture of me anywhere in the place."

"What the hell is wrong with her? I can't understand how a woman can choose a man over her kids. What did she see in him?"

"It certainly wasn't the money."

"She did it for his massive dick!" Beth says dramatically.

"Ew!" I cringe and laugh at the same time.

As I turn down Gammie's lane, the nectarous scent of honeysuckle seeps through the vents, and I roll down my window. I can almost taste its sweetness. Honeysuckle lived everywhere Gammie did. She made sure of that. I think of her every time I see or smell its sweet vines.

Gammie's house is the perfect size for someone living on their own. Its wide front steps and large wooden porch make you want to come and sit for a while. Two white swings with bright yellow seat cushions hang opposite each other on each end of the porch. The yellow door is just as welcoming.

We reach Gammie's and I can already feel a heavy weight on my chest. I go to unlock the front door and find it is already unlocked. *Strange.* Inside the door, an indescribable amount of emotion moves itself into the back of my throat—it feels swollen, making it hard to breathe. Next to the door hangs Gammie's favorite yellow sweater. I resist the urge to pull it from the hook and bury my face in it.

I put my things on the kitchen table and take Beth on a tour. Gammie moved here not long after my father ran off. Before, she had always lived next door. During my first visit, I felt like I'd been here before. There was both a newness and a familiarity to it. As you step inside, a cozy living room welcomes you, its back wall lined with shelves and a massive number of books. On the left is a kitchen and dining combo area decorated in pale, relaxing colors.

We finish our rounds and take a seat at the kitchen table.

"Let's see what young Kevan had hidden away," I say.

I pry the corroded lid open, leaving flakes of rusted debris on the table. Inside is a handmade friendship bracelet from Beth, a photograph of Gammie when she was young, and the necklace I was searching for.

"Oh, wow," Beth says as she picks up the bracelet braided from three pieces of yarn. "Didn't I make this for you?"

"Yep. I'm sure I hid it here because I didn't want my parents to find it."

I search my mind for memories of the necklace and key. The key, which looks like an old-fashioned skeleton key, must have been important for Gammie to have trusted me with it. I was in my early teens on the day she gave it to me, and I begged her to tell me what it was for. She would only say, "In due time, I promise. Make sure you hide this and don't tell anyone you have it."

"I wonder what it's for," Beth says. "Do you think it goes to something in this house?"

"I have no idea." I look at my watch. "We have time to look."

Laying the other items aside, we begin to search the house.

"I assume it's for a lockbox or some sort of keepsake chest," I say. "You can look out here while I search her bedroom."

My search begins with the dresser drawers and closet. Neither has any kind of hidden box or chest. I kneel beside the bed to look underneath; nothing is there. As I straighten up, I run my hand across the bedspread. It's white, with a blue, fluffy design. As I rub my hands over it, feeling its familiar texture, my emotions collapse. I bury my face in it and breathe deep. It smells so much like her. The entire house does. I swallow hard and try to choke down the urge to cry. After a moment, I feel able to return to my search. I open the nightstand drawer to find only small, miscellaneous items of no significance.

I go back to the living room to check on Beth.

"Find anything?"

"No, nothing hidden in here."

I look at the wall of shelves. Tucked away at the end of a row of books is a bright yellow vase with vines and a hummingbird etched in its side. Of course, the vines are honeysuckle. I hadn't noticed this before, but I remember it from my dream.

My dream, again!

In my dream, this vase was an urn. And it had Beth's name on it. I move closer to look for a name, but there is none. It's possible that my mind wrote its own big, twisted story for this little piece of decoration.

I run my fingers over the rows of books, reading the titles at random. Gammie's favorites were mysteries. She wasn't much on drama or romance. She always said that any form of drama was ludicrous and that romance was overrated. As I scan her collection, my eyes fix on one book with a blank spine. It's more like an ancient encyclopedia in appearance, only shorter and thicker. Between the vase and now this, I feel a sudden wave of déjà vu.

"This is a strange book," I say to Beth, turning it in my hands. "It's blank on the outside."

Beth steps beside me. "It looks old."

I've seen it somewhere before—maybe in a dream. I rub my hand over its cover and picture it on an old, empty shelf. Gammie may have shown it to me, but I don't remember. The book's cover is made from dark leather; its pages are edged in gold. I open the front cover and am met with the smell of cedar. It isn't a book at all. It is a box disguised as a book.

There's a wooden panel underneath the cover. Near the front edge is a leather handle and a slot for a key.

With looks of surprise, we dash to the kitchen to retrieve the key. "Maybe I'll get lucky," I say. The key fits into the slot, and I turn it in one direction and then the other. The lock opens, and I give Beth a wide-eyed glance. My heart races with excitement as I pull on the leather handle. A stronger smell of cedar greets me. Inside are several folded sheets of paper. The one on top has my name on it. Next I find two that appear to be a set of deeds. Below them is a key.

"Another key?" Beth and I say in unison.

"And the plot thickens." Beth tries to sound like Hercule Poirot. "What does the note say?"

I open the first piece of paper. There is no mistaking Gammie's handwriting.

Dearest Renee,

If you are reading this, it means I had to leave you. Just know that you are not alone. You didn't deserve the life you had growing up—no one does. Your hand of cards stacked themselves against you from the beginning. Regardless, you made the best of it and became the woman you are today. Where you came from doesn't define you. You define you.

A blurry film of tears forms over my eyes. Impatiently, I wipe them away.

I tried my best to protect you from the shitty childhood you had to endure and to be there for you into adulthood. Even though I can't be with you now, I know you'll be fine. I want you to remember the story that I told you as a child, about our connection and the gifts you possess. You will see that you are more special than you had imagined. I suspect that the things that are going to come into play in your life are inevitable, so I want you to be prepared. Whether we like it or not, our pasts always come to find us, so we must ready ourselves. Believe in your gift, your gut, and your heart. They will never steer you wrong.

You have heard me speak of my dearest friend, Dorothy. You must go see her. She has some of my belongings that she will pass to you. Do that soon, my dear. She will guide and assist you with my last farewell.

Until we meet again, take care, my sweet Renee. I love you, always.

Gammie

I hand the letter to Beth as I take a moment to process. My next words come out as a low mumble as the tears begin to flow freely. "Oh, my," I say, studying the new key as if it will tell me answers. "She didn't tell me what the key was for."

"Maybe this Dorothy can," Beth suggests. "What else is in the fake book?"

Beth and I sit on the couch and I rest the box on the coffee table. I lay the letter aside and pick up the two deeds. The first is a deed of conveyance for this house, addressed to Frances Mays. Folding it again, I open the second deed and look at the name and address. I recognize the name of Gammie's mother, but I don't recognize the address. My gut says it has something to do with the piece of property that won't stay forgotten. Once far from my thoughts, now front and center.

"Well, now I'm curious." Beth's curiosity is obvious, but mine teeters between wanting to know and the fear of knowing. "You should check it out. Perhaps this second house is where your Gammie grew up. You think?"

"I don't think she ever told me it belonged to her. But why keep that a secret? Better yet, why is someone else wanting me to stay away from it?"

"I'm sure there's a simple explanation."

"Maybe," I say automatically, but Gammie was right about gut feelings. There is always something behind them. And I had one now.

PART TWO

When one burns one's bridges,
what a very nice fire it makes.
—Dylan Thomas

CHAPTER FIFTEEN

Deloris
Summer 1953

"Leave her alone, Deloris. Hasn't she done enough for today?" Fred chides, as Marge drags her feet toward the back door.

"She still needs to feed Daisy, close the windows and doors on the outbuilding, and gather the eggs. It's supposed to rain tonight, and the upstairs windows in the shed are hanging wide open." Deloris hears Marge huff and puff out the back door of the house.

Marge has grown up overnight, blossoming into womanly curves, her breasts plump for a girl her age. Deloris saw the way Fred looked at her: differently than a father should, scanning her body from head to toe with lust in his eyes. It was especially obvious when he was two glasses into a bottle of whiskey. A year ago, Deloris wouldn't have thought it possible—not with his own daughter, anyway.

She knew he had a wandering eye. When they visited town, he gawked at the young women. If an attractive woman walked by, he rubbernecked and uttered something under his breath. Deloris also knew that when she wasn't with him, he would act on his desires. The man had come home late at night many times, smelling of booze and cheap perfume. He was a terrible husband, but up until now, she'd believed he was a good father. He'd taught Marge how to fish, how to shoot a gun, and other useful things. Deloris had never worried about them spending time alone together.

Now she sometimes feels lightheaded with fear and premonition.

"I'm going to go help her. You're too strict with her, Deloris. Let the girl be." Fred gets up from his chair and walks to the back door, his glass of whiskey in his hand.

Deloris continues to rock in her worn-out rocking chair, her fingers moving her knitting needles as quickly as if she were in a knitting contest. As worry begins to gnaw at her like a disease, the rocking of her chair becomes more aggressive. Is she being too protective? Just because her uncle tried to force himself on her doesn't mean Fred is like that. Does it? Fear works like yeast in her stomach, fermenting and expanding. Each time she glances at the back door, the sick feeling rises higher.

She lays her knitting needles aside, stands and paces the floor, then peers out the front window toward the pond. She walks to the back door and watches the stone shed. The remnants of daylight are now dark shapes and shadowed outlines. She can't see either Fred or Marge in the faint light from the small windows.

Deloris grabs her shoes and carries them through the house to the front door. Slipping them on, she steps outside. *There's no harm in just listening to make sure everything is okay*. The ducks waddle out of the pond and quack. *Shush, now*.

The smokehouse section of the building has a small window. It, along with the side window, remains almost dark. The chickens are locked in their coop and the upstairs windows are closed, which means Marge should be back downstairs. The only light glowing is in Fred's section of the building, which houses his tools and a set of stairs that leads to the loft. She tiptoes across the yard.

Standing still outside the door, she hears her husband speaking in a low tone that turns her gut feeling into a loud alarm. It sounds as if he's pleading with Marge. Deloris strains to hear better, but the night creatures seem to echo louder, making it difficult. Her heartbeat thuds in her ears, competing with the night sounds, forcing her to put her ear against the door. Bile makes its way to her throat. *Please, let this be my imagination.*

She presses her ear to the door more firmly and covers her other ear.

"Shhh, Marge. It's okay. It's supposed to be like this. You're becoming a young woman. It's all a part of growing up."

Deloris hears Marge's pleading response. "Please, Daddy, the steps are hurting my back."

Fred lets out a moaning sound. "Come on, Margie, I promise it'll be okay. It's okay."

"Please, Daddy, stop. Let me up," Marge pleads.

Deloris looks around on the ground, searching for something—anything. Sitting on the ground is a rusty iron skillet that has become a scrap bowl used to feed the dog. She picks up the pan and feels its weight. She eases the door open and peers across the dimly lit room to the wooden stairs. Her husband and daughter are lying on the steps—Marge's legs on either side of Fred's body as he lies on top of her. He reaches down between them, fumbling with the button on his pants.

Deloris steps forward, anger shifting into madness, blocking out everything else. Fury and adrenaline raise the iron skillet high, slamming it down on the back of Fred's head. His body goes partially limp as he rolls himself onto his side, leaning back against the wall.

"Fuck!" he swears under his breath.

"Run outside, Marge. Now!"

Marge stumbles down the steps and rushes toward the door. She pauses, her voice timid. "Mom?"

"Go back to the house." Deloris's voice sounds scary-calm as she turns to look at her daughter—her wild eyes unseeing. "I said *go*," she says, stressing each word.

Deloris turns back to Fred. His head is swaying as he tries to focus his eyes on his hand after touching his head, his body still limp and stretched on the stairs. The door closes behind Deloris. She takes one more glance to make sure Marge is gone, and then she walks closer to Fred.

"No! Deloris, please!" His plea is little more than a whisper. He holds up his bloody hand in an attempt to block what is coming.

With the skillet clutched in both hands, Deloris raises it over her head and brings it down with the force of someone pounding an object with a sledgehammer. Again and again and again. The thuds echo around the tall room, followed by silence.

Out of breath, she steps back and stares at her husband, rage still poisoning her veins. His chest rises and falls, but his body remains otherwise still. She knows what her mother would do right now. She wouldn't stop here. Her mother would say, "Kill the bastard."

Finding a piece of cloth, Deloris rips off a long strip and uses it to tie Fred's hands together behind him. She then looks at the ceiling and along the walls. High on the ceiling are a pulley and rope that were once used to hang slaughtered livestock to drain them of their blood. She catches the end of the rope and makes a crude noose. She slides it up and down and then yanks on it, testing its strength.

Deloris uses a handful of Fred's hair to lift his bloody head from the step, sliding her noose around his neck, adjusting it for a snug fit. Fred moans, and this only fuels her anger. She lets go of his hair, letting his head thud down. As she steps back, Deloris grabs the other end of the rope and pulls until she feels tension. Using all of her body weight, she leans back as she steps away from Fred. She watches as his head rises and then his shoulders. She tugs and steps in short increments, struggling as his weight pulls harder against her. His hips rise and his body rocks back and forth, and she can see that his pants are undone. The sight of it sends a new wave of blinding rage through her body, and she heaves harder, this time moving him until his feet dangle. His whole body sways forward toward her, and she raises him even higher. Strange sounds gurgle from his throat, and his eyes pop open. He twists wildly but cannot free his hands to claw at the rope. He stares in horror at Deloris, his eyes locked on hers.

"You fucked with the wrong woman," Deloris declares.

Fred's eyes shift from horror to defeat as urine stains the front of his pants. With one more hard heave of the rope, his body swings back and forth as she ties the rope's end through a hook mounted into the floor. She nods her last goodbye and walks out of the building, closing the door behind her.

After nightfall, once Marge is asleep, she will move his body to the kiln out back.

CHAPTER SIXTEEN

Kevan
Early Summer

After searching Google Maps for the address on the second deed, I find very little regarding its location. GPS seems to be as confused as Google, as it takes me down a narrow road and then tells me I've reached my destination, even though I'm in the middle of nowhere. I get out of my car and stand inside the door as I determine how to reach my destination exactly. There are no markings. It's as if the place doesn't exist. At least not so that anyone can find it. This must be close to where it *should* exist.

The path is overgrown with brush and briars and looks like a breeding ground for snakes. A strange truck, minus its driver, is parked near the side of the road, furthering my decision against trekking through. Deciding that it must be the same place Gammie took me to when I was young, I decide to backtrack and use the path I knew as a kid—which means sneaking past my mother's house.

Just like before, seeing my childhood home hits like indigestion and a cold in the head. I park down the street close to Gammie's old residence. Even from this distance, a heaviness floats in the air like an invisible poison. Nobody seems to be home at Gammie's old place. Their fenced-in backyard has access to the woods behind as well. The neighbors and my mother are not friendly; however, they seem to like me and have said that I am welcome anytime.

The lawn is neat, with no resemblance to a junkyard. The siding is painted, unlike the peeling eyesore my family lives in.

A short distance into the woods, I find one of Gammie's trees with the X mark left years ago. The growth of lichen and moss has camouflaged the X's. My recollection of the path is foggy, but ahead is another of her trees, and beyond that one, a third. The walk seemed much longer as a child.

The clearing is the same. Except for the work done by neglect and time, the old property is just as I remember it. Why didn't Gammie tell me she possessed the deed? After we stopped coming here, she never mentioned this place at all. It became another thing of the past.

Around the pond, weeds are higher than my knees. The pond gives me a strong sense of déjà vu. At its edge, the feeling turns to anxiety. As if on cue, something splashes, followed by the small ripples. My eyes widen as I search for a frog, then a necklace and key. My mind is trying to conjure a recent dream to life.

Shaking it off, I walk toward the old house. From the front steps, there is a better view of the dilapidated dock. Confusion fogs my mind as I squint, blink, and repeat. I know I'm not dreaming.

A girl is standing on the dock. Her face is flawless, pale, and her eyes reflect sadness and confusion. She wears a white sundress with one strap sagging down her upper arm. She clutches a thin doll that hangs upside down, its long, yellow hair moving in the breeze. She points to the pond and then looks back at me. Fear speeds in and parks itself between us. She looks familiar, real, and yet translucent—like a ghost, but alive.

"Hello?" The word is in my head, but no sound escapes. I try again. "Hello?"

As slow as a sloth, I try to move but can't seem to make my legs work. The girl looks into my eyes imploringly, as if she wants me to help her. I turn my head in micro-movements, side to side, scanning the area for others. When I look back, she's gone. Was I seeing things? I am alone. Taking a moment to gather myself, I take a deep breath to calm my nerves. I turn back toward the house, but not without reservations about going in. Climbing the steps, I glance over my shoulder at the dock once more—relieved to see nothing.

Though the old porch boards hold my weight, it seems less safe, or maybe it never was. I think about the key Gammie left me. Since the door rests on the floor, it would be useless.

A sense of longing permeates this house. Déjà vu returns. Dreams of this place come to me, and the emotions from the dream surface and are frightening. A familiar smell of damp wood and mildew wafts through the drafty house. I pause, disconcerted, as I realize something. Dream aside, this house is familiar for a reason. It is a skeletal replica of Gammie's current house. The living room with its shelves on the far wall. The kitchen on the left. Gammie built a very close replica of this house. *Why?*

This house must have been her childhood home.

What used to be a kitchen triggers more details of my dream. The one closed cabinet now stands open. Inside are loose boards but nothing else. Apprehensive, I look in the upper cabinets, but they too are empty.

I tiptoe around weak spots in the floor and enter an open door off the living room. In this room, I find another open door, to an oblong closet. I ease inside. A damp, musty smell makes me cough. The flashlight on my phone shines on the wooden walls and ceiling. Hanging halfway to the floor is a partial stepladder. I test the bottom step—it's sturdy enough. I look at it for a moment with apprehension, then decide I want to explore. Apprehension is the mother of all instincts. It tries to warn us what our gut already knows.

But, after all, I never listened to my mother.

I return to the kitchen and retrieve a piece of an old chair. The top part is bent downward, but the bottom seems to be strong enough to hold me. Standing on it makes me tall enough to grip the opening in the ceiling. As my fingers curve over the attic ledge, I feel grit and dust underneath my fingertips. Ignoring the willies that shiver through my body, I use my arms to hold most of my weight as I raise one foot high and place it on the first step of the ladder, testing it once more. It feels as though it will hold, so I climb a second step and then hoist myself the rest of the way up. My face and shoulders part sticky webs that threaten to make my arms buckle under their invasive spread. I ignore the thoughts of the creatures that put them there.

My jaw drops at the sight before me. The room is large and bright. More so than I'd expected. The light comes from two windows built into the ceiling. Or roof. They look like actual windows. *How odd*. It's like a secret room, as it isn't visible from the outside.

The room contains some dust-covered furniture and few derelict boxes. Sitting near the far left corner is a child-sized rocking chair. Next to it stands a small dressing table with a mirror and a cushioned bench. I stroke my fingers across the surface of the table, leaving lines in the dust. The table's center is lower and larger, and on each end are two taller surfaces with drawers. Underneath is one long, narrow drawer that spans the width of the table. I pull open one of the small drawers, wood sliding against wood, making a slight squeal as it moves. Inside is a small, handmade yarn doll. Sewn *X*'s, like the *X*'s on the trees, form the eyes, nose, and mouth, and it wears a handmade floral dress. The doll reminds me of a creepy doll from a horror movie. I open the other drawer and find a small hairbrush and several pieces of ribbon.

The long drawer underneath won't move. Brushing the front with my palm, I feel a keyhole. It's locked. Could the key I found in Gammie's house fit this lock? Fingering it, I think it's too small to match. I rummage through the drawers for a key. Nothing. As I'm pressing the doll back into its drawer, I feel something hard underneath its dress. Threaded through the yarn is a tiny key, its end shaped like a heart. I remove the key and try it in the hole. The sound it makes pierces my ears like nails on a chalkboard, but it works.

Inside are two tiny, worn notebooks. The outsides of the books are black, their spines tattered and worn. I begin thumbing through the first, which contains childlike drawings and a few words. I slide the book with drawings inside my backpack and lay the other on top of the desk, opening to the inside cover, using my phone's flashlight to look at its contents.

The first page is a sketch of a tree with several branches drawn out on both sides—each branch labeled with names. The bottom two branches have the names of Gammie's parents, and written across the trunk of the tree is the name *Frances*.

I keep paging through the book. The rest is a diary dated in the early 1950s, spanning several years. I stuff the diary into my backpack.

The rest of the room contains miscellaneous items, but nothing of significance. The floor is creaky and loud when I move back toward the ladder. With caution, I descend, one step at a time. Just as I am stepping on the last step and making my way down to the chair, the ladder breaks loose from the ceiling and I come crashing down hard, one foot slamming into the chair, the other hitting the floor. I try to catch myself with my hands, but I end up sprawled on the floor. It sounded as if the entire ceiling had come crashing down inside the closet. Stabbing pain shoots through my right wrist and my left ankle. My bottom hurts as well, but not as badly as my wrist and ankle. I attempt to stand, putting weight on my bad foot, and pain splits across the side of my foot just below the ankle.

"Fuck!" The word comes through clenched teeth; then I scold myself, "You idiot!"

CHAPTER SEVENTEEN

Marge
1957

"Don't be such a wimp, Dotty," Marge chides. "You can do this. Just jump."

Dotty squeezes her eyes shut, takes a deep breath, and counts to three inside her head. On three, she opens her eyes, runs toward the cliff's edge, and halts a few feet from it.

"I can't do it, Marge," Dotty whispers as she turns around. A whole crowd of partygoers and thrill seekers stands behind Marge, screaming and encouraging her to do it.

"Come on, you chickenshit," Jimmy yells. The spoiled, rich loud-mouth clucks like a chicken and gets a laugh from the bystanders.

"Shut the fuck up, Jimmy!" Marge flips her head around. She places both hands on Dotty's shoulders. "You got this, Dotty. All you have to do is jump." Marge's swimsuit drips a steady stream of water down her legs. She's already jumped into the lake several times. "I'll jump with you."

"Me too." A handsome stranger walks toward them. Neither has noticed him before now.

"We don't need you," Marge snaps.

"Marge," Dotty scolds, "he's just being nice."

"We don't need some guy trying to rescue us. We can do this on our own. Come on, Dotty."

"Easy for you to say, Marge, you're an expert swimmer. I hate going underwater."

"My name's John," the guy introduces himself.

"I'm Dotty."

"I think it would be cool if a bunch of us jumped in together. What do y'all think?" John speaks to the onlookers behind. Several yell back. Everyone else has already jumped off the famous rock cliff.

"See?" John looks at Marge. "I still haven't caught your name." He's pouring on the Southern charm.

"Who said I wanted to give it to you?" Marge rolls her eyes.

"She's Marge," Dotty offers.

"Dotty!"

"Nice to meet you, Marge. What do you say? Form a line with us?" John waves others to join. Two guys and three other girls sprint up to them.

Marge takes a deep, annoyed breath and says to Dotty, "Will *this* make you jump?"

"Come on, we'll put you right in the middle. You won't be alone," John says.

"You gotta do it now, pretty girl," a dark-haired guy says to Dotty. He flashes her a smile.

Dotty blushes and looks down at the ground.

Marge gives a huge eye roll. "You ready?"

With a long, loud exhale, Dotty agrees. "Okay."

John waves to the crowd. Four more join them, and they all form a line at the edge of the cliff. Marge and Dotty place themselves in the center.

"You count, Dotty," John says.

As Dotty gazes at the water below, she breathes in long and counts slowly, "One, two, three!" She takes a swift step forward, and the others follow. They leap from the edge of the rock and sail through the air. Dotty screams the whole way down, and just before she hits the water, she sucks in a deep breath and closes her eyes. After they plunge in, John releases her right hand and she paddles upward, not letting go of Marge. They break the surface and scream at the top of their lungs. The bystanders at the edge of the cliff cheer and clap.

Marge and Dotty float in place, wave their arms back and forth, and laugh.

"I knew you could do it," says the guy who had called Dotty pretty. "I'm Tom."

"We know who you are." Marge hisses the words, then turns her body away from him. "Come on, Dotty."

"I kind of want to float awhile," Dotty says.

"With him?" Marge eyes Tom.

"Why not with me?" Tom asks.

John swims over and hovers next to Marge. "You want to do it again?"

"I can jump all by myself, thank you." Marge's face shifts into a deeper frown.

"Oh, I know. I've seen you do it over and over. I just thought it might be fun."

"You should do it, Marge," Dotty says.

"I'm not leaving you here alone with him." She nods her head in Tom's direction. Marge hates the idea of Dotty hanging out with Tom. She's heard the rumors and knows that he's a snake. More than one rumor has surfaced with him taking what he wants, anytime he wants it.

"I'll be fine," Dotty assures Marge. "Go jump. You know you want to."

Marge looks up at the cliff for a long moment. "I'll be back." She swims to the water's edge. John swims behind her.

"I didn't say I wanted to jump with you," she says once she has climbed out of the water. She then attempts to ignore John as she wrings water out of her hair.

"Well, I guess I'll just have to jump by myself, then," John says.

"Suit yourself." Marge climbs the path that leads back to the top.

"Why do you want to be like that?"

"Like what?"

"Like you're better than me."

Marge stops and turns. "I'm not doing that. I just don't want some creep following me around."

John laughs. "I wanted to jump off of a cliff for you. Most women would kill for that type of man."

"Not this woman." Marge looks him in the eye. She glances down at the water where she left Dotty and sees her splashing and wrestling with Tom. Her eyes narrow and turn hateful. She turns and stomps up the path even faster. Once she reaches the top, she walks straight to the edge and looks down at the two below. She despises seeing them together. Men with thick charm never prove to be anything more than scum. She knows that Tom is one of those men.

"Come on, now. Let me jump with you."

Marge turns to John and says again, with a shrug, "Suit yourself." She leaps far out toward Dotty and Tom. John leaps a second after she does. Marge lands in the water only a couple of feet from Tom, close enough to cover his head with water, forcing him to paddle harder to stay afloat in the ripple of waves.

"What the hell?" Tom flips around to see who has landed so close. "Hell, Marge, you could have landed right on top of me. Why did you do that?"

"Aww, you scared?" Marge fake-whines.

"Marge. That wasn't very nice," Dotty says. "Why did you do that?"

"I'm just having fun."

Dotty swims to shore, and Tom follows. Marge treads water as John swims up beside her.

"I get the feeling you don't like Tom," he says.

"He's a jerk."

"Oh, yeah. Big asshole," John agrees.

"I thought you guys were friends."

"We are. But I don't like the way he treats girls. As long as he's not dating my sister, then I can tolerate him."

"I don't like the idea of him sniffing around Dotty."

"You want me to kick his ass for you?" John gives Marge a full-teeth smile and winks.

"If I have to, I can."

"I don't doubt that."

Marge's lips move, one corner of her mouth shifting upward into a half smile. Then she turns and swims to shore. She grabs her towel, climbs up the side of the rock, and lets her legs dangle over the edge. John, without asking for permission, follows and sits next to her. Marge spreads her towel out on the rock behind her and lies down. John sits, looking out over the lake.

She looks over and spots Tom and Dotty sitting side by side on the cliff, arm touching arm.

"You don't have to worry about her. There are too many people around."

Marge snaps out of it and diverts her gaze up to the sky. "Well, you don't know Dotty. She's naive and trusts everyone. She always falls for the bad boys."

"Well, you have him pegged."

John lies back too, looking up at the darkening sky, and spots the first star.

"Do you know what that star is?" he asks Marge.

"Everyone knows it's not a star."

"I'm impressed. What is it, then?"

"It's Venus."

John rolls his head back onto his forearm and smiles. "Guess I'm not the only one who gazes up at the sky at night."

Marge lets her guard down as their conversation leads one direction and then another. The warm glow of the campfire casts outlines and shadows. Marge feels a chill, and John wraps his towel around her. They talk a while longer, unable to see each other in the darkness.

"I'm cold. I think we should head up close to the fire," Marge says.

As they reach the top, they see that the crowd has doubled in size. Marge looks for Dotty. John follows close behind. At every dark edge of the cliff, boys and girls plaster themselves to each other, necking. John and Marge comb through the party and find Dotty and a very drunken Tom standing in a crowd gathered around the fire. Tom leans on Dotty with his arm draped around her shoulders, swaying, unable to stand still.

"Your friend is fucked up," Marge says.

"What's new?" John replies, not surprised. He walks toward the two and says, "I'll take care of Tom. You grab Dotty." John walks around beside Tom. "Hey, Tom, why don't you save some drinks for the rest of us?" John smacks Tom on the shoulder.

"Just doing my part," Tom slurs, staggering around to look at John.

"Come on, Dotty. It's time to go." Marge grips Dotty's arm and pulls her away from Tom.

Dotty pulls away, annoyed. "I'm not ready to go yet, Marge."

"Yeah, Marge, you've been such a bitch all evening. Stop acting like you're Dotty's mom," Tom snaps.

"Tom, cut it out," John scolds.

Tom puts his arm around Dotty and whispers in her ear. "What do you say we swim and get away from these people?"

"Forget it, Tom," John urges. "You're too drunk to go swimming right now. Let's just hang out here."

Tom pulls on Dotty with the arm that he has wrapped around her. "Come on, Dotty. Ignore them."

"Maybe we shouldn't go," Dotty says.

"You heard her." Marge steps in front of Tom.

Tom stops, but his body sways back and forth. He slurs, "Here comes your mommy again, Dotty, telling you what to do. What's the matter, *Marge*?" Tom stresses her name long and loud. "Didn't John satisfy ya? Maybe you should take a dip with me and Dotty. I'll show you what a real man can do." Tom staggers one step forward, reaching his hand out to grab a lock of Marge's hair.

Marge shifts her upper body backward and slaps Tom's hand away. "Keep your damn hands off me." Marge stares him down for a moment, then grabs Dotty's hand. "Time to go, Dotty."

"Cut it out, Tom," John snaps.

Tom reaches for Dotty's other hand, but she yanks it away. "Not now, Tom. Maybe some other time."

"You gonna let this bitch tell us what to do?"

"She's not a bitch. She's my friend. I don't like it when—"

Marge cuts Dotty off. "Call me a bitch again, Tom, and I'll put you on the ground."

"Go ahead, bit—"

Marge balls up her right fist and punches Tom in the nose before he can get the whole word across his lips. He bends forward, grabbing his already bleeding nose. Without acknowledging the pain in her hand from the blow, she follows the punch by shoving her foot into Tom's side, sending him crashing to the ground. John wraps his arms around Marge's waist.

"I think you made your point." John turns Marge's body away and sits her down on the ground, but without releasing his hold on her. "I'll let go when you calm down."

Marge tries to turn and look at Tom, but John keeps a tight grip on her. She puffs a few more breaths. "I'm good."

"You sure you're calm?"

"Yes."

John releases his grip on Marge, and she turns to Dotty. "Now, are you ready to go?"

"I guess," Dotty agrees, but turns to Tom and whispers, "Sorry."

CHAPTER EIGHTEEN

Nathan

A loud crash echoes through the air, accompanied by a woman's muffled scream. I'm certain that the noise came from somewhere inside the house. It can't be. There isn't anyone around here. I stand still just inside the cellar and listen for more sounds. Then I hear the woman curse. Either I'm losing my mind, or someone is definitely inside the house.

I abandon the cellar and walk back through tall weeds. I stop inside the door to see if the noise will reveal its source. Farther into the house, I hear a rustling sound, so I ease across the room with caution.

"Hello?" I call out as I take a few more steps. The sound ceases. I call again, a little louder. Still nothing. I tiptoe a few more steps. Everything looks just as it did before. I call one last hello as I step through the doorway of the room with the open closet. A woman stands there, with a broken chair held high over her head. Before I can react, she hurls it at me. I step backward, out of range, and the chair slams against the doorframe.

"What do you want?" the woman yells. I hear more rustling, only this time it takes on a frantic sound.

"Whoa, whoa!" As if to wave a white flag in surrender, I hold my hands in front of me. "I only came to investigate after hearing a loud noise."

The woman appears agitated as she searches for something—another object to throw, I imagine. Then a wave of realization hits me as I really look at her for the first time: it's the woman who's been parading through my mind since I met her at the spirit store. This time I stutter when I try to speak. "Um, I was just exploring the property when I heard a loud noise."

"What are you doing here? This is private property!"

"Oh—uh—I didn't know. I . . . I'm not sure." I continue to stutter, like a teenage boy on a date with an older girl. "Long story short, I haven't been here in years. Not since my sister disappeared somewhere around here many years ago. I just got to thinking about her and decided to revisit the area, and that led me here." I take a breath, then finish. "By private property, you mean someone bought it?" I continue to hold my hands in front of me, palms out.

"I—I mean—it belongs to my grandmother," the woman replies, stuttering as well.

"I'm sorry. I didn't know." My mouth has turned to cotton, and I try to work up enough saliva to speak again. I search the woman's face and see that she remains on guard. I smile warmly, hoping to calm her uneasiness. "Has it always belonged to her?"

Waiting for her reply, I realize that the two dolls I slid into my back pocket earlier are sticking out above my waistband. I casually reach around to make sure my shirt is hanging down over them. I don't want her to question why I am carrying dolls.

She seems to relax a little. "I'm not sure. I mean, I suppose. Just since her recent passing, I found out that it belongs to her. I wasn't aware of that before. The house has been vacant for a while. Even when Gammie first brought me here, it was long abandoned. She never talked about having any connection to it." The woman swallows and continues. "We used to come here a lot, but I haven't been in a while either."

Her long red hair is partially pulled back from her face, showing off her fair complexion. My eyes dart over her body, taking in her fitted jeans and T-shirt. I rush to correct myself and bring them back to her face. My gaze settles into her big, brown eyes. They are beautiful.

"I'm sorry to hear about your grandmother." I peer around the room. "I thought I heard a loud crash earlier. Is everything all right?"

"Yes, I just twisted my ankle," she says. "And my wrist," she adds, massaging it.

"May I ask what the loud crash was?"

"Oh—yeah. It was me falling from the ceiling." She laughs and points toward the closet. Her smile reaches her eyes, making them brighter somehow.

I smile back. "So, I'm guessing you tried out the scary piece of ladder? Brave!" I raise my eyebrows. "I saw it earlier but decided I didn't want to break a leg."

She laughs again, rolling her eyes playfully. "I guess I let curiosity almost kill the cat." Continuing to rub her wrist, she asks, "What was your sister's name?"

"Gracie," I say, relaxing a little and leaning against the doorframe. " Well, that's what I called her."

"Was she ever found?"

"No. That was more than twenty-six years ago. I suppose I haven't really let it go. Every so often I think about it, and this time I wound up here."

"How old was your sister?"

"Seven, almost eight."

"Oh, my."

I'm struggling not to stare at this woman, partly because I'm so curious about her and partly because of her beauty. My mind scolds me into realizing that I'm that creepy, gawking man again, and I attempt to cover any awkwardness. "I'm Nathan, by the way."

"I'm Kevan," she says. "Sorry I tried to kill you with that chair."

CHAPTER NINETEEN

Marge
1962

"It's about time you two lovebirds showed up," Dotty says, smiling, as she opens the front door. "Everyone is in the backyard. Make sure you grab yourself a drink in the kitchen. I have any poison you want."

"I'm ready!" Marge grins. "John, you go on out back and I'll bring you something to drink. What would you like?"

"Cold beer will be just fine, honey." John kisses Marge on the cheek before turning to head outside.

"Aww, look at you two. Married more than two years now, and you still act like newlyweds," Dotty says, smiling as she watches him leave the room. "Come on, Marge, I'll help you fix the drinks."

She grabs Marge's hand and leads her to the kitchen, where they find Clara standing next to the tall table, mixing whiskey and soda in a short, fat glass. "I guess we'd all better catch up with your man, Dotty," Clara says. "Tom is drinking us all under the table."

"What the hell else is new?" Dotty sighs loudly with disgust. "Is that his drink you're mixing?"

"Hell, no, this is mine." Clara laughs as she adds a handful of ice to the drink and heads toward the back door.

"Good, I'll mix his. It's time to mix them weak."

"That's just sad, Dotty. If he can't hold his liquor, then he shouldn't be drinking." Marge knows she has mentioned this to Dotty before.

"You try telling him that. You know how pissy he gets if I say that while he's drinking."

"Yeah, well, the next time he lays a hand on you, you should just pick up whatever you can find and knock the holy old hell out of him. I trust him about as far as I can throw him. I don't know why you put up with him, Dotty."

"Marge, let this go for right now. I just want to have fun."

Marge tuts and huffs, giving Dotty a disgusted look. "All right—but we will have this conversation sometime."

"Deal," Dotty agrees.

Dotty and Marge step into the backyard to join the others. Several guests sit around a table smoking cigarettes and cigars while Tom, John, and two others play horseshoes out in the yard.

"It's about time you brought me my drink," Tom barks as he walks heavy-footed toward Dotty. He snatches the drink from Dotty's hand and then wraps an arm around her waist, yanking her against his chest. "I thought I'd have to hunt you down." His tone shifts into a gentlemanly one as he turns on the fake charm.

Marge gives Tom a hateful glare and looks away. For Dotty's sake, she wonders just how evil it was. She doesn't care—she doesn't find him charming at all. She tolerates him only because of Dotty. She knows Dotty loves him, but she can't understand why. Marge takes a deep breath and makes the choice to support her friend and try to be civil to Tom tonight. Maybe try to find a good quality in him.

The evening moves ahead as the drinks flow freely, everyone becoming loose, happy, and carefree. As dark creeps in, the party moves indoors to the large living room, with music, dancing, and card games. Dotty and Clara partner up to beat John and his partner for the second time in a game of hearts. Marge and Tom stand on the sidelines, blowing smoke from their own cigars into the cloud hovering around the ceiling. All evening, Tom has stayed near Marge, showing her a sweeter version of himself. After a few too many drinks, she laughs at his jokes and sees a smidgen of what Dotty sees in him. He does have a charming side.

"Look over there," Tom whispers as he puts his arm around Marge's shoulders and nods his head toward the couch. Clara's husband has already found his spot there for the night, and his snoring is getting a chuckle out of everyone. "That would usually be me," Tom laughs.

As the night wears on, Marge begins to feel the room spin, her buzz louder than she wants it to be. She sneaks out the back door for some fresh air. As she walks a short distance into the backyard, she hears the door behind her open. When she turns, her body feels a little top-heavy. Tom is coming down the steps. She rolls her eyes and turns back around, feeling as if her head and her body aren't in sync. Tom walks up beside her, his voice smooth as creamy butter.

"What's the matter? Too much fun in there for you?"

"Just needed some air, that's all."

"Too much to drink?"

"No, that would be you." Marge tilts her head toward him in a teasing manner.

"You got me there."

They laugh together.

Rocking back and forth on his heels, Tom looks up at the sky and asks, "You know Dotty better than anyone. Can I ask your advice on something?"

"You sure you want it?"

Tom laughs, and Marge sees his softer side again.

"No, really." He rubs the back of his neck, looking like a schoolboy unsure of himself. She has never seen this side of him before. "I bought Dotty a gift for her birthday, but I'm not sure if she'll like it. Can I show it to you and see what you think?"

Taking a deep breath, Marge eyes him hard.

"It's in my shed." He points to the building that sits back a hundred feet or so from the house. "Will you come see it and tell me what you think? I really want her to like it."

"Since when do you buy thoughtful gifts?"

"I know. I'm really trying to do better."

Marge looks back at the house and then agrees, "Hell, why not?" She staggers on the first couple of steps, and to her surprise, Tom takes her elbow and steadies her.

"You sure you're okay?"

"Yeah, I'm fine. Let me see it."

Tom releases her arm, pausing to make sure she is steady, and they walk to the shed. He takes a set of keys out of his pocket and unlocks the door. He steps into the dark room first and pulls a string hanging from the ceiling. A faint light illuminates the center of the room; the corners remain somewhat dark.

"I had this place wired for electric the other day. Makes it easier when I work in here." Marge steps inside as Tom points to the opposite corner of the room and says, "There."

Marge walks to the corner to search for what he's pointing at. She hears the door close behind her and then hears the lock turn. As she whips around, the room spins, forcing her to stare at a fixed point, waiting for it to stop. Tom slams his body into hers and places one hand over her mouth. He wraps his free arm around her waist, squeezing her against his body. Her heart jumps into overdrive as his sour, hot breath moves close to her face.

"I've seen how you've been looking at me. You've been begging for this all evening. You shouldn't tease a man."

"Let me go, you son of a bitch," Marge mumbles, the words barely audible. She is very little match for Tom's strength as he drags her across the room to another dark corner and slams her down on a cot. With little effort, he presses Marge onto her stomach while pinning one arm behind her and then uses his other hand to press her face into the cot. He places a knee into her bent arm and back, and she hears him unbuckle his belt. Marge presses her other hand into the cot, fighting back against him, but can't budge.

"Keep fighting, bitch! That just makes it even more fun." His voice is cold and evil.

Shame, horror, and a multitude of questions scream inside Marge's head. *Why did I get into this situation? Do I scream? Do I stay quiet and hope it's over soon? Why did I have to wear a dress? I made this easier for him. How can I stop him?*

Marge continues to press her hand into the cot, bucking against him with her shoulders, but it's like trying to raise a rock wall. Tom stretches her panties aside and forces his way inside her. Lying there, Marge answers her own question by allowing her body to go limp, waiting for it to be over. Time seems to slow down as shame takes hold of her. He grunts under his breath and staggers backward, pulling his pants back into place. The sound of his zipper tells her it's over.

She sees him in her peripheral vision, smoothing his hair and tucking in his shirt. He puffs his chest and fixes his cold eyes on her. "If you tell anyone, I'll make sure you never see Dotty again. I'll kill her, then I'll come for you. Got it?" Tom's voice has distorted to match the monster he is. It sends fear slithering down Marge's spine like a poisonous snake. She believes him, but even though she's terrified, she turns and looks him dead in the eye.

"It will be me who kills *you*."

Tom laughs, seemingly unaffected by her words. "I'd like to see you try." He turns and walks out the door, closing it behind him.

The aftermath brings humiliation. *What should I do?*

Choking back sobs, Marge looks around the shed for anything to clean herself with. She finds a roll of paper towels. Wrapping several around her hand, she wipes vigorously, trying to scrub away what has just happened. Her mind spins in a whirlwind of confusion. *If I go in and say something, John will kill him. That's what he deserves, but what would happen to John then?* Still fighting back tears, she takes a deep breath and straightens her clothes. *I could say something to Dotty, but what if Tom carries through with his threat to kill her? Or what if I say something and Dotty just doesn't believe me? I would lose my best friend for good.*

Her thoughts spin, and they always lead back to the same conclusion. She will have to take care of this herself.

Right now, she knows she has to go back, or John will wonder where she is. Marge cracks the door to peek out into the yard. There's no sign of Tom. Stepping into the night air, she pulls as much oxygen into her lungs as she can. The humidity forces her to choke out a cough. Her emotions are high, and she is not ready to face John or Dotty, so she darts behind the shed and collapses against the wall. Mind spinning out of control, she closes her eyes for a moment and makes a choice to pretend that nothing happened, even though she doesn't intend on forgetting it. She promises herself that she will make the bastard pay.

Coming to terms with her decision, Marge opens her eyes and sees in the moonlight a small mound of dirt. Squinting, she sees a stack of stones with an opening in the center.

"What are you doing out here?" Dotty asks.

Marge jumps, her hand finding her chest. She forces herself to gain her composure to speak.

"You scared me!" Marge says, turning only slightly to face Dotty, afraid that her best friend will see the fear and hurt in her eyes. She knows she has to keep her composure and pretend that everything is okay. She turns back toward the cave-shaped structure. "Just out here getting some air." Marge then looks down at the stones, remembering a structure similar to this, only much larger.

"Not much air out here tonight," Dotty says. To Marge's relief, she appears to be clueless.

"Guess I had too much to drink."

Dotty walks to stand beside Marge; Marge can feel Dotty's eyes staring into her. "You sure you're okay? You look a little flustered. Did someone upset you? 'Cause if they did, then I'm going to kick some ass."

Attempting to make a joke and distract Dotty, Marge says, "I thought I was the one who kicked ass and you were my sidekick." She fake-laughs. "Like I said, I drank too much. So, that pile of rocks there —is that a kiln?"

"Yes. My mother had a pottery hobby a long time ago. See all the flowerpots around?" Dotty points as she rotates her body. "Those are her handiwork. I never picked up the skill. Wasn't my interest. It's just been sitting here all this time, unused."

"Have you ever seen the one that's out by my cellar at home? The one my mother had? It's big enough to fire a life-size statue. It's grown over, so I'd forgotten all about it. Maybe I should open it back up," Marge says, distracting Dotty from looking at her face.

"I think Tom has used this one twice."

Marge feels her insides turn cold at the mention of his name. Dotty must have seen the change in her expression; the moonlight is too bright to hide it. Marge breathes in deep and turns away.

"Marge, what's wrong? I can see it. It's written all over your face. Someone has done something to you." Dotty leans in, trying to look into Marge's face. "You may as well tell me, because I'll find out eventually."

Marge chokes down a sob, forcing herself to keep up the lie. "It's getting late—I'm just tired. I should find John and head home. Thank you so much for this evening. We had fun." Marge chokes on the last words. She wants nothing more than to go home, bathe, and bury herself under the covers. How will she hide this from John? Marge worries he will never look at her again if he finds out.

She walks back toward the house, and just as she is reaching to open the screen door, it swings open and there Tom stands. Her heart shifts to a deafening thud in her ears. She steps back, avoiding his eyes, and calls around him, "John?"

Tom steps around her, glaring at her out of the corner of his eye as he passes. She avoids his glare, for if she looks at him, she might not be able to hold herself together.

Dotty walks up and asks, "What are you doing, Tom?"

"Looking for you. What have you two been doing out here?" Tom asks with a fabricated sweet tone. He swoops one arm around Dotty's waist, grabbing her ass with the other hand as he picks her up off of the ground.

"Cut it out, Tom. There are people around." Dotty is half serious and half teasing. She looks at Marge. She then presses away from Tom with both hands and says, "Let me go, Tom!"

Tom drops Dotty. "What the hell is wrong with you?"

Marge turns and hurries into the house, Dotty not far behind.

"Marge, wait!"

CHAPTER TWENTY

Kevan
Early Summer

"My name is Nathan, by the way," he says.

"I'm Kevan. Sorry I tried to kill you with that chair."

He lets out a pleasing chuckle. "You have excellent aim. Remind me not to challenge you in an ax-throwing contest."

I return with my own full smile. Standing in his presence, I feel my uneasiness start to fade, but I'm still nervous, not least because this is Mr. Tall, Dark, and Handsome from the spirit store, and I've just nearly beaned him with a chair. I want to get off that subject, and I'm still curious to know more about his sister and about him in general, so I ask, "Did you and your sister come here often?"

"I didn't. I'm not sure about my sister. They weren't sure whether she was here before she vanished. Our mother allowed her to roam the woods, providing she didn't wander far and made it home before dark. I guess back then there wasn't as much fear of someone snagging one of us. My mother regretted it later." Nathan's eyes dart to the floor as he rubs the back of his neck.

"My parents were the opposite. If I wanted to leave, I had to sneak out." As I chew my bottom lip, I try to figure out why I shared this with him.

"My mother was always very trusting. Maybe too much."

Nathan looks out the window when he speaks of his mother, then pauses for a long moment. I am never good with the slightest hint of awkward silence, so I break it quickly.

"What year did your sister disappear?"

"It was the summer of 1996. They found her backpack a couple of days after we reported her missing. They believed that whoever had been involved in her disappearance must have ditched her backpack beside the road a short piece from here. Her backpack was the only clue that she had been close to that spot. She's been a missing person ever since."

"That's so sad," I comment, struggling with my words. "If she was almost eight in 1996, then we're close in age—I mean, would have been. Um—" I stutter, trying to redeem myself from sounding so nonchalant about it. I move on quickly. "Gracie was her name, you say?"

"Yeah. Well, Grace. I called her Gracie," Nathan answers. He chuckles and adds with pride, "She was my little squirt. I picked on her a lot, but I suppose that's what big brothers are for. She was a spunky little thing. Spoke her mind and was very outgoing for a girl her age."

Hearing the way Nathan speaks of his sister, I imagine that he was a good big brother.

"What will you do with the place?" he asks.

"I have no idea. Still trying to figure that one out. I already have my own place, so I wouldn't move back here."

"Ah—this booming little town? Why not?" Nathan laughs, then says, "This place needs a lot of work."

I gaze around the room from ceiling to floor and wall to wall. The thought of fixing it up hadn't entered my mind. "So, where were you when you heard me fall?"

"I was nosing around out back. There's a pretty spooky cellar," Nathan says as he steps toward the window and points. "Have you checked it out?"

"No, not since I was a kid. My Gammie didn't really want me wandering around everywhere." I limp over and join Nathan at the window, getting closer than I had intended because I'm hobbling in place to favor my ankle. His woodsy, masculine scent wafts around me, and I inhale more deeply.

"Looks like you really injured your ankle," he says.

"It's not bad. I've done worse. Would you join me to look around?" I ask. I inhale his pleasing scent again and feel my stomach flip-flop. Everything about this man sends me into adolescent mode.

"You feel like walking out there?" He seems dubious.

"Piece of cake," I respond, trying to appear casual but still feeling nervous. What is it about this man? "My wrist hurts worse than my ankle does."

I hobble out the back door behind him, getting a good view of his backside. When I realize I've raised an eyebrow in appreciation, I look away quickly before he catches me. As we walk to the stone building and cellar, I follow close through the tall grass. I look in all directions, trying to remember this from my childhood, but I remember little more than the house and pond.

A large stack of stones grabs my attention. I stop and stare at the jagged pattern the stones create. There's a cave-like opening in the center that looks like a perfect spot for a small bear to hibernate. Suddenly, I realize this is a kiln. It reminds me of my ceramics days in college, only this kiln is larger than any I've ever seen. It piques my interest, and I wonder how hard it would be to make it functional again.

Nathan continues to walk, and I catch up. As we enter the stone building, he warns me that the stairs aren't safe to climb, and I listen. I wonder what I will do with this building. With any of this.

Next we descend the stone steps to the cellar. Nathan turns on his phone flashlight, and I step in beside him.

"What do you think?" he asks.

The room gives me a chill—more like a vibe than a physical sensation. The corners are dark by nature, but they seem to loom more than they should. I feel I want to leave the space. It seems suffocating.

Tapping his toe on the rough wood floor, Nathan says, "I'm

surprised by the type of floor in here. A dirt floor would be better. Wonder why someone would add this?"

I shrug. "It does seem odd. I'm not a fan of dark places, but this room just gives me the creeps."

"I have to agree with you—it feels heavy, somehow." Nathan says, making me feel less embarrassed for being such a wuss. We walk from the cellar back to the house and pond as I listen to Nathan talk more about his sister.

I look toward the dock, and I feel my blood turn as cold as water that drips from an icicle. My breath catches as I see the little girl, doll still in hand, staring at me. Hesitant, I glance at Nathan, then look back again. He doesn't appear to see her. My expression must have shifted, though, because he stops in mid-sentence.

"What's wrong?"

He follows my gaze, but he clearly does not see her. Tearing my eyes away, I ask with apprehension, "What did your sister look like?"

My question seems to catch him off guard.

"She was about average height for a child that age, with long blond hair. Her eye color was like mine."

I stare at the little blond girl, focusing in on her blue eyes. What the hell? Something about the little girl is familiar as he describes his sister. In fact, she looks similar to Beth as a child. But I knew lots of girls with blond hair when I was a kid. My school was full of them. What if I saw his sister here but don't remember? I blink, letting my eyes stay closed for a split second longer than a normal blink. When I open them, she is still there. I hear my Gammie's voice in my head telling me I have a gift.

If this is my gift, I don't want it. Seeing missing or even dead girls doesn't seem like much of a gift. It's bad enough seeing my brother Tommy at random moments, but it doesn't make sense that I'm now seeing a girl I didn't even know.

CHAPTER TWENTY-ONE

Marge
1962

Marge checks the lining of her panties for the eighth straight day, hoping that her period will be there. Again, there is no blood. She is never late. Every morning she wakes with nerves stretched as tight as the strings of a violin when she goes for her morning pee. She and John have tried for years to get pregnant, but she isn't excited. *Why now? What if it's—*

She stops that thought, but she still begs under her breath that it isn't now.

She has only talked to Dotty a handful of times since that night. It's the longest they've ever gone without seeing each other. She's terrified that her face will give away that she is hiding something and that her sheer hatred for Tom will cause her to commit an extreme act. She hates him—worse than ever. Every time he hits Dotty, it only makes Marge's hatred boil hotter. Now the malice that she feels for Tom has buried itself deep into her core, and she can't dig it out.

More than once, she's tried to convince Dotty to run him off.

Dotty claims he would end up getting everything her family worked so hard for. A judge would rule in Tom's favor and she would lose her family's estate for good. The sad thing is, she's right. A woman never wins in these situations. And if a judge gives him the estate, Tom will more than likely lose it in a hand of poker during one of his long binges.

Each day that passes, Marge's fear of being pregnant grows, making her desire to get rid of Tom grow. What was once a hypothetical scenario inside her mind is now an overwhelming need. A need growing so pungent that she can taste it. She knows that for men like Tom, karma will visit, but not before their damage takes its toll. For men like him, karma needs a swift kick in the ass to get its job done and done right. Her mother taught her that without ever saying it. Now it's only a matter of convincing Dotty.

Two days ago, Dotty called, saying that Tom had gotten pissed because he didn't like what she had fixed for dinner. He'd slung his plate across the kitchen, barely missing her head, and told her he wasn't eating her nasty slop. When she'd retorted that he'd have to starve until morning, he had backhanded her so hard that it blacked her eye. When Dotty had told Marge about it, Marge had struggled to hold back her words. She'd warned Dotty that the next time would be worse and that one day he might not stop until he had killed her.

Feeling guilty for not going to see Dotty when she had called her so upset, Marge decides she has to put her feelings aside and be there for her friend. She has to visit her eventually or Dotty and John will suspect something is wrong. As if the universe knows, the second she makes her decision, the phone rings and it's Dotty.

"Hello."

"Marge," a quiet voice says on the other end.

"Dotty? What's wrong?" Marge hears only breathing for a moment as she waits. "Dotty, is that you?"

"Can you come over?" Dotty's voice quakes.

"I'll be right there." Marge slams the phone down and runs from the house, shouting over her shoulder, "Dotty needs me. I'll be back soon."

"Wait—" John calls out.

"I need to go, John. The bastard did it again."

"I don't like this, Marge. Let me go with you."

"I'll be okay. I promise." Before John has a chance to say anything else, she is gone.

Marge speeds across town and straight to the front of Dotty's house. Her gut instinct toys with her heart rate as she throws the car into park. She races through the front door without knocking. Dotty sits at the kitchen table, a glass of bourbon and ice in front of her. Without saying a word, Marge walks over to a cabinet, grabs another glass, and sits in a chair next to her. She looks at Dotty's swollen lips and at the black eye that had been fading to a greenish-brown halo but is now dark purple from a second blow.

"What the fuck, Dotty? How long will you allow him to continue? He's going to get worse!" Marge pleads with Dotty, sympathetic yet pissed as hell.

Dotty picks up her glass and takes a large gulp while Marge attempts to bring herself under control. Marge picks up the bottle and pours herself a large shot.

"I don't know what to do, Marge."

"I know what to do," Marge says matter-of-factly. "We figure out how to get rid of him."

"You tell me how. It can't be 'we.' I'll do whatever you say, but you can't be involved."

"Hell, Dotty, I'm your best friend. There's no way I'd let you do something like this alone," Marge says and begins laying out a plan.

At first, Dotty is only partially on board. Marge continues with carefully thought out details of how and when it should happen, hoping to persuade her further. The plan is ironclad. As she talks, she's sure she has Dotty convinced. Marge stands and looks out the window toward the backyard. Tom's shed is there. As she looks at it, her stomach churns. Pausing, she waits for the churning to subside, but instead she feels a need to retch. She dashes out the back door and loses her stomach's contents. Dotty follows her.

"Marge, are you all right?"

"Yeah. I guess the bourbon isn't agreeing with me." Marge glances toward Tom's shed again and wonders if he's in there. It hadn't occurred to her that he might be. The urge to puke rises again, and she bolts back into the house to quell it and to avoid the possibility of seeing him. "Let's go for a walk down the front drive. It's a beautiful day," she says, not slowing down as she stomps through the house.

"It's, like, ninety degrees out there!" Dotty scurries behind.

"Not yet. It's still early in the day. We'll be back before it gets that bad."

Marge leads them out the front door and down the tree-lined lane toward the front of Dotty's property. Soon she realizes that Dotty was right; it's sweltering. Marge fans her face with her hands as they walk along under the trees. The nausea doesn't fade—it only grows stronger. She feels her face flush, and she becomes lightheaded. In the heat, the air seems thin, even though the path is shaded. Marge decides this was a bad idea. The farther they walk, the more disoriented she feels.

"Marge, your color doesn't look right. We should go back inside."

"I'm fi—" Marge tries to say, but feels the ground rising to meet her.

"Marge!" Dotty wraps her arms around Marge, easing her to the ground.

"I'm okay, just give me a second," Marge says, resting her elbows on her knees, supporting her forehead in the palms of her hands.

"I'll go see if I can find Tom. He can help get you back to the house."

"*No!*" Marge's voice comes out high-pitched, but she forces it to calm. "I mean, I'm fine. Just give me a second."

"You don't look fine. You catch some kind of bug?"

"Yeah, I guess," Marge says with slim hope that it is nothing more.

"Maybe you're pregnant." Dotty beams. "You and John are still trying for a child, aren't you?"

Marge ponders whether she should say yes. "We aren't trying to prevent it," she says. "So, maybe." Dotty mustn't suspect that Marge's possible baby could belong to someone other than John. Marge makes an attempt at convincing herself that it could only belong to John— futile, but she tries anyway.

"That would be wonderful. You've been waiting for this! I say we make an appointment with a doctor right away," Dotty says, her excitement obvious.

"We should get back to what we were discussing earlier. None of this erases what Tom did to you."

"We need to concentrate on this. If you're pregnant, we have a lot to plan for. Besides, we need to take care of *you* now."

Marge doesn't have the strength to argue at the moment.

CHAPTER TWENTY-TWO

Nathan

Reluctantly, I leave Kevan behind and head straight to town, to the police station. Before I left, our conversation ended with the amount of work the property would need to restore it. I used the opportunity to talk about my professional background, and I told her I could put her in touch with some contractors. It worked, because she gave me her phone number.

I'm still thinking about Kevan as I park in front of the small police station and step inside. As the door opens, an electronic chime signals my entrance. When I was a teenager, a bell hung above the door and served the same purpose. The small office smells of old cardboard, paneling, and tacky air freshener.

Sheriff Kenny sits at a desk behind a tall counter, his glasses resting far down on his nose.

Kenny Woods has been the sheriff for almost as long as I can remember. Every four years, he wins the election by a landslide. Kenny is the kind of person who represents all that is fair. If you screw up, and if you can admit that you did, he'll let you off lightly. If you give him an attitude, with no sign of regret, then he takes care of the problem.

During his early years as sheriff, crime seemed high for such a small town. Several people were reported missing, most of them female; my sister was one of them. The sheriff made a name for himself with his contributions to those cases. Some disappearances are still a mystery—one being Gracie's. Her case has grown cold, but the sheriff still searches for answers. I think he does it mainly for my sake. He was only on the job two years when my sister vanished. He'd had a hard time filling the shoes of his predecessor, who was a legend around here. With hard work, he thought, maybe he could make a name for himself too. With my sister's case, he hoped he could provide a joyous outcome, but it didn't happen. Still, his years of service have labeled him as the big-hearted, small-town sheriff, and over the years, we've become good friends.

"Well, hello, Nathan. How can I help you?" He tosses his glasses on the desk, stands, and holds out his hand to shake mine.

Kenny is a tall man and a large one; his signature suspenders hold his khaki pants just below his potbelly. As he stands tall behind the counter, he hooks his thumbs inside his suspender straps and then interlaces his fingers in front of his chest. I remember him standing the exact same way when I was a teenager, though without the belly. I'm not sure why he wore suspenders then, but I don't believe I've ever seen him without them.

"I wanted to show you something I found today. You know that abandoned property—the one close to where my sister's backpack was found? I decided to go check it out again."

He flashes a questioning frown. "Really?"

I pull out a napkin, careful as I unfold it, and show him the braided candy wrappers. "This was inside a cabinet, buried in some debris. You remember Pop Rocks candy?"

He nods.

"These are candy wrappers braided into a bracelet. My sister did this a lot." I pull the two dolls out of a plastic bag. "I found these underneath some loose boards in the same cabinet." I hand the dolls over.

He rotates them in his hands, examining them from all angles, one eyebrow raised. He lays one doll on the counter and proceeds to lift the dress on the other doll.

I cock one eyebrow and flash him a crooked grin. "Hobby of yours?"

He lets out a belly chuckle and says, "Very funny. I had a little sister who liked to write her name on all of her toys. Maybe this person did the same thing."

As he inspects the doll, he finds what he's looking for. He turns the doll around to show me, and I feel a slight boost in my adrenaline. Written in faded ink in the center of the doll's back are the letters *G. E. H.*

"Grace Elizabeth Hill. It *is* hers!" My voice hits a different octave.

He examines the boy doll and finds initials there too: *K. R. M.*

"Any idea who this one belongs to?" he asks.

"Nope. Don't think so."

"We need to locate the owner of these initials."

"At some point, my sister was there, and this proves it."

"Yes, it has to. Thing is, back then we questioned all of her classmates. None of them had been anywhere with your sister outside of school recently. I questioned older students as well, and we got the same responses. Do you remember the names of your sister's friends?"

"I can't recall. Especially not after all these years."

"What about her personal items? You still have any?"

"I'll have to do some digging. Her stuff has been packed away for years."

"Go through her toys—maybe some will have names instead of initials. It's worth a shot."

I tap my knuckles on the counter a few times. "It can't hurt. I'll check and get back to you soon."

"Sounds good. I'll bring up her box up from the basement and search through it again. Who knows?"

"Thanks, Sheriff. I'll be seeing ya."

Out on the sidewalk, I glance down the street to the rest of town, feeling optimistic. A rusted Ford truck drives by with more brown than blue, and only a handful of people walk along the sidewalk in front of the city building.

The town has changed little since my childhood, except for additional stoplights or the facelift of a building here and there. My mother's old diner at the opposite end of town still serves the same country-cooked meals as it did when she worked there. The daughter of the original owner runs the business now. At the very end of the row of buildings is an L-shaped structure, the Bitterton Inn. It remains in business as well—old, but clean.

I walk down the street to the locally owned hardware store to pick up a few items that will finish out the list Dorothy has laid out for me to complete. I push open the glass door, and it slams against a bell hanging from the ceiling. I'm met with the smells of motor oil and rubber. Over time, the store hasn't changed. The floors creak underfoot and slope toward the back. The low ceilings have yellowed from years of allowing smokers to keep up their habit while shopping.

"Can I help you?" says a voice from behind me.

"Uh, yeah. I'm looking for some replacement bulbs for porch lighting."

The man is at least six inches shorter than I, with messy reddish-brown hair and a plump belly.

"Right back here." He squeezes around me and walks down the narrow aisle. "Here they are. Do you know what kind you need?"

"Yes, Matthew," I say, looking at the name tag pinned crookedly to his shirt pocket. Underneath the large, bold letters of his first name, in smaller lettering, is the name *Mays*. "Thanks for your help. I think I can figure it out from here."

"Suit yourself. I'll be around if you need anything."

Matthew Mays walks away but leaves behind a faint scent of booze. I look at my watch, curious to see if it's even noon yet. It isn't. He must be having a bad day.

I locate the bulbs, walk across the sloping floor to the front of the store, and stand in line behind another customer. The gentleman has a complaint about the prices in the store; he says they are highway robbery. Matthew leans over the counter and speaks in a lower voice. "I have a part at home that's close to what you need. Of course, it isn't new, but I don't guess it needs to be. I sell all kinds of used items for cars, outdoor equipment, just about anything. If you're not in a hurry, I'll check for you when I go home on my lunch break."

"Can you give me a better deal?" the customer asks.

"Hell, yeah. About a quarter of the price. Why don't you give me your number, and I'll call you and let you know." Matthew looks over his shoulder, then back at the customer, and speaks even more quietly. "I can meet you somewhere."

The man nods, punches the number into Matthew's phone, and hustles out.

I step up and lay the bulbs on the counter.

Matthew's face has a smug expression as he watches the man leave. With a *huh* under his breath, he looks across the counter at me. "Looks like you found what you needed. So, are you using these big-ass bulbs inside or outside?"

"Porch."

"Only two places around here require these special bulbs. The Ivymond place and the Lansdown property. Which one is it?"

"Well, that would be Ivymond."

"Yeah, that old place requires a lot of these. You work around there?"

Matthew isn't just a guy making small talk, and something about him rubs me the wrong way.

"You make a habit of taking your boss's customers?" I ask, nodding my head toward the door where the previous customer just exited.

Matthew stutters, "Oh, that was just me helping a guy out. No, not a habit, just seeing an opportunity to help someone else." Matthew hands me my change and picks up his large tumbler of coffee with a slight tremble in his hand.

"I'm sure the boss man wouldn't see it that way."

"What's it to you?" Matthew tips his chin upward as if stating his masculinity.

"Oh, nothing. Have a nice day, Matthew," I say with a smart-ass grin, exiting the belled door.

CHAPTER TWENTY-THREE

Marge
1962

Marge sits in the exam room, wringing her hands, waiting on the results of her blood test. With her nerves in a tangled mess, she's glad Dotty stayed in the waiting area.

"It looks like you're going to have yourself a baby," the doctor says as he walks through the door.

Panic hammers its way into Marge's brain, causing instant pain, and then nausea bubbles in the pit of her stomach. A flood of different emotions sweeps through, and she doesn't know which one she should allow herself to feel. Love for her husband. Hatred for the man who might inadvertently have given her what she'd wanted for so long. She wants to give her husband a child, but not like this. Not if it isn't even his.

She fake-smiles. The doctor says something about the next steps, but his words bounce off the walls of her consciousness. Another part of her brain screams and drowns him out.

Marge walks out of the examining room in a daze.

"Aww, I knew it! How wonderful!" Dotty beams and stands with her arms outstretched.

Marge forces her face into the phoniest of smiles and asks, "Can you please keep this a secret until I tell John?"

"It'll kill me, but of course. When do you plan on telling him?"

"Soon. I want it to be just right."

Days pass, but Marge can't bring herself to tell John. As soon as she tells him, Dotty will feel free to tell Tom. Marge worries about what Tom might do. The sick bastard is evil enough that he might try to claim the child as his. He might even say that the act that produced the child was consensual. She doesn't trust him. She will lose Dotty and John if he stoops that low.

Dotty pays Marge a visit, eager to find out if John knows yet. They sit down at Marge's small kitchen table, each with a coffee cup in hand.

"I want to wait until the risk of miscarriage is slim, so I'm going to wait until I am a little further along," Marge tells Dotty.

"Oh, Marge, tell him. He would want to know."

"I want to wait a while longer."

Dotty chews on the inside of her cheek and then says, "Please don't be mad at me, but I told Tom the news last night—"

"Dotty! You promised."

"I am so sorry. I just couldn't wait any longer. He says he won't tell, but you'll never guess what else the son of a bitch said." Dotty's voice cracks with obvious aggravation.

"With Tom, who knows?" Marge tries to sound passive.

Dotty relates her conversation with Tom, using his exact words and tone. "'Good for John. Guess he is a man, after all.' Then he said, 'Or maybe your friend Marge there is spreading her legs somewhere else.'" Dotty swallows hard as if she's struggling to go on. "Can you believe him? I asked him why he said that. You and John are perfectly happy together. You know what he said after that?" Dotty pauses, her eyes wide, as if she is waiting for Marge to respond.

Marge doesn't.

"He said you were a tease and he wouldn't be surprised if the baby didn't belong to John. He claimed you came on to him." The more she speaks, the more her voice quavers.

Anger flows through Marge's veins like lava. She bites her tongue to keep from saying what she really wants to say. "What do you see in him, Dotty?" she blurts. "He is so mean and just evil." Marge stops herself from saying any more as tears burn the corners of her eyes, threatening to multiply.

Dotty's eyes fill with tears too. "He didn't stop there." Her breathing becomes hard and fast as she tries to speak in between gasps. "I'm so sorry, Marge. I'm so sorry. What did he do to you? I'm so sorry!"

Confused at Dotty's words, Marge asks, "What are you apologizing for, Dotty?"

Words and sobs mesh as Dotty tells her the rest. "He said the baby you're carrying is his. Please tell me! What happened?"

Marge's face grows cold and numb, as if the temperature of her blood has dropped. "What do you mean? Why would Tom say that?"

"He runs his mouth far too much when he's drunk. He said that it was me who was keeping us from having a child. Then he said he could prove it."

Marge stares at Dotty in horror.

Dotty closes her eyes and breathes out long between parted lips. When she has calmed herself somewhat, she says, "He was in a good mood earlier. I knew he'd been drinking, but I didn't realize how drunk he was. He persuaded me to have sex with him, and when it was over, he turned as cold as a whore's heart. Next, he said I was useless and that my pussy was only good for a quick fuck." Dotty relates Tom's next words using a tone that he might use: "Guess who has a good pussy? Marge!" Shifting back to her own voice, Dotty says, "Then Tom grabbed his cock, shook it at me, and said, 'Yeah, I got me some of that Marge pussy, and now I'd bet my left nut that the child she's carrying is mine.'"

Dotty turns her face away for a moment, obviously working on her composure. The room grows silent. Dotty turns her head slowly and looks into Marge's eyes.

"He raped you, didn't he?"

Speechless, unable to answer out loud, Marge nods her head, feeling as if it has detached itself.

"I knew it! It was that night you all were at our house. I saw it all in your face. You've been different ever since. Why didn't you tell me?"

Again, words won't form. Marge closes her eyes, trying to control the tears of anger, confusion, and relief.

"He's done it to me many times," Dotty says. "If I refuse to have sex with him, then he just takes it."

Through clenched teeth, Marge asks, "Why do you put up with him?"

"What choice do I have? You know how it is. The day I married him, everything that was mine became his. My whole family's estate! If I try to divorce him, he'll get all of it. We women don't get shit! I'll be damned if I'll walk away and let the bastard have it."

Marge's voice becomes dead calm. "Let's figure out how to make it all yours."

Dotty's eyes widen, and Marge isn't sure whether she reads disbelief or just straight-up fear. "I'm not sure I'm capable of what you're suggesting," Dotty says in a low voice.

Sitting forward, bringing her face closer to Dotty's, Marge says in an even lower tone, "Getting rid of the bastard is the only way."

Dotty's face turns pale. "There has to be something else we can do."

"Aren't you sick of his shit yet?"

"Yes. Especially now, after what he did to you. I want him gone now more than ever, but to kill him?"

"The bastard has hurt us both. I believe that when it comes right down to it, it'll be easier than you think. Just let me work out the details. I won't let him come after me and John. We can do this, Dotty. When it's done, it will be a secret we'll take to our graves."

CHAPTER TWENTY-FOUR

Kevan

Early Summer

I continue to be aware of the girl on the dock. As Nathan leaves, I divert my gaze—anywhere. When I gain the courage to look back, she is gone.

Was she a figment of my imagination, or was she real? Either way, I don't wish to see her again. But I can't stop thinking: If she was real, why was she there? Why was she motioning to me? Did she want to show me something?

I venture closer to the pond, stop at the edge, and part a cluster of cattails and weeds. The dock is empty. Murky green water prevents me from seeing more than a couple of inches below the surface. I'm alone and I want to run like hell. I step away and turn my back, remembering myself in my dream, as I emerged from the pond and walked across the prickly ground. As I stare, upset and confused by everything that's happened, more of my dream becomes clearer: the menacing man. My eyes follow the overgrown path that Nathan departed through, and a horrible realization hits me. I remember who the man in my dream was.

My father.

I never think about him when I'm awake. Why here? Why now? I hated the man. I try to pull more of the dream to the surface. Though it's fuzzy, I remember that my father was pulling or carrying something. I've never seen him in this place, but that part seems like a memory instead of a dream, as if at some point I was standing here watching him.

The more I try to remember, the less I want to. *It must be a dream. I haven't been here in years.* I shake my head as if that will remove my thoughts just as a dog shakes water from its back. *He's dead, and it isn't real.* I repeat this in my head. It's fruitless, but I do it anyway. Gammie believed that my dreams were more than my mind inventing stories while I slept, and she always said it was wise to pay attention to them. My inspiration as an artist has come from my dreams, imaginary stories that only I have been a participant in. What is memory and what is imagination?

Something compels me to walk back to the house. I stand inside the doorway and look across the old kitchen. The dream resurfaces. The urn with Beth's name on it. The urn was one that Gammie had described to me several years before as the one she wanted her ashes to be placed in. I remember she said it was yellow, her favorite color, and that it had a pattern of honeysuckle and hummingbirds. I realize that maybe she purchased this vase as an urn for herself. I now know what prompted this part of the dream. Why did it have Beth's name on it, though?

I ponder for a long time as I roam through the house. Eventually, I give up and walk back through the woods.

Back in town, I feel relief. No member of my family saw me. I go to Gammie's house to see if her replica home has a secret attic. The smell inside Gammie's front door drags sadness back into my consciousness. The sofa invites me to flop down and have a good cry. Instead, I walk into Gammie's bedroom, feeling as if a discovery awaits me in the closet. I turn on the closet light and look up. Nothing. And I've seen no attic access anywhere else in the house.

Disappointed, I drop onto the bed and stare up at the ceiling. Maybe I was wrong. A big inhale, and on the exhale, my emotions find their way out. I succumb to the realization that I will never see Gammie again.

"Are you okay?"

I bolt upright and put a hand to my chest.

"Sorry. Didn't mean to scare you," Beth says. "I thought I'd find you here. You all right?"

"I'm fine. It just hits me sometimes."

"Well, then, let's find your Gammie's booze. You need a stiff drink right now."

Relieved to have Beth's distraction, I fling myself from the bed and lead her out of the bedroom. "In the kitchen. I'll show you."

"Did you go visit the old property?"

"I did. It's changed a little since we were kids. But guess what? The attic had a hidden room! I discovered that this house is pretty much identical to that one, too. I searched for an attic access here, but I haven't found anything." I retrieve two small books from my backpack and lay them on the table.

"What are those?" Beth asks.

I open the smaller book and look again at its contents, taking more time than before. The childlike drawings continue throughout, with stick-figure people, trees, suns, houses, and strange-looking animals. Gammie must have been tiny when she drew them, but although they're simple, the subjects and objects are recognizable. I slide the book forward to Beth and let her scan it as I pick up the second, thicker book and open it again, turning a sheaf of pages, then another. The curves of her handwriting change and straighten between 1949 and 1953. I feel happy touching this paper, because I know she touched it too. It's a treasure.

I turn back to the beginning. Three pages in is a brief entry:

August 9, 1950

Dear Diary,

I plan to sneak through the woods tonight to meet Dotty and Clara. Mom and Dad say that I am way too young to go to this party, but I am going anyway. Fingers crossed that I don't get caught.

Marge

Gammie had told me once that everyone called her by that name back in the day. She didn't start going by her birth name, Frances, until she got married and became a mother.

Another entry is dated much later than all the others. The hand-writing's neater. It's dated July 11, 1964, and I pause before I read on. My grandfather was killed on that day. My father was a boy then. Gammie spoke of it often. When she talked about Grandpa John, her eyes lit up.

Dear Diary,

I am grown now, a wife and mother. I never dreamed I'd be either. In fact, I despised the idea. According to my mother, a woman doesn't need a man. But I think she was wrong. I met John, and he showed me that there are good men out there. They aren't always easy to find, and I am one of the lucky ones. I only wish my mother were alive to see just how good he is. He loves me and our son. Yes . . . OUR son. No one will ever know any different. It may not be his blood that runs through Clyde's veins, but he is teaching him to be a good person. I know that with his love, Clyde could never be like his real father. Bad genes can't win above good teaching. I am so happy now, and it has everything to do with John. Life is good!

Frances Margarette

I hold my breath. My father wasn't Grandpa John's biological son! I feel shock and disbelief. Whoever my real grandfather was, it's obvious that she despised him. This could explain why my father was such an asshole. I always wondered why my father couldn't be more like the grandfather Gammie described.

CHAPTER TWENTY-FIVE

Marge and Dotty
1962

Marge leans down closer to Tom's face, eye to eye, and declares, "I told you I would kill you." She straightens again, towering over him, and turns to Dotty. "You ready to finish this?"

Dotty's voice is serene even though she is doing the unthinkable. "I am." She looks down at her husband. "It's time to go to hell, Tom."

They straddle his body: Marge at the head and Dotty at the feet. They grab the rug and struggle to drag the body toward the side of the house to Dotty's car. They drop Tom just below the bumper. Panting and sweating, Dotty releases the trunk as Marge returns to the shed to retrieve an empty milk jug and a short rubber hose. Together, they tug, lift, and roll Tom into the trunk. Marge throws the other needed items on top of him. They exchange a silent glance of relief, shut the trunk, and climb into the car.

The act of ridding the world of this human seems to open the clouds and calm the storm. The full moon lights up the night once more. They don't speak; there is no need. Dotty drives along back country roads and turns down Marge's gravel lane. She eases her tires across a ditch, drives into a field, and kills her lights. By moonlight, she drives behind the stone building and parks in front of the stone face of the massive kiln.

They get out of the car and carefully shut their doors. Marge's husband is asleep inside their house across the field. Earlier, Marge had phoned him to say that everything was okay and that she was going to spend the night with Dotty. To ease his fear, she'd also told him that Tom had left with some of his friends and probably wouldn't return until morning.

As they raise the trunk lid, the smell of whiskey and blood wafts upward. A wave of nausea goes through Marge. They drag the rolled-up rug fifty feet and drop it to the ground. Marge returns to the car to retrieve the milk jug and hose as Dotty works to line the bottom of the old furnace with chunks of wood.

Marge opens the gas tank hatch on the Buick, slides one end of the hose down into the tank, and places her mouth over the other end. She sucks on the hose several times until bitter liquid shoots into her mouth and she pulls away, spitting gasoline. She picks up the jug and inserts the hose, letting gasoline gurgle into it. Once it's full, she holds the hose up until the liquid falls back into the gas tank.

She joins Dotty in front of the kiln, then soaks the rug in gasoline. Fumes fill the air and coat the insides of their nostrils; their throats burn. When the jug is empty, Marge tosses it aside and they move the body one last time, into place on top of the wood. When they finish their cremation chamber, they place more wood on top of Tom's body and stand back to assess their work. To shed any evidence, they strip off all their clothes and toss those in on top, leaving nothing on except their bras and underwear.

Marge pulls a small box of matches from her bra. "Let's finally get rid of this bastard."

Dotty takes the box, opens it, and hands a match to Marge. "I think we should both have the pleasure of doing it. You have as much reason to hate this son of a bitch as I do."

Taking the match, Marge adopts a mischievous smile. "On the count of three?"

They strike their matchsticks against the box and say in unison, "One, two, three!"

Flames blaze upward and out, filling the kiln with blinding light and heat. They hold their hands up in front of their faces, but they don't look away. Orange flames dance, filling the kiln with such heat that the smoke becomes barely visible. They watch the pile burn. However hot, the fire cannot burn away all the ugliness this human caused in his life, but at least he can cause no more. They are free. Their lives can begin anew.

CHAPTER TWENTY-SIX

Nathan

I return to Ivymond and complete the list of chores Dorothy requested. Then I head home to search through my mother's and sister's belongings. When my sister disappeared, my mother couldn't bring herself to move anything out that belonged to Gracie. Mother tidied up Gracie's room, made it all set for her return. A return that never happened. Neither Dorothy nor I can bring ourselves to change anything here either. In fact, I rarely enter either of their rooms. It's not unusual for Dorothy to wipe up dust and refresh the bed linens, but that's it.

I open the tiny closet door and see my sister's clothes still hanging on child-sized hangers there. Two shoeboxes sit on the top shelf, and a large storage bin sits on the floor. A weight seems to press into my chest. I slide the bin free from the closet and remove the lid. I find toys, dolls, clothes, and books that were my sister's favorites. One item at a time, I search under clothes and turn over toys to search all sides, looking for writings or markings. Gracie has carved or drawn her initials or first name on everything. Every item in this bin belonged to my sister.

The shoeboxes on the top shelf belonged to my mother. I open the first, a faded red box stuffed full of school achievement certificates and braided items my sister had made. The second box is blue, and the possessions it holds are akin to the items in the other box. Neither proves to have information that would help me investigate Gracie's disappearance.

I sit on her bed and wonder if maybe she had a hiding spot in her room. I did as a boy. Mine was at the bottom of my closet floor, underneath loose boards. Surely my sister had things she didn't want our mother to find. As I crouch at the edge of the closet, I rub my hand over the floor, feeling for loose boards. Everything is solid. An eight-year-old girl wouldn't be able to pry boards loose from the floor.

I try to mimic a similar thought pattern to that of an eight-year-old girl. Difficult for a forty-something man. I'm imagining a hidden diary or something similar. Of course, I check the obvious by sliding my hands between the mattress and box spring, certain that they have been searched before. I rub the palm of my hand along the back of the headboard. Still nothing. Next, I remove the dresser drawers to look underneath and behind them. I start to think maybe my sister had nothing to hide.

As I sit on her bed again, I stare blankly at the wall, where there's a canvas picture of different-colored butterflies. Curious, I tap on the front surface of the picture. The canvas bounces. There's a hollow space on the other side. I take it off the wall and find a thin book taped to the back. I try not to damage either piece as I remove it from the canvas. My heart pounds faster with excitement.

The book is homemade, with loose-leaf notebook paper stapled between covers made from green construction paper. I open the front cover and a Polaroid picture falls into my lap. It's two little girls, heads tilted together, arms draped across each other's shoulders. One is my sister, and the other is a girl who looks similar in age, with red hair and dark brown eyes. I can't recall seeing this little girl before, either in person or in a photo, but her eyes are familiar. The background in the photo makes my heart skip a beat. It's the old house where I found the dolls. Now I know she didn't always play there alone; at least once, this little girl went too.

I lay the book on the bed next to me, opening the first page, where I see in childish handwriting my sister's full name. As I turn the page, I read the typical misspelled words and incomplete sentences of an eight-year-old.

Deer diry, me and renee had fun. I tot her how to make a neklis. We playd dolls. She is so fun. I cant wat to see her agin.

I turn the page and continue to read.

Deer diry, me and renee played with dolls and drood with roks on the dok. She is my best frind.

Deer diry, renee did not come to day. I miss her.

Deer diry, renee did not come to day agen. I hop shes not mad at me.

Deer diry, renee got to com and play. she wuz in trubel and cud'nt com and see me befor.

On one page, she writes that she's angry with me for picking on her. She even hates me sometimes. She also writes about our mother; Gracie was often upset with Mom, but her entries focus more on all the nice things that they did together. Mostly, though, she writes about Renee. Again I look at the photo of them together, and again something tugs at my memory. Do I know this red-headed little girl from somewhere? Did I meet her back then?

After I finish reading through the tiny diary, I remove my phone from my pocket, search through recent calls, and find the Bitterton Police Department. There's a chance Kenny is gone for the day, but I call anyway. He answers after two rings.

"Hey, Sheriff. It's Nate. I think I might have found something. Will you be there for a while?"

Sheriff Kenny tells me to come on over, so I head back into town. Hope builds that long-awaited secrets will unfold like the palm of a hand. I might discover the truth. After years of dead ends and disappointments, I've learned it's best to try to avoid hope; I don't want to be disappointed again. Today, though, I can't help it.

As I enter the tiny police station, the sheriff is sitting at his desk, a phone attached to his ear. He waves me on in and holds up his index finger, letting me know he won't be long. I look at old photographs hanging along the paneled walls of the office. The people in them are years' worth of law enforcement, protecting our little town. There's a new picture every time a new sheriff is elected. It's all men in the photos until the last one, the one with Sheriff Kenny.

The sheriff hangs up the phone. As he's getting up from his chair, he pulls at the top of his pants and says, "So, you think you might have found something among your sister's things?"

"I did. She had a hidden diary stashed behind a painting. I didn't think about her having this before. When you started talking about your own sister, it got me to thinking. She writes about a friend named Renee, and she also has a photograph. I assume that the girl in the photo is the same as the one she names in her diary, since the diary and photo were hidden together." I hand over the photo. "This picture proves my sister had a friend with her on that abandoned property."

"I wonder if this is our K. R. M.?" Sheriff Kenny looks at the photograph and then thumbs through the little green book. "I have a copy of a school yearbook from the year your sister disappeared, as well as one from the year prior." The sheriff pulls a box from the floor behind his desk and places it on the counter. He pulls out two paper-back elementary school yearbooks and hands one to me. "You look through this one, and I'll thumb through the other one."

I find the class my sister would have been in. As I look over the tiny faces, I only find one boy with red hair and brown eyes, no girls. I work backward to classes before hers, then forward, but come up empty. As I give up and close the book, I ask, "Anything in yours?"

"Nope, afraid not. Maybe this little girl attended another local elementary school," Sheriff Kenny says.

"How would they have known each other?"

"I don't know, but I'll drive out to the other schools and search for her in their yearbooks." Sheriff Kenny slides the Polaroid toward me. "Take a picture so we both have a copy. We may get lucky and find she still lives here."

CHAPTER TWENTY-SEVEN

Kevan
Early Summer

I awake from a deep sleep, nestled down into the covers of Gammie's bed. I still feel groggy and not quite rested. It seems these days I live my life upside down and backward. I wake up still tired, and when I lie down, I am wide awake and jittery. Images from my dreams remain at the forefront of my thoughts even though I wish for them not to.

Last night I dreamed of the little girl on the dock. Only in my dream she wasn't standing. She was underwater, face down. I, too, was immersed underwater, only deeper, looking up at her, panicked and paddling to reach her. Her blond hair was feathered out all around her, floating with the surface of the water. Her mouth was frozen into a scream and her eyes were wide open with fear. My first thought was, *Is this Beth?*

I tried to paddle faster and harder, determined to get to her, but my movements did nothing. Something, or someone, was holding me down. The weight turned from heavy to a tight grip, fingers digging into my flesh.

The rerun makes me edgy, so I try to push it aside. I've tried my entire life to ignore dreams and what seem to be out-of-nowhere stories that play out in my mind—occurrences that Gammie said were a gift. Since Gammie's death, something has only ignited these episodes more. *Why would I dream of such a horrific scene?* I shove the thought aside, bury it, and sink deeper into bed. I wish I could fade away—even from myself.

My eyes remain closed as I breathe in the sweet scent of Gammie. Grief holds me like a corset. I suppose when you have a bond like we had, the hurt carves itself in deep and bores a hole that will remain forever. I wonder if I actually knew the real Frances. She didn't tell me everything about herself.

I'm still in shock from what I read in Gammie's childhood journal. Finding out that John wasn't my real grandfather only proves that Gammie had secrets. Makes me wonder if there were any others. She had a wild side then. She enjoyed sneaking out through the woods to her friend Dotty's house and then sneaking from there to wild parties. She was much wilder than I was at that age. Society would have considered me an angel and her a hussy.

Gammie wrote of her father's disappearance in her journal, and something about it disturbed me. Her mother claimed that her father had run off after a huge argument, but Gammie didn't believe it. She suspected her mother had forced him to go, or something much worse. She even hinted that her mother had killed her father and gotten rid of the body. I'm not sure if she was serious. Maybe she was angry at her mother and she wrote what came to mind at the time. Teenage girls are like that. However, her father's disappearance affected her greatly. Afterward, she grew reckless.

Taking a deep breath to clear my thoughts, I force my eyes to open and look at the phone resting on the pillow next to me. I heard two text alerts during the night and now see that both are from Kyle. If he were in bed with me right now, I would fuck these thoughts out of my mind by burying my body underneath his.

I open the first message, which reads, *Hey gorgeous.* I smile and open the second one. It's a selfie showing his bare lower torso—just low enough to tease me. I smile and welcome the naughty thoughts to mask the effects of my current state of mind.

Letting out a long breath, I raise up, propped on my elbows, and look at the closet door. The idea of a secret room still toys with me. Why wouldn't Gammie have copied that part of the house too? I throw back the covers and spring from the bed. The closet door squeaks, and I step inside to look at the ceiling, already knowing what I will find there. Just a ceiling. I think about Gammie trying to climb a ladder at her age. She was tough, but it would have been difficult.

Is there another way to the attic? I search the walls, knocking and sliding my hands across. I tap at the far end of the closet and it sounds hollow. There aren't shelves on this wall. I tap again and then shove some clothes aside. There's a small handle and, just below it, a lock. Bingo. I pull on the handle but it doesn't budge.

The key!

Careful not to wake Beth, I go to the kitchen and retrieve the key from my backpack. I feel anticipation, as if I'm about to embark on a treasure hunt. Like a child turning the handle on a coin machine full of toys, I shiver with excitement to see what's behind the wall. The key fits the slot. I turn it with a click, pull on the handle, and am met with the smell of cedar. The hidden door reveals a set of steep stairs leading upward.

I flick a switch just inside the door, and the stairs and room above are illuminated with warm light. I stick the key and my phone in my back pocket and climb the stairs. Compared to the old house, the ceilings in this attic are taller. Natural light floods the room from evenly placed skylights along the ceiling. From the outside, I assumed these were just solar panels to help heat the house. Similarly to the other house, the walls have no windows. The room is hidden from the world outside.

I'm transfixed and captivated. The walls and ceilings are covered with horizontal boards made of light cedar, shiny with varnish. Spaced all around the room are hanging wall lanterns that give the entire space a dreamy glow. From where I stand, I feel as if I've walked into an art museum merged with a cozy living room. Gammie's studio.

Various forms of art fill the room; some are propped up, resting on the floor, while others hang on the walls. I knew she liked to draw and paint sometimes, but it's obvious she spent a lot of time here. Most of her time, maybe. Why wouldn't she have shared this with me?

A massive painting looms on the opposite end of the room. Even from this distance, I recognize a self-portrait of Gammie. Everything else in the room fades away as I walk toward it. She has painted herself in a likeness that I have never seen before. It is her—but it isn't her. In fact, she's menacing. Her hair is wild and free, flowing about her on the canvas. Her eyes are even wilder, almost dangerous. She wears a red dress, as if she's the devil's mistress. Her nails and lips are blood-crimson. There is a dark feeling behind the painting.

I'm filled with shock as I stare at the painting. This is not the Gammie I knew. The Gammie I knew was kind and gentle. Sure, she was strong, but not menacing. Maybe she wanted to be this person. I stare a while longer and then shake myself and my thoughts.

I turn, and my eyes widen in wonder as I take in the rest of the room. They stop on a three-paneled, hand-painted paper screen, a shoji. Each panel completes a nature scene of the woods that Gammie and I walked through many times to visit the old property. Trees begin on one panel and their branches finish on the next panel. Birds fly and land on the branches. The trifold panels allow me to see the whole beautiful scene of the woods that gave me solace and escape as a child. It is breathtaking. It is like stepping back in time.

The next painting to catch my eye is of Gammie, John, and my father as a baby. This woman's eyes are full of love—soft and gentle. Her smile is genuine. This is the way she always smiled at me. If you compared the self-portrait to this one, you would see a devil and an angel.

Two doors catch my attention. The left door reveals a very small closet with walls painted black, a space for removing film to prevent exposure to light. The second door opens to a larger developing room, well stocked with chemicals and supplies to process photographs. Apparently, my interest in photography came from my grandmother. I wonder why she never talked about it. Looking at all her artwork now, I can see she was talented. The world should see this talent. For a moment, I feel a hint of anger that she didn't share any of this with me.

I close the door and stroll around the room, stopping next to a large easel, canvas, and rolling cart with many containers of paint and brushes. She must have been working on this particular piece when she died; the brushes stand in containers full of water that hasn't yet evaporated. As I step around to face the painting, I feel the blood drain from my face. I stumble backward, my hand stifling the sound that escapes my mouth.

Familiar blue eyes stare back at me.

CHAPTER TWENTY-EIGHT

Frances
1964

Frances places her son in the crib that was once her own. After she has rocked him for more than thirty minutes, he's finally given in and fallen asleep in her arms. She looks out across the yard to see John squatted down and working on his tractor.

She and John moved into her childhood home just after they were married, and he has worked tirelessly ever since to make it their own. They are making newer, happier memories here. While Clyde sleeps, she decides to look for her mother's jars in the attic. She pulls down the ladder in the closet and smells a hint of woodsmoke caused by the stove in the house when she was growing up. She doesn't visit the attic as often as she did when she was young; back then, it was her personal space and play area. Her mother had stored things in the attic, but Marge had laid claim to it from the first time she climbed the ladder on her own.

She steps in front of the little dressing table and bends her knees slightly to look in the mirror. Her reflection has changed since she looked in it last. She sees the tiniest of lines in the corners of her eyes and two permanent parallel lines between her eyebrows. She tries to smooth them out with her index fingers, but they come right back.

One day she will show this room to Clyde and make it his. She believes every child should have their own refuge. This one had been hers. Her mother and she had gotten along well enough, but at times her mother hadn't been very kind. Frances had assumed it was because times were tough without her father's income after he ran off one day. At least her mother always said he had run off. Deep down, Frances knows his disappearance was much more sinister, but she brushes the idea away now as she always has. No point in thinking about that after all these years.

Frances slides one of the table's little top drawers open and pulls out a handmade doll. She lifts the doll's dress to reveal a key and uses it to unlock one of the table's lower drawers, which holds her childhood diary. It has been years since she's looked at it. She thumbs through it and reads a couple of pages, then searches for a pencil. She finds it and then sits down on the tiny bench. Opening to the next blank page in the book, she makes an entry and signs it, this time as *Frances Margarette*. She then locks the book back in the drawer and hides the key in its place.

Clyde stirs downstairs, and she makes her way down the ladder. She glances out the window and sees John wrapping one end of a thick chain around a large sycamore. He hates that old, dying tree and has been wanting to get rid of it before a strong storm brings it crashing down on their house. When he'd first told her of this plan, she had been terrified, telling him that it couldn't be done safely. He'd laughed at her, saying he had to do it now because she'd said he couldn't. Of course, he'd been teasing, but he was convinced it would work.

Stepping out onto the front porch with her toddler's hand in hers, Frances watches John, hoping he will look in her direction, but he's far too engrossed in his work. Picking Clyde up and propping him on her hip, she walks in his direction. A loud cracking sound echoes through the air, and the top of the tree shudders and sways. Frances freezes in place, teeth clenched so tight that her jaws burn. Another loud crack bounces off the trees around them. She sees the tree waver for just a second, and then it begins to fall.

Her heart stops as everything seems to move in slow motion. She screams John's name, but the sound of the tree, as it fractures and descends, drowns out her cry. John looks up, stands, and leaps from the tractor on the opposite side of the tree's trajectory. The trunk lands on the tractor. Branches cover John's body. Frances exhales, hopeful that his injuries are minimal. She sets her son on the ground and says, "Stay here, Clyde. I'll be right back."

She approaches the tree and steps through the large branches, continuing to say John's name, still sure he is okay. He doesn't make a sound. She sees him now, lying face down, a branch draped across his shoulders. The branch isn't huge. She lets out a relieved sigh as she squats down beside him. Then she sees a pool of blood forming around his neck and head. A sharp, tiny limb protruding from the branch has pierced the side of his neck. Frances panics and screams his name. "John! John!" As she examines more closely, she sees that the blood mostly isn't coming from his neck but from the side of his skull. His head has landed on the thick end of a splitting maul.

Fear and adrenaline drive her now to free his body from the piece of the tree that lies on top of him. She attempts to the lift the branch, but she can't lift it and drag his body out from under it at the same time. As she continues to try, there is no response or movement. She keeps trying, but she still can't move either the branch or the man. After several attempts, she runs to the house to dial zero for the operator.

CHAPTER TWENTY-NINE

Nathan

I awake to the sounds of rustling in the kitchen and the smell of bacon cooking downstairs. This might alarm someone who lives alone, but I know exactly who it is. I peel my face from the pillow, roll from my stomach, and look at the clock on the bedside table. 6:02 a.m. With an audible exhale, I slam my face back into the pillow. There's no doubt Dorothy is here to be nosy or spread gossip. The nosy part is what I'd put my money on.

Here, Nate, I made you a bracelet.

My head jerks from the pillow and I look around the room as the giggle fades. I sit up in bed and scope the whole room again. This occurrence of hearing my sister's voice is becoming more frequent. It isn't the least bit soothing. I remain still, listening, then rub my face with both hands and shift my focus back to the aroma coming from downstairs.

It isn't unusual for Dorothy to sneak into my house and fix me breakfast. Especially if she feels left in the dark on any aspect of my life. She seems to always know when I'm hiding something from her. I haven't told her about finding the dolls with my sister's initials, because I don't want to get her hopes up. She loved my little sister and treated her like the granddaughter she'd never had. I roll over on my back and ponder it for a moment. Would telling her do any harm? She's dealing with the death of her friend, and it might give her a distraction.

A deep growl interrupts my thoughts as the scent of bacon prompts my stomach to voice its hunger. Dragging myself out of bed, I get dressed, splash water on my face, untangle my hair, and head downstairs.

"Good morning, Miss Dorothy." I say the words with more energy than I feel. I head straight to the cabinet, grab the largest cup I can find, and fill it to the rim with coffee. "What brings you by?"

"Well, can't I come and fix my godson some breakfast?" Dorothy comes off with her usual tone, grumpy yet loving.

"Absolutely. You know I love your cooking."

"I laid a list of jobs on the table to get your workhands started today."

"Will do." I pick up the piece of paper, fold it, and stuff it into my T-shirt pocket.

"Where were you yesterday afternoon?" she asks.

There it is. The reason she's here. I decide I should tell her about my find. If I don't and she finds out later, I'll never hear the end of it. "So, I told you I went to visit the old property?"

"You may have mentioned it. That abandoned place just beyond our woods?"

"Uh-huh. I snooped around harder and found two old Barbie dolls in one of the old kitchen cabinets. I took them to the sheriff, and during his inspection, he discovered initials scribbled on them. Two sets of initials."

Dorothy turns from the stove and gives me her full attention—the kind that only a true busybody can give. Something about her expression makes me pause. For a moment, I detect something besides curiosity. I continue.

"The initials on one doll belonged to Gracie, but the other doll had different initials."

"What were they?" Dorothy ignores the sizzling bacon on the stove.

"K. R. M."

She pivots and gives her attention back to the stove, but not before I detect a rapid shift in her expression. She looks troubled now, but in a guarded way that warns me not to ask why. I pause again in my words and wonder if I should go on.

Finally I say, "I brought them to the sheriff hoping to find out more about them."

"Oh, good." Dorothy doesn't turn back around. Her voice has taken on a passive tone.

"I left them with the sheriff and checked Gracie's room for clues to the other initials. You'll never guess what I found." I wait for Dorothy to turn around or at least speak, but she doesn't. "I found her diary."

She drops the spatula and steps back to keep it from landing on her foot. She curses under her breath and retrieves the spatula, taking it to the sink to rinse it off.

"Are you okay, Miss Dorothy?"

"Oh, yes. Just clumsy, that's all. Go on, I'm listening."

"I found a Polaroid of Gracie and another little girl tucked inside that diary. She wrote about a girl named Renee, who I assume is the girl in the photograph with her. I took a picture of the Polaroid." I stand, remove my phone from my back pocket, and open it to the photo as I hold the phone in front of Dorothy.

"She doesn't look familiar." Dorothy whips her head away as if she's disgusted by the photo. "That was a long time ago." Her actions and tone shift, making me question her words and her behavior. She spits out the last words. "My memory isn't what it used to be."

I sense a complete withdrawal of Dorothy's need to know any more. This only prompts me to continue in order to see her reaction. I move away from Dorothy a few steps and lean my backside against the counter. From here, I can continue to observe her profile.

"The strangest thing happened while I was in the house. I met the granddaughter of the owner. Her name is Kevan. Her grandmother passed recently and left the property to her." I assume that telling her this will bring out her irresistible urge to know more, but she never looks my way. She continues flipping bacon that she has already flipped several times. I frown at her as she continues to gaze downward. *I must know why she's acting so strange.* "Did you know who owned the property?"

Dorothy's eyebrows furrow and she bites her bottom lip. She remains silent, as if she's debating whether to answer the question. She replies, but still offers no information. "It has been vacant for years, my dear. So, what's prompted you to dig up bones now?"

"What do you mean?"

"I mean, your sister's disappearance was so long ago. I thought you had accepted that what happened to her would always be a mystery."

I frown, taken back by her comment. "I'm not sure I ever accepted it. There were never any leads until now." I feel irritated at Dorothy's lack of support or enthusiasm. Her behavior is completely out of character for any conversation about my sister or mother.

"I just think you're setting yourself up for another disappointment. Getting your hopes up about something that's impossible to solve. That's all."

My voice fights my attempt to keep it under control. "I will never give up on solving this." I put myself in check, take a breath, and finish by responding in a calmer tone. "Surely you haven't."

She turns to look me in the eye. "No, no, my boy. It's just hard to relive it sometimes, that's all." Dorothy's eyes are sincere, and I wonder if maybe I was misreading her earlier. Perhaps her seeming insincerity was only an attempt to avoid being hurt from disappointment.

"I know I asked you this once already, but I'm still curious," I say. "Did you know who owned the property?"

She takes a deep inhale as if she realizes I'm not going to let it go. "I did—but she has passed away, so it doesn't matter."

I suppose it doesn't, but I am beyond intrigued by the woman I met today, which makes me want to learn more about her. After seeing her in the store and in the old house, I wonder if fate has a plan. What would be the odds?

"This Kevan lady said she'd visited the property often as a girl, so I hope something will jog her memory about my sister. She and Gracie have to have crossed paths."

As if she is done with this conversation, Dorothy's tone shifts more. "Dear boy. I hope you find some answers, but please don't pin all of your hopes on this. I don't want to see you disappointed again. Don't live your life waiting on answers that may not come. Getting stuck in the past is no way to live."

Something in my gut tells me I shouldn't let it go. Finding the dolls has flicked a switch I can't turn off. Someone knows what happened to my sister. "I understand your concern, Miss Dorothy. If no leads come from the dolls, I'll do my best to move on."

"Good, Nate." Dorothy hands me a breakfast sandwich, all wrapped up, and a fresh cup of coffee. "Make sure you eat this before you get started this morning."

"I will. Just leave the dishes—I'll get them later."

"I will not," she tuts. "I'll clean up and lock up."

"Thank you, pretty lady. See you later?"

I kiss Dorothy on the cheek, as I have done many times, and stroll out the back door, feeling her eyes on me as I leave. I can't shake the feeling that Dorothy knows something she isn't telling me. Her entire disposition changed when I showed her the photo of my sister and the little red-haired girl. Could Dorothy be hiding something about my sister's disappearance? I try to convince myself otherwise.

Why would she?

This question continues to burn a hole in my thoughts through the morning, and I can't seem to let it go. I mustn't let it go.

CHAPTER THIRTY

Kevan
Early Summer

I stare at the painting, motionless, yet the hair on my arms and neck rises to peak level. It is the girl on the dock. Her eyes are innocent and absent of the beseeching look she had yesterday. Her long blond hair flows outward as if floating on the breeze. She stands near a pond, her lower body turned toward the water, her upper body turned as if she is looking at the person painting her. She appears relaxed and at peace. Again, this girl reminds me of Beth in both my memories and the photo I looked at recently. I wish I had the photograph with me to compare.

Gammie met Beth a few times in our secret place, but she didn't know her well; surely she wouldn't have been painting Beth after all this time. So, who is this girl and why would Gammie paint her? Better yet, why am I seeing her when no one else can? I can't seem to pull my eyes away from the painting.

The painted pond in front of her is the same except for the weeds and cattails. In the painting, they are thin and only knee high. The dock appears strong, and the water is painted in many clear shades of blue and green, devoid of algae. It looks just as it did when I was a little girl.

Breathing out through parted lips, I tear myself away with the need to explore more. I step in front of an easel that holds one canvas, while another rests on the floor against it. The canvas on the tripod is a watercolor of my father. I catch my breath as I stare into his eyes. I hold my breath as if I'm trying to hide from him. His eyes are cold, menacing, and just as I remember. He is wearing all black, and draped across his hip bone is a silver chain that runs from his front belt loop around his hip and out of sight. I know what Gammie has drawn here: the ugly black wallet that was always chained to his person so that no one could rob him. I shiver at the sight of it and decide not to linger on it any longer.

I turn to the painting that rests on the floor at the base of the easel. It is also of a man, and his eyes look the same as my father's, but his hair is a shade lighter. He stands with the same threatening posture. He is a complete stranger, yet he isn't. I no longer wish to look at him either.

I look behind the paintings in search of a description or explanation. Each has a card taped to the bottom with Gammie listed as the artist. The title she gave to the painting of my father was *Monster*. The card on the back of the other painting reads, ***T**he **O**ther **M**onster*.

I take note that the first letter of each word of the second title is in bold type, and I realize those first letters spell the word *Tom*. Against my desire to walk away, I feel compelled to examine the painting again. I look at them both carefully: first my father, then "the other monster." The resemblance between the two monsters is remarkable. Is this man my real grandfather? I shake myself, literally, and walk away.

As I walk the rest of the room, I find many canvases, done in a variety of art styles and forms. Gammie knew how to do it all. Her talent far exceeded my own. In fact, I feel a little insecure about my own abilities to create art as I look at hers. I push negative thoughts aside, remembering that we are all artists in our own unique ways. Gammie believed that, and she instilled that belief in me. I wouldn't have made it to where I am today without her.

I walk slowly, taking in each piece. Eventually, I find a painting of Gammie and myself. It's painted in thin brushstrokes and unusual angles. We are seated on the dock in our secret place, which isn't much of a secret anymore. It's a place full of mystery, a place that I am finding meant a lot to her. I decide right away that this painting will hang in my study.

Looking back and forth at our matching eyes, I feel mine moisten with tears. My throat tightens and I choke down a sob. This forces me to move on.

A drawing table similar to mine is located in the corner. As I approach it, I recognize that a collage covers the entire table. A collage that is eerily familiar. The closer I get, the more I realize just how familiar. Gammie's collage includes several visual elements that make up a farmhouse, a stone building, and a pond. The outline of the house is the same as the one in my collage. The stone building and cellar are easy to see.

Just out from the cellar is a small, stone-faced cave I recognize as the kiln. Instead of her entire collage making the outline of a house, like mine, she placed her pieces separately, but it's clear the two pieces were inspired by the same place. In the bottom right corner, Gammie wrote the year. Her collage was started at least seven years ago, long before I began mine.

She mounted her collage on a lightweight panel board; like my own, the weight of it comes from the materials she used to create it. I tilt it up and slide the bottom back to lean it against the wall. Once it's secure, I step back to eye it from a short distance. Viewing it as a whole piece, I see the differences and similarities between hers and mine. Details that would only be obvious to someone viewing it up close.

My eyes focus in on several blemishes that seem out of place. The clipped door of the stone building has a blackened smudge on it, resembling a face. It looks as if Gammie changed her mind about putting something there and erased it, but with a cheap, dirty eraser, leaving the smudge behind. Then I realize the stone building isn't the only place there's a smudge that resembles a face. Both the kiln and pond have them. In fact, the pond has two. And while the faces are indistinct, they're undoubtedly there.

I feel a sudden chill as my eyes remain glued on them. Something about them is haunting.

I move onward to the house. I view every inch, but nothing there seems out of the ordinary. I try to convince myself that the weird smudges are nothing more than mistakes that couldn't be corrected. They must be.

Deep inside me, though, something questions this.

Now that I have seen the smeared images and what look like human features in them, I can't unsee them. It's like a puzzle that wants you to look for the image of an old man or a frog. Which one you see will be determined by the person you are, and once you see one image, you can't let go of it. Backing away, I pull my phone from my back pocket and take a picture of the collage. I will compare the two when I get home.

The room around me still puts me in awe as I rotate one last time to take it all in. Gammie is the one who deserves her own art show somewhere. This work is beyond amazing. A lump forms in my throat and I decide it's time to go—for now.

Climbing down the steep stairs, I lock the door and slide the clothes so that they hide the secret door. I go to the back bedroom to tell Beth about my discovery. When I enter the guest bedroom, I find an empty, made-up bed. Assuming that Beth had an early morning, I overcome the dread of leaving and go home to compare the two collages.

CHAPTER THIRTY-ONE

Nathan

There is an elephant in the room, even though I'm standing outside. This overwhelming feeling that Dorothy is hiding something won't go away. I'm preparing to complete some maintenance work at Dorothy's house when I get the urge to look at my phone again. I open the picture of my sister and the Jane Doe seated next to her. My jaws clench as I remember Dorothy's out-of-character behavior. The conversation we had plays again, and I search for something that will ease my negative suspicion over the way she responded. The elephant seems to get bigger and heavier, and I can't find any way to dismiss my conviction that Dorothy knows something she isn't telling me. I bury the thoughts for now and stuff my phone back into my pocket.

One item on her list of chores involves tightening the hinges on a few doors throughout the house that aren't closing as they should. I decide to complete this task first, while Dorothy remains preoccupied with cleaning up the breakfast dishes in my kitchen. Entering through the back door of Dorothy's house, I head toward her kitchen, pausing as I consider entering her sitting room. I'm not sure what I expect to find there. I was never curious before now.

Like a sneaking child, I remove my shoes and step in. I stand in the middle of the room, pausing to examine. The picture in the silver frame catches my attention again, and I spend more time observing the red-haired girl in the photo. My eyes more open, I take out my phone and step in for a closer look. Comparing the redhead in this picture with the redhead in the Polaroid from Gracie's diary, I see that their eyes match, as well as their hair. Similar thoughts cross my mind as on the night I sat in this room and Dorothy spoke of the red-haired friend. Both girls remind me of Kevan.

The journals Dorothy was holding are next to her favorite chair, and I note the name again: *Frances M. Mays.* As I look back at the picture on my phone, a strange feeling stirs, telling me that everything connects somehow. Is it a coincidence that Dorothy's friend Frances and Kevan's grandmother both just passed away? Or were they the same person? And why is Dorothy hiding the fact that her friend owned that old property?

Playing the role of a sneaky child again and not wanting to get caught, I leave the sitting room to make sure Dorothy hasn't returned home. I decide to give Sheriff Kenny a call to see if he can look up Dorothy's friend for me. He answers on the second ring.

"Sure, Nate," he responds to my question. "What are you interested in learning about this Frances Mays?" Sheriff Kenny is willing to help with my sister's case anytime I call.

"Anything. Is she connected to the property where I found the dolls?"

"I checked out ownership years ago in the search for your sister. Records for the property are lost. No one knows who actually possesses the deed. Once upon a time it belonged to a Fred and Deloris Clark—I think. Rumor was that Fred ran off, leaving his wife and child. After that, the paper trail goes cold. I believe their daughter lived there some after Deloris died, but it's been abandoned as long as I can remember. It's possible the owner transferred the deed to someone else."

The sheriff pauses for a moment, and I wonder if he is thinking back on something.

I break the silence. "So, you never found out who it belonged to when my sister disappeared?"

"No, but here's what I think happened. Someone got rid of the property through a pocket deed transaction. The person who now possesses the deed never had it recorded. There's no way of knowing who owns the property. I searched forever when your sister disappeared, but that seems to be the only explanation."

"Is that legal?"

"Sure. As long as it was notarized and the owner signed the deed. They are under no obligation to have it recorded officially. The person who has the notarized and signed deed in their possession can claim the property whenever they want. But the dumbass who has it owes a shitload of back taxes."

I flinch slightly. "Huh. Well, I'm pretty sure I know who owns the property. While snooping around, I ran into a woman who claimed that her grandmother had just passed and left it to her. Everything I'm finding out points to that grandmother being Frances Mays. Is there anything else on her or on her granddaughter?"

"Let me look. You hang on the line and let me get to my phone next to the computer."

"I'll be right here."

As I wait, I notice my clenched jaw and the tightness forming in the muscles of my neck. I force myself to relax a bit, but my head still spins with questions concerning Dorothy's secrecy about her friend, especially after everything I told her about what I'd found in the old house. The chances of her knowing Kevan's grandmother continue to grow, and there's something she isn't telling me.

Waiting for the sheriff to confirm what I'm figuring out, I debate how to approach Dorothy with my concerns. I can either confront her or dig a little deeper.

"Nate?" I hear on the phone.

"Yeah, I'm here."

"Okay. Let's see here. Let's start with Frances Mays. You say Dorothy knew her?"

"Yeah."

"Of course she did. Who doesn't she know?" The sheriff laughs, and I can hear him pecking on the computer one-finger style. I visualize him using the middle finger of one hand to tap the keys. As he's typing, he says each letter as his finger hits the keyboard. "F-r-a-n-c-i-s M-a-y-s." Next comes the sound of his heavy breathing as he waits. "What are we looking for in particular?"

"Maybe see if someone has claimed the property in the recent past." I wait as he mumbles what he's reading, skimming over one document, then the next.

"Nope. Still not seeing her name tied together with this property."

"What about the granddaughter? Kevan Copeland." I offer the name I found on the college website a couple of days ago.

"Worth a shot. Okay. K-e-v-i-n C-o-p-e-l-a-n-d." Listening, I laugh under my breath, thinking that while I am no speed demon with typing, I want to help him through the phone.

"Yeah. Here we go. Kevan—with an *a* instead of an *i*. Her maiden name was Mays, so I guess this Frances must be her grandmother after all," the sheriff adds. "Full name, Kevan Renee Mays. Born September 1, 1984. Married. Divorced. She—"

"Wait! So, Kevan Renee Mays? The initials on the doll—"

"I'm right there with you, buddy. K. R. M.," the sheriff confirms.

"My sister wrote in the diary about playing with a Renee. I bet the girl in the photo is Kevan." During my research on Kevan through her college's website, her middle name hadn't registered. I suppose then I wasn't searching for answers about my sister—just about a beautiful mystery woman. With everything coming to light, I have to keep going. I'm pretty sure both of their dolls ending up in the same spot wasn't a coincidence. Kevan has to have known my sister.

"Nate?"

"Yeah."

"I know this is fresh evidence, but it's possible it could lead to a dead end. I'll check it out for you, but don't get your hopes too high."

"You just call me if you have anything else."

"I will."

"Thanks, Sheriff." I end our conversation with a courteous tone, but I'm still frustrated. I wish everyone would stop telling me not to get my hopes up.

CHAPTER THIRTY-TWO

Kevan
Early Summer

I can't get the images out of my head: Gammie's self-portrait, my
father, the strange man who looks a lot like my father, and the little girl
from the dock who looks far too much like my best friend. They flash
through my mind on a constant shuffle, with questions that scroll on
their own loop, like closed captioning. I force myself to hit pause and
send my mind elsewhere.

Though I've lived on my own for years, my house seems lonelier
now. Even though Gammie only visited a few times, something about
her being gone makes me feel more alone here. Eleanor runs into the
room to greet me, her motor sounds vibrating my legs as she rubs
across them. I pick up the very healthy cat and rub my cheek against
hers, letting her soft fur soothe my aching emotions. She tolerates my
affection for a moment but then squirms to break free. They say
animals take on their owners' demeanors as time progresses. I believe
it. Eleanor only tolerates affection when she invites it, and only when it

serves a bigger purpose. For her, at this moment, that purpose is food. I give her what she wants.

Removing my shoes, I grab an apple from the fruit bowl on the counter and head to the study. The first thing on my agenda is to revisit my collage. Now that I've seen Gammie's, I feel I should reboot my brain and look at mine through clearer eyes. Something about seeing hers makes me want to understand my purpose a little more. What compelled me to make the collage? I rarely question my art—I just do it. However, I question a lot of things these days.

I take a seat on the floor, crisscross style, in front of my collage. Laying my phone on the floor in front of me, I open it to the picture of Gammie's collage. I take a big bite of the apple and view both of them, noticing how they are eerily similar. How two people could create such similar works without discussing it is beyond me. The juxtaposition of the objects and their similarities tells a complex story. I'm unsure what that story is. I play this question, rewind, and play it again as I continue to compare the two.

My collage is one large house, enclosing smaller houses and objects, which is the layout of a story. Looking at all the images in a different context, I see it more clearly now—it's Gammie's old property, as I have never seen it before.

Or it's the way I saw it as a child.

I had noticed the pond before, but not the stone building. This part of the collage, as well as the house clippings and objects that form the stone kiln and cellar, take shape and make more sense. It's as if they've come to life. I was writing a story while making Gammie's childhood home. What story? The strange part is, I hadn't been there in years, but apparently it was lurking in my subconscious.

I use two fingers to zoom in on the object that represents the kiln in Gammie's collage and on the painted dark shadows that look like human faces. I stand and move closer to my own collage and focus on these parts there as well. Nothing in my collage resembles a face or anything similar. I know I must be missing something.

They say art is subjective, existing only in the mind of its creator. But when someone else looks at it, thinks about it, doesn't it belong to that person as well? So, what is really here? What I notice: Gammie's collage has objects and shapes that resemble people in some form or another. In those same areas of my collage are individual letters, in disarray. In the area that represents the old kiln, I find several letters cut and pasted at random, including *r, m, o, t, s, n,* and *e.* I unscramble them to see if they make a word.

The word they make is *monster.*

I stare at it for a second longer and say aloud, "Shit!"

There is also a random number: 2. I'm not sure if I meant to put it there or if it happened by chance.

I move my finger across the phone to zoom in on the area of Gammie's collage that seems to represent the pond. When I focus on the smudges there, I catch my breath. Up close, they look even more like faces. I suck in another breath and hold it as I look back at my collage. There are no smudges or faces, but the ephemera and newspaper clippings seem to form patterns and words. I hadn't noticed this before.

The first name I'm able to see is attached in a circular pattern. It's my own name, but not my first name; it's my middle name—*Renee.* I find it odd that I incorporated my middle name into my collage without realizing it; as far as I know, I've never done anything like this before. Feeling as if I'm missing something, I continue to search. Soon I realize I didn't stop there, and a sudden flash of one of my dreams crosses my mind.

It's the dream of finding the yellow urn. The name that was engraved on it. I am looking at the name here. The letters form a zigzag pattern, and it reads *Beth.* I look away and back as if looking at it hurts my eyes. When I look back, I can't unsee it—it is there to stay. I stare at it, and as I do, I see another word forming.

Confused more than ever, I say this one aloud: *Jackie.*

PART THREE

And now here is my secret, a very simple secret:
It is only with the heart that one can see rightly; what is essential is invisible to
the eye.
—*Antoine de Saint-Exupéry,* The Little Prince

CHAPTER THIRTY-THREE

Kevan
August 19, 1996

Kevan stands in water, pants rolled past her knees, as she tries to scoop up minnows. The sun reflects off the water, creating blind spots from the glare, making the minnows seem as if they disappear and reappear out of nowhere. She doesn't have any plans for them once she catches them; she just likes the challenge of being faster than they. She holds her hair back with one hand and crouches, ready to strike, as a school of minnows swirls in a circular motion. With one quick dip of the old rusty can, she scoops one up. Looking in the can, she says out loud, "Caught one!" She sticks her fingers down into the cylinder and tries to grab the tiny fish, but it swirls around her fingers. It's too fast. She gives up and pours it back into the pond.

Her backpack of dolls and toys lies on the ground behind her as she waits for Beth to emerge from her side of the woods. With a hand perched over her eyes to shield them from the sun, she looks to see if Beth is there. Her shoulders sag when she doesn't see her. As she returns to playing with minnows, she spots something metallic a little

CHERANN WRIGHT

farther out into the water. She tosses the can onto the bank and grips her pant legs with both hands, pulling them higher and stepping deeper. She's careful where she steps, because she knows that at a certain point the pond's bottom drops and the water is way over her head. Swimming isn't in her plans today.

As she steps her feet down onto the squishy bottom of the pond, little swirls of mud circle up and around her shins and calves. She reaches her hand into the water, nearly to her shoulder, and picks up the object. When she pulls it up, she's holding a funny-looking key hooked on a necklace. It doesn't look like any kind of key she has seen before. It looks ancient—like a skeleton key. The key reflects the gleam in her eye, and she can't wait to show it to Beth. She sticks it into her pocket and tiptoes around the edge of the pond to search for more hidden treasures.

Growing antsy, she looks for Beth again, and this time she sees her skipping across the field, her backpack bouncing up and down. Kevan steps out of the water, squealing with excitement, and they both skip toward the old house in search of shade to play in.

They plop down in the middle of the floor, remove their dolls and toys from their packs, and set them up in a circle. After they have everything ready for their pretend classroom, they play their favorite game: school.

"Oh, yeah, I almost forgot," Kevan says with excitement in her voice. She stands and pulls the key from her pocket, then flops back down on her bottom as she hands it to Beth.

Beth's eyes grow large as she takes it, turning it over in her hand. "Cool. Where did you find it?"

"In the pond. I can't wait to show Gammie."

"Show me what?"

The girls jump and look to the missing front door. Relief floods both their faces as they see Gammie. Neither one heard her sneak in.

"I found this." Kevan jumps up from the floor and takes the key to Gammie. "Isn't it cool?"

"That is super cool," Frances says, taking the dirty necklace and key into her hand and holding it up toward the doorway. "I think I've seen this before. In fact, I know I have. If I'm correct, this has been missing since I was a little girl. It goes to a secret box that looks like a book. The box belonged to my mother. I think I still have it somewhere, but I could never get it open. Miss Renee, would you mind letting me take it home to try it out, and then I will give it back to you for safekeeping?"

"Yeah," Kevan says, excited at the idea of a secret box. "Can you show it to me sometime?"

"I sure can. Thank you, my dear. I promise it will come back to you one day to keep."

"What are you doing out here, Gammie?"

"I took a walk and thought I'd check on you, but it looks like you have your little friend here, so I'll catch up with you later. You two have fun and stay away from the areas we talked about. This place is not stable."

"Okay, Gammie," Kevan says, already sitting back down on the floor.

"So, where does your mom think you've gone?" Gammie asks her.

"She went to town to run some errands, so she left Matthew in charge. He thinks I'm just in the woods playing. He don't know. Matthew just stares at the TV." Kevan bounces one of her dolls around in the air as she speaks, as if the doll is doing the talking.

"All right, then. Don't stay gone too long. I don't want you to get into trouble."

"Okay, Gammie. I won't."

Kevan and Beth play inside the run-down house most of the morning, the interior significantly cooler than outside. Each has brought a pair of Barbie dolls to play with. Kevan's include a Barbie with a pink dress and a Ken wearing a tight blue shirt and blue jeans. Beth has only Barbies, both wearing yellow dresses: one with pink flowers, the other with blue.

As they begin to pack up, Beth makes a suggestion. "I have an idea. Why don't we each hide a doll here? That way, if we forget to pack any, then we will each have one here to play with."

"Yeah. Good idea. Where should we hide them?"

The girls rummage through the kitchen cabinets, looking in one, then another. Beth squats down in front of a cabinet and says, "What about this one?" She picks up some loose boards on the bottom. "We could hide them in here."

Holding up her two dolls, Kevan asks, "Which one do you want me to leave here for you to play with?"

"Duh, the Ken doll," Beth says, rolling her eyes. "How about you—which one?"

"That one." Kevan points to the doll with pink flowers.

Beth reaches into her backpack for a marker. "Here. Put your initials on your doll. I always put them on my toys—it's how I keep up with them."

Kevan does as she requests.

They lay their dolls in the bottom of the cabinet and conceal them by placing the boards back in place. Kevan pulls a candy wrapper bracelet from her backpack and tosses it into the cabinet, saying to Beth, "I'll leave this for you." Beth smiles.

Kevan attempts to shut the metal door on the cabinet, but it catches and won't close. Beth kicks it, slamming it shut. They look at each other, eyes wide. Kevan attempts to open it again, yanking on the handle. Each attempt ends with a metallic thud, but it won't open.

"Now what?" Kevan asks.

"Let's just leave it until we come back next time," Beth suggests.

"Okay. I guess I'd better go before Matthew knows I'm gone," Kevan says with a sigh. "Can you come back on Saturday?"

"Yep!"

"If you get here before me, wait for me. Okay?"

"Okay, and you have to wait for me if you do."

"Deal."

CHAPTER THIRTY-FOUR

Dorothy
Early Summer

I can't stop staring out the window after Nathan is out of sight. Can't he just leave the past where it should be: in the past? My entire existence is sitting on a foundation that's ready to crumble around me. I should have talked to Nathan about everything that happened. Explained what I did back then. What *we* did. If Frances was correct, everyone would forgive and put it behind them. Surely those we love would realize we did what we had to. That there was no other choice.

With no motivation to move, I wait at the window until my thoughts come to a screeching halt when a bird crashes into it. The bird hits with a loud thud that threatens to break the glass; then it falls to the ground, out of sight. Had it not been for the piece of glass between myself and it, its landing spot would have been my forehead. Out of instinct, I jerk my head backward anyway.

What are the odds of such an omen happening now, with everything else that's going on? Like my mother, I've always believed that a bird slamming into a windowpane means something bad is coming. She always said that when this happens, prepare yourself for the hard days ahead. It's even worse if the bird dies in the crash. Then, everything that you love and value is at stake.

I wobble outside to check on the bird and find a gray dove lying on its side, its small body expanding and contracting in tiny movements. As I watch it, I take in deeper breaths as if I am trying to breathe for it—encouraging it to live. My joints creak as I lean forward and scoop it up from the ground and carry it inside. Wrapping it in a small towel, I set the swaddled bird down on the floor so that if it wakes, it won't fall from a tall surface. I turn to look at it many times as I finish cleaning Nathan's kitchen, and each time I plead with the bird, encouraging it to live.

As I scrub the last of the bacon grease from the stove, I hear a tiny noise behind me. The bird stirs. I fetch it and take it outside and set it on the ground. The bird breaks free and attempts to fly away as soon as I unwrap the towel from its body. It only makes it a short distance and flops back down. Still shaken, it rests there while its dazed eyes watch me. I feel relief that the impact didn't kill the bird, and I hope things won't be as bad as I fear. Maybe Nathan's search into his sister's disappearance won't lead any further.

I decide I can't stall here any longer, so I go home, hoping to avoid Nathan for now. In the refuge of my sitting room, I plop down in my chair, more exhausted than usual, and look at the journals. It seems I may have to give up the notebooks sooner than expected. Frances isn't even cold yet, and secrets are already emerging. This means mine will emerge as well.

"Damn you, Marge, for leaving me."

Trying to quiet the fearful chatter in my head, I pick up one journal and open it to a random page. I stare at the words on the page, not really reading, just in a daze.

Time is a fickle thing. The way it twists and turns, sometimes shaping itself into a selfish thief—robbing a person of happier times. It doesn't matter whether life is simple or hard; it all goes by so quickly.

Bringing my focus back to the words on the page, I go back to a time when Frances mourns her husband's death and talks of her fears of raising her son alone. It wasn't just her dream to have a child, but *their* dream. She didn't dream she would be raising a child alone. Especially if it wasn't even John's. She's doing her best to love Clyde despite the possibility, but his defiant behavior is making it difficult.

Frances's words are tainted with uncertainty and fear. She seems unlike the strong woman who advised and aided me through disturbing, dark days.

September 8, 1967

I'm not built to be a parent. It doesn't seem to matter how much love I try to give Clyde. He returns it with disobedience and pure defiance. I keep thinking that if John was still alive, Clyde might be different. Maybe John would have taught him better than I. Taught him to be kind. I try, but he doesn't seem to respond to me. Seven years old and already he knows how to lie and manipulate. His temper has gotten out of control. Today I received a call from his teacher saying that he had murdered the classroom goldfish. At first, I thought she was exaggerating. Maybe he wanted to pet it and held it from the water too long. But that wasn't the case. Clyde removed the fish from the tank, placed it on the floor, and stabbed it with a pencil multiple times. I don't understand where he has learned such things. I have never shown ill will toward him and I have especially never shown violent behavior in front of him. Clyde is shown nothing but kindness and I have worked very hard to teach him patience and love. Why does he behave this way? I fear he is turning out to be just like his real father.

I feel a spark of anger that comes out of nowhere. My hatred for Tom brews even now, hotter and more foul than a witches' brew. Any thoughts of him force my temperature to rise.

I flip through a thick section of pages and open to another entry about Frances's battles with her troublesome son. In this entry, Frances describes Clyde hanging their cat. She looked out her kitchen window as she was washing dishes and saw Clyde throwing a rope across a branch. Then she observed him hoisting something attached to the rope's end into the air. When the object came into view, she saw it was white and furry, flipping and convulsing out of control. As she realized what it was, it slowed down in its movements. She ran outside, saving the cat's life.

I raise my eyes from the journal and remember the day this happened. Frances called me and informed me she would be over soon and to have her a strong drink ready. When she got here, she brought the cat with her, finding it a new home. The cat lived to be ancient—safe in my care.

The pages from this journal are a testament to Clyde's insubordinate behavior, chronicling all the horrible things he put Frances through. On another random page, Frances's patience is shrinking as her fear grows toward her out-of-control son. The school has expelled him for being intoxicated on campus and for inappropriate conduct toward a female. On another page, the sheriff has escorted him to her front door because he was trying to break into the local hardware store, along with a friend. In yet another event, the parents of his girlfriend have presented him with a restraining order because of physical abuse. Many pages in the journal are entries about Clyde being escorted home by police because of public intoxication and disorderly conduct. All before he was sixteen. When the local police grew tired of dealing with his behavior, he had to spend time in a juvenile detention center, giving Frances a short period of relief.

Heart aching with grief, I lay the journal aside and look out the window. The things my best friend endured were enough to send anyone over the edge. But somehow she always held it together, and her patience far exceeded anyone else's. Toughest woman I will ever know.

Tears flow as I grieve and miss my best friend. I inhale and pick up another journal—the one that could change everything. The one that reveals a part of our past that I would rather remain hidden. The one that I have debated on destroying rather than handing it over to Frances's granddaughter. I promised to give it to her when the time was right. Is that time now? Will it ever come?

I gently brush the cover with my fingertips, knowing that if this journal could talk, the stories within it could destroy so many lives. Unable to stop myself, I open the book. It sends me back in time, and I feel my throat tighten. All my life, Frances was my go-to person for everything. Now I am left alone to face our past. Holding my breath, I place a thumb midway among the closed pages of the journal and open the book wide. My eyes fall upon the date and I give it a glassy stare—August 26, 1996.

CHAPTER THIRTY-FIVE

Kevan
Early Summer

I open my mouth, trying to inhale air, and it fills with thick, slimy water. The water slides down my throat and threatens to fill my lungs; then my gag reflex convulses as I try to throw it back up again. I swallow more. I force my mouth closed as I look around and panic spreads through my body. To fight against the panic, I push my way forward, trying to escape. Anywhere but here. Where is here?

I am underwater—again. I immediately look up, sure that I will see someone there. She is there. Blond hair, blue eyes, and her mouth is open as if her scream has left her, leaving nothing else behind. Green vines descend downward from lily pads and spread through the water, growing thicker before my eyes. They slither toward me like long, skinny fingers that spread across my shoulders and back, squeezing my flesh and pushing me down deeper. I flail my arms and legs from side to side, trying to break free. My efforts are all in vain as I plunge deeper underwater. My foot bumps into something hard but spongy, and it pushes away from me. I see the outline of a person. Confusion and hysteria threaten to take over. I shift my thoughts and wonder what it would be like if I were to let myself drown rather than fight it.

I look at the girl again. Her expression has changed. Somehow, I feel everything that she feels. All the sensations her body is experiencing. At first, my head pounds and I feel every cell in my body cry for oxygen. I know I can't go much longer without taking a breath. I mimic her and we take a deep breath together. It doesn't hurt the way I thought it would. We begin to sink, but it's almost peaceful. The girl sinks deeper, faster, fading into the darkness of the pond, no longer fighting. She says something as she fades, and it's as if she is whispering inside my head.

Don't be scared. You won't drown.

I hear her words loudly, then I feel them, so I fight as something grips my arm. It pulls on me hard. I can feel the vines coiling around me. They no longer hold me down, but pull me from the water. The sudden gift of air prompts me to cough and gasp as I realize I am in complete darkness. It is so dark that I can't see my hands as I hold them in front of me.

A noise shifts my focus to a loud ping on glass, and then another and another, until they are coming so fast and loud they hurt my eardrums. Something is hitting the glass with such force that I wait for it to shatter. I cover my face with my arms, trying to avoid what must be coming.

Suddenly I realize I'm holding my eyes closed. I open them. It is no longer dark, and the rain outside falls sideways as the wind howls. The passing storm breaks me the rest of the way from the dream.

As I open my eyes, they set themselves on the collage across the room. Wiping a tiny droplet of drool from my cheek, I realize I've fallen asleep lying on the sofa, staring at the piece of art. The answers I was hoping for still haven't emerged. Why do I keep having similar versions of this one dream? I lack the energy to sit up as the weight of dread forms in my chest. I fear my dreams are trying to become real, just as they did when I was a little girl.

The collage seems to scream at me as I stare at it. But what is it trying to tell me? I don't understand why I created it in the first place. When I was a kid, we had a next-door neighbor, Jackie, who had a thing with my father behind my mother's back. I don't think my mother ever found out. But why would I put Jackie's name on my collage? She was no one to me. In fact, she hasn't entered my thoughts from then until now.

I bury my face in the sofa, trying to make the loop of questions stop. It's possible I am reading too much into the two collages. I have to make one last observation, even as I think it.

This time something scratches like tiny insect legs inside my head. Light tickles of thoughts or memories, trying to dig their way out. The entire piece of art takes on a dark and disturbing appearance, and I want to just forget it altogether. I wonder if I've just had a dream of a memory, rather than a memory of a dream. Maybe it wasn't a dream at all.

I remember sitting beside a pond, soaked, and someone wiping a slimy gunk from my eyes. Someone pushing hair out of my face and squeezing me. I close my eyes and almost feel it. I am being hugged close in someone's embrace as they sway back and forth, moving me with them.

Renee, you're going to be okay. It's okay.

It is a woman's voice. Then I hear another woman's voice, but it isn't close. I can't make out what she's saying, but she isn't speaking to me. Her voice is familiar, but something about it is unexpected. The collage monopolizes my whole being as I move to sitting, trying to remember more, but it's as if I'm trying to see it through a shattered windshield. Images broken into unrecognizable pieces that no longer fit together. At some point, someone submerged my body in murky water. It wasn't something I did on my own. Someone put me there. Someone tried to drown me.

I break free from my dark trance and feel myself breathing heavily. I have been holding my breath.

I feel myself teetering on the edge of a full memory. I'm not sure I want it. I make another attempt to convince myself that this all stems from a dream, but I know differently. The details are far too vivid. Once time has passed, it's impossible for memories from a dream to return as a complete puzzle. Something tells me that more is coming, whether I want it to or not.

CHAPTER THIRTY-SIX

Frances and Dorothy
August 26, 1996

"What do you mean, you don't want to go? Come on! Let's go be fun Dotty and Marge, instead of boring old Dorothy and Frances. We'll do a little gambling, play some games, and get ourselves a happy little buzz. I'll have my driver take us and pick us up."

Frances sighs. "I'm not in the mood."

"Come on, Frances. I need to flee this big house for a while —unwind."

Frances sighs again, letting out a long breath. "I guess, but I'm not staying out all night."

"Deal." Dorothy's voice shifts from begging to pleased. "I'll come pick you up in an hour."

The two women step out of the car as Dorothy tells the driver to hang close by in case they decide to go somewhere else. They walk into the locally owned bar and grill. Over the years, it has expanded from one small space to tearing down the walls between several connected buildings to offer a variety of entertainment, including pool tables and gambling machines. When they step through the door, Alan Jackson blares on a jukebox and a cloud of smoke fogs the room. They go to the bar and order themselves Long Island iced teas and then make their way to a corner booth with a view of several pool tables.

"Think you're still good at it?" Dorothy asks, nodding her head at the closest pool table.

"I can still kick your ass," Frances teases. "Let's go hit a couple of slot machines before we catch a buzz and lose our defenses. I don't want to gamble with real money after I've had a couple of these." She takes a huge gulp.

A voice across the room sparks an immediate negative response that dampens Frances's mood. She knows that voice, and she also knows that she shouldn't be hearing it here.

"Is that who I think it is?" she asks.

Dorothy leans her upper body over to the right to peer around Frances and nods. "Yep—and he has some brunette floozy with him."

Frances feels her face flush red; heat radiates from her skin. "That bastard!"

"Now, Frances—don't you dare allow that asshole to ruin our night out."

"Oh, I'm not. I just want to witness his 'deer caught in headlights' look when he sees me."

"I'll go with you," Dorothy says, her nosy nature not allowing her to pass it up.

Frances slides out of the booth first, and then Dorothy follows. Frances's eyes narrow in anger and disgust when she sees her son bent over a woman and a pool table, one hand clutching a pool stick and the other the woman's ass. Frances steps to the end of the pool table and hears Clyde say something perverse in the woman's ear.

"You think flaunting your affair with the neighbor's wife gives you enormous balls?" Frances taunts.

Clyde lifts his eyes from the table, but not his body. He stares at Frances, then exhales and rises defiantly into his usual hostile stance.

"What the fuck is it to you?" he says. "Seems to me you're out whoring around yourself. Guess the apple doesn't fall far from the tree."

"Oh, you are correct on that one, dear son." Frances squints in the woman's direction and says. "So, Jackie, do you think your husband would approve of your company?"

"Why don't you mind your own fucking business, *Mom*." Clyde overenunciates the last word mockingly.

"Maybe we should—" Jackie begins to say before being cut off.

"Shut up," Clyde barks as he steps in front of Jackie, shoving her aside with the back of his hand.

"Oh, honey," Frances warns Jackie, "you don't know what you're getting yourself into. You better run while you can."

"Come on, Clyde, let's just go," Jackie says as she turns to face him, placing her hands on his chest as if to push him along.

Clyde grabs both of her upper arms, gripping them as he slides her aside. "Why don't you shut up and go get us another drink?" he says. Jackie gives Frances a sheepish look, then walks toward the bar.

"Why don't you take your ass home where you belong, Clyde?" Frances makes it more of a suggestion than a question. "How many days have you been gone? Three? Four?"

"I'll go home when I get good and damn ready. Why are you here, Mother? You and your whore friend tired of humping each other? Looking for some dick?"

"I'll give you about thirty seconds to get out of here, find somewhere to sober up, and go home. Or pack your shit and move away from here. Everyone would be better off."

"Or what?"

"Or I pick up a pay phone and call your wife and let her know where you are."

"Go ahead. After a few days she'll forgive me. She always does. Remember—she's not allowed to leave. She'll go to hell if she does." Clyde's lips form into a twisted smile, his head tilted into a cocky position as if he's winning.

"There are other ways of taking care of your ass, Clyde."

"That a threat?"

Jackie reappears, carrying a beer in one hand and a whiskey in the other. She walks warily in Clyde's direction as if testing the waters.

"There you are, sexy," Clyde says calmly, displaying a rapid shift in mood.

He's always been good at turning on the charm, just like his father, Frances thinks bitterly.

He grabs for the shot glass as he wraps the other arm around Jackie's neck, squeezing her against his body. "I'm tiring of the crowd here. What do you say we take this party somewhere else?" He doesn't give Jackie a chance to answer; rather, he drags her with his arm still clamped around her neck as he downs the shot of whiskey and slams the shot glass on the pool table.

"I am warning you, Clyde," Frances calls behind him.

As Clyde is walking away, he tilts his head upward and back in Frances's direction and says, "Goodbye, mother dearest." The last thing Frances sees is his free arm held high and his middle finger pointing toward the ceiling.

Frances lets out a long, disgusted exhale. "I can't believe I gave birth to such a sorry piece of shit."

"Maybe we should follow them. I'll go outside and find my driver."

"Good idea. I know I shouldn't give a shit, but I have a feeling Jackie doesn't have a clue what she's getting herself into. Who knows what he might do tonight?"

Pouring their drinks into throwaway cups, they climb into the back of the car. Dorothy instructs the driver to ease out of the parking lot, but before he does, they spot Clyde and Jackie leaned up against Clyde's car with zero space between their bodies. At first, their closeness looks like affection, but upon further observation Dorothy and Frances realize that Clyde's body language appears to have shifted again. His face is close to Jackie's, but he's not kissing her. He looks threatening.

"Should we do something?" Dorothy asks.

"Maybe that's the way she likes it." Frances shrugs. "She isn't that stupid. She's lived down the street for years, and she knows he's an asshole."

"You know how he is, Frances. He weasels his way into or out of everything."

They watch him open the driver's side door and shove Jackie into his car as he climbs in behind her, forcing her to climb over the console.

"I say we follow him," Dorothy says.

They fall in behind the swerving car and follow it to the edge of town, to the Bitterton Motel. The building is an L-shaped, single-story structure with outdoor entrances into the rooms. Clyde parks in front of the motel and staggers out of the driver's side door. Swaying his way around the car, he makes a poor attempt at opening the passenger door as if he's some sort of gentleman. The switch has flicked again, and he appears charming and gentle as he holds her hand, escorting her to room number seven.

"What do you think I should do?" Frances asks. "Should I warn Edith?"

"How many times has she turned a blind eye? Forgiven him?"

They stare at the door for ten minutes until Frances gives up. "I wasn't in much of a party mood, anyway. I'm ready to go home."

"Okay," Dorothy says with a sigh. "I'll take you home."

CHAPTER THIRTY-SEVEN

Kevan
Early Summer

The boisterous storm outside quiets, and the sun takes its turn. I walk to the window and look out across the back lawn. The clouds promise that the rain can return anytime it wants to. The uneasy feeling deep in the pit of my stomach has taken up homestead and I am restless, as it seems to keep growing in size. I fear that until I figure out the purpose behind Gammie's art and my own, that feeling won't go away. I pace from room to room, pausing to look at the collage. Eleanor, crouched on the side table, watches me with half-opened eyes as I continuously exit and enter the room. It is getting me nowhere.

Impulse decides for me, and I snap a picture of my collage before heading out the door. With all the latest occurrences, the only place that may give me some answers is that stupid piece of property I wish I could just forget. The one that now belongs to me.

It takes an hour and a half to drive there, but I have no awareness of doing it. I don't come back to myself until I'm easing past my mother's house, still hoping not to be spotted. Again, I park in front of the neighbors' house and ease through their backyard. Following the over-grown markings, I find it easier this time. During my walk, I give myself a pep talk about how I will respond if I see the little girl again.

You won't be scared. You'll walk up to her—talk to her, I tell myself.

I step from the trees into the clearing, and an ominous feeling forms in my chest. When I was a child, I anticipated Beth waiting for me. Now anticipation has become something else. I hesitate for a moment, second-guessing my decision to come and wondering if I should just vacate the premises. I should have requested Beth come with me; then I wouldn't be alone. As I debate, taking a step forward and then another, I take a deep breath and hold it in. I proceed with a breath and a pause in each step, pushing myself to keep going. I continue my pep talk. *I'm only looking for answers.* Answers to what, I am not sure. *There's no one here who will physically hurt me. I've faced worse things in my life and been able to overcome them.*

Picking up the pace, I scan my surroundings, avoiding the dock. My thought process from my walk returns, and I tell myself that if I encounter the girl, I'll push through my fear and won't run away. I still avoid looking.

I walk toward the house and pull my phone from my pocket, opening the picture I took before I left home. I compare the objects of my collage to the layout before me. As I eye every detail, tiny hairs stand on the back of my neck. I feel like I'm walking through a dream, but the view seems different. In my dream, everything was dead and haunting. Now everything is alive, but there's still a feeling of some-thing out there, waiting for me. Could a memory be lurking in my subconscious? There is something deep and, I fear, dark as well.

A breeze blows sideways, and I have to brush my hair away from my face. A chill, along with a sense that I am not alone, consumes me. I stop in my stride and look straight ahead.

The girl must be there.

With apprehension, I slowly rotate my body until the dock is in view. It's empty. I would have wagered that I wasn't alone. Shaking myself, I turn back to the house.

"Get a grip, Kev!" I say aloud.

I detour around the outside of the house and walk toward the stone building and cellar. Remembering Nathan's words about the instability of these structures, I opt for standing just inside the door of the stone building. Something about the space feels much colder than the outside. It feels as though eyes are watching me as my own eyes scan the stairs. I shudder and step back outside. I move down the stone steps to the cellar door, use my shoulder to shove it open, and stand just outside the creepy, hollow entrance. Both give me three kinds of willies. I stick one foot through the opening and tap my toe on the wooden floor. Nathan pointed out that it was odd for someone to spend money or time on putting a wooden floor in a cellar. A dirt or stone floor would keep the space cooler. I guess our ancestors had their reasons for doing things the way they did.

I walk through the back field, trekking through tall grass, scanning the perimeter of the property instead of looking down as I walk. My foot slams into a large rock, sending immediate pain to three of my toes, and I topple forward. I catch myself with both hands. Intense pain shoots into my wrist for a second time while visiting this place. I roll over onto my bottom and find myself looking at two large, misshapen stones. Their location is strange; are they here for a reason? I fold myself to rest on my knees, and I rub my hand over one of the stones. Something is chiseled into its face, although time and weather have eroded its surface, making it difficult to determine what the markings are. The other stone has similar markings. As far as I can tell, the carvings on the rock on the left resemble the letter *B*. The rock on the right has impressions I can't quite decipher. Do these rocks indicate that something is buried here? If so, what?

I spot a movement out of the corner of my eye, and fear spreads through me like the chill that comes after a fever. My heart races at the peak tempo of a Mozart sonata as I avoid turning my head to look in that direction—the direction of the pond. I'm one hundred percent sure this time that someone is standing there.

CHAPTER THIRTY-EIGHT

Frances and Dorothy
   August 27, 1996

Frances opens her eyes, but her body voices its desire to rest longer. She turns to squint at the window, where only a hint of light promises the sun will arrive. Birds chirp outside, but their redundant songs only threaten rain. She has awakened with an uneasy feeling this morning, and she fears that something horrible is waiting on the horizon.

It's Saturday morning, so she doesn't have to go in to work today, but her speeding thoughts about nothing won't allow her to sleep in. She rolls her weary body out of bed and goes to make a pot of coffee. Once it has finished brewing, she pours a cup and phones Dorothy.

"What are you doing up so early on a Saturday morning?" Dorothy asks rather than saying hello. Dorothy is always up early, directing her godson on the daily jobs that keep her large plantation running smoothly. This time of year, she hires extra help to take care of her huge tobacco and corn crops so that she has a lucrative harvest in the fall. Most plantation owners have crops as their primary sources of income, whereas Dorothy uses them as supplemental income or even donates the earnings to charities.

"How'd you know it would be me?" Frances asks.

"Too early for banks, bill collecting, and beggars. You all right?"

"I suppose. I have a nasty dread, though. Like something bad is waiting to happen."

"Oh, I'm sure it's only because of that no-account son of yours," Dorothy says.

"No. This feeling is distinct, somehow. I feel it in my core. You know how I get sometimes. But this time I can't shake it."

"You should come over for some coffee. Get yourself distracted."

"Let me check on my grandchildren first, and then I just might. Before I come, I'm going to give Sheriff Kenny a call and let him know my son is on one of his binges again. Remind the sheriff that Clyde is still the same drunken asshole son he's always been. Help him catch the bastard in case he gets behind the wheel."

Frances hangs up the phone and calls Sheriff Kenny, then showers and gets dressed for the day. She puts on her walking shoes and heads down the street, past the houses that divide her own house from her granddaughter's. Her on-edge feeling didn't go away with the distraction of a shower. Maybe it will fade once she sees that everything is still and quiet at Clyde and Edith's house, she tells herself.

Frances knocks on the front door and then comes inside before anyone invites her in. She steps into the living room and finds James and Matthew half-sitting, half-lying on the couch watching TV. She still looks for Tommy playing on the floor, seated with his legs bent in the shape of a *W*. Her heart aches every time she realizes she will never again receive one of his bear hugs when she comes to visit. It doesn't seem right that he has been gone for almost two months. His death was tragic, and she knows it could have been avoided.

Tommy died from what the doctors called a horrible stomach virus —but Frances knew that "virus" was really the stupid military punishment given to Tommy, and the other children, by Clyde. She couldn't prove it, but she knew it had to be true. Clyde must fear this himself, because he hasn't forced the children to drink castor oil since then. He subjects the children to other forms of military punishment, such as duckwalks or scrubbing the floor with toothbrushes. At a certain point, Frances had believed that Clyde's time in the military might fix him, but it had only given him new ideas for hurting those he claimed to love.

"Where are your mother and sister?"

"Don't know." Matthew shrugs.

"Mom was in the kitchen," James says without removing his eyes from the television. "Kevan went outside a long time ago."

Frances walks through the kitchen and peers out the window. Swinging the screen door open, she surveys the backyard and doesn't see either Edith or Kevan.

"Maybe Mom is in the work shed." Matthew rises slightly from lying on his back, glances at Frances for a quick second, and then flops back down in his same lazy position.

Frances can guess where Kevan has gone, and she doesn't care about Edith's whereabouts. She and Edith rarely see eye to eye, especially in regard to Clyde and the children. Frances wants nothing more than to see her daughter-in-law kick her son to the curb—religion be damned—son be damned. That isn't going to happen. Edith believes she will go to hell if she is the one to leave her husband.

Telling the boys goodbye and that she will check back in on them later, Frances walks back home, gets in her car, and drives to Dorothy's. As the morning wears on, Frances's outlook remains as gloomy as the cloudy sky above. She sits down at the kitchen table as Dorothy pours her a cup of coffee. Dorothy sets the cup in front of her and then walks to the liquor cabinet and retrieves a bottle of Kahlúa. She pours a shot into Frances's coffee.

"You look like you could use this. It isn't strong, but it's enough to take the edge off."

"Thanks." Frances stares at the cup of coffee, hugging it with clutched hands as if someone might take it away from her. Several minutes pass as Frances continues stroking her fingers up and down the side of the cup, never taking a sip.

"You going to drink it or fondle it all day?" Dorothy cuts in on Frances's gloomy reverie.

Frances lifts the cup to her lips and chuckles. "My hands haven't fondled anything in a long time."

"Well, there you go—maybe that's your problem." Dorothy teases. "So, has that son of yours made it home yet?"

"Hell, no! I stopped by to check on the kids this morning, but my girl wasn't there. I'm guessing she's out wandering my old place."

"Then let's take us a walk and get some fresh air."

"Good idea."

Frances and Dorothy stroll beyond the back fields of Dorothy's plantation, exiting through the gate to the woods. The woodlands behind Dorothy's property are home to massive cedar, ash, and oak trees extending long branches that jut out in all directions, preventing much undergrowth. Walking through these woods brings back memories of the wilder days when Frances would sneak out of her mother's house to cross through the same woods to Dorothy's house. They each knew this path well.

Frances hasn't used it since that moonlit night when she made her trip to Dorothy's house to remove a major thorn in both of their sides.

As Frances stomps down the old path, she feels almost physically sick, expecting something ahead. She realizes she is holding her hands into fists so tight that her nails are almost breaking the skin. She shakes her hands vigorously in front of her to loosen them and relieve some of the tension she's feeling.

"What is it?" Dorothy asks.

"I don't know, but something's wrong. I'm not sure which direction we should go, ahead or back home."

"What do you mean, something's wrong?"

"I can't describe it, but I've gone from worrying that something bad is about to happen to feeling that something bad has *already* happened."

"What do you want to do? You tell me and we'll do it."

"I think we need to pick up the pace."

Their strides become much more rapid. They cover more ground quickly, reaching the clearing in the woods. They walk out into the open, taking a few steps toward the old house and pond. When the realization of what they are seeing sinks in, time stops. They look at each other—then run.

CHAPTER THIRTY-NINE

Dorothy
Early Summer

There was no choice. We did what we had to do . . .

I read the last words of Frances's diary with tear-filled eyes, mourning my best friend. The lines on the page begin to blur and run together, and I squeeze my eyes shut, forcing the tears to stream down my face. Frances has written every detail of that horrible day. The memory of it is vivid and harsh—worse than ever. I know her words are true when it comes to the reasoning behind everything we did that day.

We had to do horrible things over the course of our lives in order to survive. That day was the worst. We knew we'd done the right thing, but making others understand that would be something entirely different.

I shut the journal, placing it on the table, and look out the window again. The sky emanates a wide array of colors as clumps of thick, gray clouds move swiftly into view. I try to dig inside myself to find courage to face the past. Now my fear is like the sky, which grows and shifts into a gloom, moving over the sun, sending a large, dark shadow to consume this room.

Restless, with my nerves on edge, I can't bear to sit any longer. I leave by the back door and walk across my manicured lawn toward the back of my property. Birds move rapidly overhead while others stay perched on tree limbs, singing their assortment of tunes. The noise in my head keeps me from enjoying the sound. After I stroll outside the perimeter of the backyard, the restlessness only grows. I continue to walk across the neatly mowed fields with their sporadic, massive trees. I wander past outdoor staff who pay no attention to me, continuing with their chores. My steps seem to take on a sporadic pattern, much like my thoughts, as I walk along the neatly graveled lane that circles the property. It's been years since I've walked this path. Actually not, since Frances and I walked it together on that terrible day.

Nathan is up ahead. He throws up a hand in a hello gesture, but I'm nearly oblivious to my surroundings, and I barrel ahead, barely acknowledging him. I pause at the edge of the property, in front of an iron gate set into a stone wall. I stand for a long moment, debating, and then I open the gate and slip through, closing it behind me. The uncluttered woods haven't changed. My mind is on fire, even more than my aching joints and muscles from the fast pace of my walk. I know where I'm going now. If I visit the place where all those terrible things took place that day, maybe I can figure out what I should do. I move with urgency, my feet making a swooshing sound through the leaves with each step.

A chaotic rustling behind me, a noise louder than my own, causes me to jump.

A chipmunk scurries from its hiding spot in last season's leaves. Patting my chest, I exhale a long breath. I continue, only this time I walk faster. As my pace quickens, so does my mind. The closer I move to my destination, the more my mind rewinds. Like a chopped film, clips and flashes of that day spotlight and disappear. That day I walked alongside Frances after having morning coffee together. Frances was frantic and sure that something was wrong. She was right.

It seems as though each time my foot strikes the ground, an image of that day opens just behind my mind's eye, then closes again like the shutter on a camera—each image worse than the next. The white cloth drifting down below the surface of the water—gone. Strands of blond hair floating upward, swaying in the water like thousands of tiny threads—gone. The woman and her dark, matted hair—gone. The wide-open eyes, hollow and staring in horror—gone. The girl with pale, bluish skin—gone. The bad man—gone.

I stop to lean on a tree. This break finds me more out of breath, which I think is fueled just as much by the images as by the trek through the woods. I cough to remove an irritation in my throat. As I breathe in slowly to ease the coughing, the sound of a twig snaps behind me and I cease my movements. Turning my head to look, I spot someone quite a bit larger than myself darting behind a tree. Heart racing now, I try not to sound alarmed. "Who's there?"

Nathan slowly steps out from behind the tree with his hands up, as if surrendering in a gunfight. "It's just me."

"Whew." I let out a relieved sigh. "You scared me, Nate. What are you doing?"

He approaches with a smile. "Hi, Miss Dorothy. I saw that you were going for a walk, and I just thought I would check on you—make sure you're okay."

"Well, now, you know that I'm perfectly capable of walking by myself." I try to camouflage the annoyance in my voice that comes more from the fact that Nathan is following me to this place than from him checking to see if I am capable of walking on my own.

"I do know that, but I just thought I would check anyway. You headed anywhere in particular?"

A debate begins its frenzy inside my mind. Should I take Nathan by the hand, lead him to what he needs to know, and get it over with? He is all I have left in this world. How can I risk losing him over the secrets and lies that I've kept to protect him? The thought speeds through my mind on rapid play all the way to the end—an ending where he no longer looks at me as a loving godmother but with sheer hatred.

I continue to look mutely at Nathan, the debate still raging inside my head so loudly that I feel my temples pulse. Now could be my chance to put an end to so many unanswered questions. But how could I ever begin to explain? I will have to go back—all the way back.

CHAPTER FORTY

Kevan
   August 27, 1996

Even though Kevan's eyes are closed, she knows there is light coming through the window, because it makes the inside of her eyelids glow. Her eyes pop open and she springs from her bed. Her plans are to fly through her chores as quickly as possible, make it known to her mother that she is finished, and then sneak away to meet Beth. Easing her bedroom door open, she peeks into the hallway and then sticks her head out as well. She tiptoes into the hall but stops cold, her face draining of color. Tommy stands motionless in the mirror at the end of the hall, looking out with a pained expression. He is normal—not sick —not dead. The last time she saw him, his clothes drooped from his body. Now his striped shirt and khaki shorts fit as they are supposed to. This can't be real—he *is* dead.

She continues to stand and stare at him, waiting for her imagination to stop lying to her. Rubbing her eyes, she looks again. He is still there.

"What do you want?" she whispers—hesitant and disbelieving. Tommy doesn't move, but she sees a single tear slide down his cheek.

Remaining frozen in place, unsure of herself, she finally asks, "Why are you here? What's wrong, Tommy?"

His mouth opens as if he is going to speak and then closes again. He squeezes his eyes shut, scrunching up his face, then opens his eyes and whispers, "Don't go, Sissy."

Struggling to understand him, Kevan steps a little bit closer. "I can't understand you, Tommy."

Voice shaky but louder this time, he says, "Don't go."

Not realizing that concern has overtaken fear, she now stands only a few feet away from the mirror. "What do you mean? Don't go where?"

"Don't go to the pond, Sissy."

Forehead frowning with confusion, she asks, "Tommy, how are you here?"

"I'm here because you need me. Please don't go to the pond."

"How do you know about the pond? I never told you about it."

"It's not safe, Kevan."

"No one knows about it except Gammie and my friend. Why wouldn't it be safe?"

"He knows."

"He who?"

"The bad man."

"What bad man?"

The screen door in the kitchen slams. Tommy's eyes reflect an urgency for Kevan to listen to one last thing. "Don't be scared. You won't drown."

"What?" Kevan asks, and as the word leaves her lips, Tommy disappears.

She hears footsteps in the kitchen and darts into the bathroom, easing the door closed behind her. She leans against the door, trying to comprehend what has just happened. Tommy is dead. *It wasn't real. It wasn't real. It wasn't real.*

She repeats this over and over in a low whisper, telling herself she's only imagined seeing Tommy. It doesn't work, so she chants a rhyme. *One, two, buckle my shoe. Three, four, shut the door. Five, six, this doesn't make sense. Seven, eight, this I hate. Nine, ten, I'm scared again.* She does this until she feels calmer.

Kevan pees, washes her hands in cold water, and then brushes her teeth in record speed. As she puts her toothbrush back into the cup used to hold the children's toothbrushes, she spots her father's toothbrush and takes on a twisted grin. She grabs it, dips it into the toilet, and sticks it back into his cup. She flushes the toilet.

Cracking the door open, she listens for any noises on the other side. All she can hear is the never-ending sound of the wall clock ticking in the living room. She doesn't look in the mirror's direction as she darts to her bedroom. As soon as her feet land on the shaggy carpet, she closes her door. Shuffling around her room as quietly as she can, Kevan makes her bed, picks up her clothes and toys, and prepares her backpack. Not wanting her brothers to know that she's going outside, she tiptoes to the kitchen to find her mother so she can get clearance to go outside. She hopes that her mother is in a good mood.

Kevan walks into the kitchen without being heard, watching Edith before speaking. "Mom?" Kevan speaks in a hushed tone, testing the waters. Her mother is standing rigid at the kitchen sink, staring out the window, a cigarette in her hand and her elbow propped on her hip.

"Yes, Kevan?" As Edith turns, she blows smoke across the room.

Kevan looks at her mother's face to note her mood. Edith's mouth is cocked upward on one side in a half-hearted smile that says she is worried or stressed. Her smile is always lacking in sincerity when Clyde is gone on one of his binges somewhere. It's as if she can't muster the energy to pick up the other side of her mouth.

Unsure of herself but taking the chance anyway, Kevan says, "I've finished cleaning my room. Can I go outside and play?"

Edith looks at Kevan, but her eyes don't appear to be seeing her. Instead they are glazed over, looking somewhere into the abyss. "I guess you can—just for a little while."

Kevan doesn't want to give her mother an opportunity to change her mind, so she bolts back to her bedroom, grabs her backpack, and runs out the back door. She rides her bicycle around in circles, waiting for her mother to enter the work shed, then makes a beeline for the opening in the back fence. She races for a couple of minutes to ensure that she gets far enough away from home, lessening her chances of getting caught. Finally she slows down.

Beams of sunlight shine on sporadic sections of the woods while a dewy mist blankets the rest. Kevan's hair dampens and sticks to the edges of her face. She makes it to the wood's edge and steps out into full sunlight. Not seeing any sign of Beth yet, Kevan skips and gallops to the old house to try to open the metal cabinet where they hid their dolls. She curls her fingers and thumb around the handle, bends her knees, and yanks on the door with all her might, but she only falls backward on her bottom. Rummaging around the floor, using her foot to brush aside debris, she looks for something to wedge behind the cabinet door. She finds an old wooden spoon, its tip worn thin from use, lying in the clutter. Pulling on the door handle and getting the door to crack slightly, she slides the spoon in behind it and attempts to pry the door open. She tries it several times before breaking the bowl off the spoon.

She gives up and skips back outside to find that Beth still hasn't come. Her hopes are high that her friend will arrive soon. She opens her backpack and pulls out some pieces of chalk she's collected from school. Then she sits down, crisscross, and draws on the boards of the dock. She keeps glancing over her shoulder to see if Beth is emerging from her own part of the woods; she worries that Beth won't make it today.

The sun is rising higher in the sky and warms the top of Kevan's head. Deciding to find some shade, she packs her things into her backpack and climbs down from the dock. She makes her way underneath the wood planks and sits on the ground near the water's edge. There is only a small space of land beneath the dock, just big enough to sit on, so she relaxes her feet and calves into the water. From this position, she can peek through the opening in the steps to watch for Beth.

On her third glance in that direction, something just at the edge of her peripheral vision moves unexpectedly. Unable to determine where the movement came from, Kevan shifts her whole body and tries to see what caught her eye. She sees it now, and it makes her suck in a deep breath and hold it. A man has appeared into full view, though he's still a fair distance away. He walks, stomping heavily, straight toward the pond, like a monster walking out of one of her dreams. Something about his gait makes her heart pound faster.

The sun's glare takes its toll on the clarity of what she is seeing, so Kevan scoots herself forward to get a better view. Like the flash of a camera, the sun reflects from a shiny object around the man's hip, and then the flash is gone. With each step of the man's legs, it flashes again and then disappears. As the man gets closer, she sees what the object is, and it forces a low yelp to escape her lips.

What Kevan sees now is like a scene from a horror film. The man is carrying a large object draped over his shoulder, and something about the image sends her breathing into a paralyzed state. Her eyes fix themselves on the long brown hair dangling over his lower back. As he moves, the hair swings from side to side. It looks like a woman's hair. He turns his direction slightly, and now she can see that the hair is dangling from a woman's head. The woman's upper body is hanging, upside down, over the man's back. Her head bobs slightly with his gait. Kevan feels like a person driving by the scene of an accident. She can't peel her eyes away from the woman's discolored face.

Remembering Beth, Kevan glances between the steps once more, only this time she is hoping Beth won't be there. Her breath now shifting from a hold to a frantic pace, she sees Beth trotting out of the woods. Like a pinball, Kevan's eyes shift desperately from the man to Beth and back again. She forces back a wave of emotion that threatens to make her cry. Pushed by fear, tears well up in her eyes, blurring her vision.

She continues to switch her gaze back and forth. The man doesn't appear to see Beth, and Beth doesn't see him either. He gets scary close now, and Kevan focuses once more on what he carries. As he walks around the steps toward the side of the pond, she gets a full view. She watches the repetitive motion of the woman's upper body bouncing with each step, her long brown hair swaying in the breeze. Her arms and hands extend unnaturally toward the backs of the man's legs, brushing the tops of the tall grass. Kevan has never seen a dead person before, but she believes she is seeing one now. Rotating her body while staying low under the dock, Kevan watches as the man moves around to the side of the pond and stops about midway.

She doesn't want to believe there is something familiar about him.

She looks back toward Beth, who is now staring at the man, her whole body frozen in a seemingly uncomfortable posture. Kevan, in terror, realizes that Beth is seeing something she shouldn't see. What if the man sees her too?

Kevan remembers what her brother Tommy told her: *Don't go to the pond. The bad man.*

Crawling down to the water's edge, Kevan looks more closely at the man and then at the chain that runs from his front belt loop to his hip pocket. Her whole body shakes with fear.

CHAPTER FORTY-ONE

Nathan

A fly buzzes around my ear several times, lighting on my face just long enough for me to stop rotating on the wrench to swipe it away. It does this several times, each time landing on a part of my body where it's impossible to ignore. The final straw is when it bites into the skin of my neck, forcing me to stand from my stooped position to slap it into fly heaven. The fly has eaten its last meal.

Looking up, I see Dorothy walking down the gravel lane toward the back gate. It isn't unusual for Dorothy to take daily walks for exercise, but she usually sticks to the front of her property. I throw my hand up at her to gesture hello, but she doesn't notice. She walks in a trancelike state, seemingly unaware of her surroundings except for what is ahead, but she moves quickly; for a woman of her age, Dorothy walks at a factory worker's pace.

I watch until she's almost out of sight. Then, puzzled by what she's doing, I lay down my tools and decide to follow her. She slips through the back gate, and I hold back for a moment, then step closer to see which direction she turns. I then ease through the gate as well and begin to follow her.

Our walk into the woods away from Ivymond brings on recurring bouts of déjà vu. I have meandered around these woods before—either alone as a teen, or with friends. Especially after my sister disappeared. I searched these woods numerous times, not finding anything. What I don't understand is why Dorothy is in these woods today. The suspicious behavior she displayed this morning, my chat with the sheriff, and the direction she is going all lead to one conclusion: she's going to the deserted property I visited yesterday. The one that I discovered belongs to her lifelong friend. There's no doubt that she is keeping a secret about the place. What is it, and why?

Dorothy stops suddenly beside a tree, coughing, and it alarms me for a moment. I dart behind another tree and watch her from a distance, making sure she's okay. As I lean to peer around the tree, I step on a dried stick and it snaps, making a loud crack that seems to bounce from every tree, alerting her that I'm here. I silently curse when she asks, "Who's there?"

I don't want to scare her, so I give up and step out. "It's just me," I say, holding my hands up so as not to scare her. No longer walking with light feet, I hear the dried leaves crackle under my step as I approach her.

"You scared me, Nate. What are you doing?"

I see on her face that she's relieved it's me, but I also read something else. The same look I saw this morning. An enigmatic shift to her eyes that has made me question Dorothy for the first time. Her actions today are so out of character. She's usually straightforward and blunt, regardless of the situation. Today she is unsure, secretive, distracted.

After a little meaningless conversation that I don't think she's paying attention to, I ask, "You headed anywhere in particular?"

She stares at me as if the question is struggling to sink in. Her eyes reflect a conflict going on inside her head, as if she's debating an impossible decision. You can almost see the wheels turning, and she seems nearly beside herself.

"Miss Dorothy, you okay?"

"Huh? Yeah. Oh, yeah. I'm just giving my legs a good workout today."

"Do you mind if I join you?"

Dorothy stutters, "Uh, I don't want to take you away from your work. I'll be just fine on my own. But if you wish to walk, that's okay too." The tone of her voice doesn't make me feel welcome.

"Well, then, I think I will. I could use a change of scenery for a bit."

As we walk along in silence, I ponder asking her about her friend and about the property. Not sure how to bring it up, I ask, "So, how are you doing, Miss Dorothy? You lost a very close friend. Would you like to talk about her?"

"Aww, I could tell you many stories, I suppose. She was a stinker. Never a dull moment." Dorothy pauses, sounding winded. "She was a hoot, but she also knew when to be serious. Had my back more than once."

"Oh, yeah? How so?"

To my surprise, she continues, in a rambling sort of way. "I couldn't tell you the number of pickles we found ourselves in. Sometimes she caused them, and other times I did. I made some pretty stupid choices at times, but she always bailed me out. She kept us alive more than once—literally."

"Sounds like she was quite the friend." Thelma and Louise flash through my mind again.

"Oh, she was. Understand, Nate, that we women form a bond unlike any men. I don't believe a man can truly grasp the meaning of friendship—not like a woman. A woman would beg, borrow, steal, and yes, even kill for her friend. That was the kind of friend my Marge was. Frances, that is."

"I don't believe I've had a friend like that."

"Probably not. If it hadn't been for Frances, I would have lost everything I owned years ago. She could read people better than anyone. She could especially pinpoint a sleazy, slimy man, even if he was putting on the charm and others were fooled. I don't speak of my husband often, but he was a no-account son of a bitch from the beginning, and she knew that. She tried to warn me before I married him, but my pig-head wouldn't listen." Dorothy pauses, catching her breath, and then closes the conversation with, "Well—all that is ancient history now. I sure miss her, though."

Dorothy is right. I could count on one hand how many times she has mentioned her husband to me. The only conclusion I've come to from her comments is that he was a mean-ass drunk. Despite the abrupt halt to her story, I decide to barrel ahead with questions to see if she will offer anything on what she knows about the mysterious property and its connection to her friend.

"I have a pretty good idea where this path will take us," I say. "I found the place when I was a young lad. Doesn't this lead to that abandoned property where I found the dolls?"

Dorothy doesn't answer. She just picks up the pace.

After a few moments of silence, I press on. "Was this Frances a grandmother to the woman I told you about this morning?"

Dorothy's long silence speaks its own answer. Looking at her profile, I see frown lines of defeat forming as she exhales and speaks. "Walk with me, Nate—there's something I have to show you."

Satisfied for now, I walk in silence, taking in my surroundings. The cloudy, humid sky weighs overhead, and beads of sweat form on my face. Ahead, I see an opening in the woods, and the familiar scene seems to loom before me. I feel a sense of heaviness that I didn't feel before. I can't put my finger on it, but something tells me this visit promises something I'm not prepared for.

As we step out into the open, we both stop and stare, then glance at each other, confused. I see a distraught look consume Dorothy's face, but relief appears as well. I know that whatever she's been hiding is about to be set free. She walks toward the woman kneeling by the pond, and I follow a few steps behind.

CHAPTER FORTY-TWO

Kevan
Early Summer

Time stops for a moment. All I can seem to focus on is the sound of my heart pumping blood through my ears, forcing a swishing sound like a noisy ceiling fan. Episodes like this are becoming a regular occurrence in my world. I still can't make myself turn my head. In my mind, I chant the words of a childhood rhyme, as I've always done to calm myself. *One, two, buckle my shoe. Three, four, shut the door. Five, six, pick up sticks. Seven, eight, lay them straight. Nine, ten, a big fat hen.*

You're not going to be afraid of her, I tell myself.

One, two, the sky is blue. Three, four, sing some more. Five, six, stop playing tricks. Seven, eight, it's not too late. Nine, ten, look again.

I repeat the chant three times, pumping myself up. Then I turn my head toward the pond, expecting to see the little girl. Instead, Beth stands there, with her back turned. My shoulders relax, but I'm confused. I walk toward her, and as I approach, I call out, "Beth? What are you doing here?"

She doesn't turn, just stands statue-still, gazing at the water. Katydids, frogs, and crickets sing, carrying with them a memory from the time when Beth and I were little.

We're running down the steps of the dock, around the edge of the pond, to the other side. Tiptoeing into the water to our knees, looking for the frog we spotted while playing on the dock. A dorsal ridge runs down its back, and its bright green head stands out in a spot of algae it has surrounded itself with. To our surprise, the frog doesn't scare away but instead swims toward us, parting the algae with its sprawling legs.

The memory's image merges with an image of a dream, only this frog did not bear a gift.

Beth reaches down and picks the frog up and holds it between her cupped hands. We both hop out of the pond and squat down near the edge to look at the frog more closely. When Beth opens her hands, the frog just sits there. Its throat expands and contracts as if it is curious about us, instead of the other way around.

As if someone has used a hand to swipe the image to the side, out of sight, another scene slides into play.

Beth trots across the field to my left. I have walked here from the old house after looking for the dolls we hid there for later use. I've come outside to look for her.

As if trying to see the scene outside my mind, I turn my head in the direction Beth was walking in my memory. When I do, I see the little girl from before. This time, I see her more clearly. She looks just as Beth did at that age, walking toward the pond.

She is not a memory. She is very real.

I look back at the grown Beth to see her watching the little girl, who now halts and stands perfectly still. She is not looking at Beth or myself—instead she's staring just beyond the dock. She looks frightened. Noticing movement in my peripheral vision, I turn back to Beth. She's facing me now. I look back at the little girl, and like a hologram she fades away, leaving only an outline in my mind's eye.

I look at Beth again, and she smiles at me.

Confused and a little dazed, I try to shake it off while making sense of it all. "How did you know I was here?" My voice cracks and doesn't sound like my own anymore.

"I've always been here."

What she says doesn't quite register in my brain, and I look to my left again; no one is there. Puzzled, I ask, "What do you mean, always been here?"

"I'm always wherever you need me to be. You know that."

"Beth, I'm confused."

"You see her, don't you?"

"What?" I instinctively turn and look again for the little girl—she is still gone—and then I breathe a sigh of relief. "You saw her too? I thought I was losing my mind."

"Do you remember the story your Gammie told you when you were little?"

"Gammie was full of stories."

"The story about what you're capable of doing? About what it means?"

I look at Beth, puzzled. Why has she brought this up now?

"Yes—of course I remember. It seems to be all I think about these days. Her far-fetched stories about me having some sort of gift. I always thought it was all myths and old wives' tales. Even seeing that little girl—I can't explain it, but I can't believe that it's because I have some kind of magical powers. I mean, you can see her too."

Ignoring my comments, Beth asks, "Which part do you think is a myth?"

"What do you mean?"

"I mean, which part do you not believe?"

"Well, pretty much all of it."

"You see your brother Tommy sometimes, don't you?"

I stare, shocked at the turn of our conversation. At no point have I ever mentioned my recent hallucinations of my little brother. "How did you know that?"

"I know whatever you know."

"What? What do you mean?" Now I feel myself becoming defensive. I'm afraid of where this conversation is going.

"You saw him the other day when you went to visit your mother."

"I didn't tell you that, so how did you know?" I insist again.

"Like I said, I know what you know."

"Well, I know we've always been close, and sometimes it seems we read each other's thoughts, but that still doesn't explain how you know that." My voice comes out even more flustered than I feel.

"I see everything you see. I feel everything you feel."

"Beth, you're not making any sense."

"I always know when you retreat somewhere inside yourself, whenever you don't want to face something. You've done it our whole lives. Remember that time when that jerk cheated on you in college and I drove forever to come to you, or when that professor told you your art sucked and I came and threatened to beat her up? I've always been here anytime your life got tough."

"I've never asked you to do any of that."

"You don't have to, because that's what I'm here for. I have been since we were eight years old. Your need for me began back then, and I've been with you ever since."

"Yes, I know, but it still doesn't explain how you know I've been having visions of my brother."

"You've started seeing other things too. In your dreams—"

I interrupt. "Well, we both know that I've always done that. Now you sound like Gammie." Frustration alters my tone of voice.

Beth smiles. "Not like now. In your dreams, you're seeing—remembering things you buried a long time ago. I guess you could say that I've helped you bury them all these years. That's what you wanted. But, like it or not, not everything can remain buried forever. Your Gammie knew this."

For a moment, I picture myself sticking my fingers in my ears and ignoring her, like a bratty child.

"I don't understand why you're saying all this. I just do not believe in all this stuff!"

"You haven't only dreamed about events of your past, you've told the story yourself in your art. The girl, the woman—the monster. The other monster, whom you've seen through your Gammie's eyes. And you don't just see events of your own past; you see things from your grandmother's past as well. Like you, your Gammie found a way to deal with the things of her past through her art. A way to release any hold that her secrets had on her. You do the same thing with your art."

I turn my eyes to the pond, but I no longer see the view in front of me. Instead, I see Gammie's painting of the little blond-haired girl who looked like Beth. I see the painting of my father—*Monster*. And I see the painting Gammie called *The Other Monster*. They're superimposed on one another, shifting back and forth in a pattern I can't decipher.

Somehow, Gammie's art is all a part of the story of this place. But how? And how does Beth know? For the first time, I experience anger with her. "I didn't tell you about Gammie's art!"

"You didn't have to," Beth says calmly.

"Now you're just freaking me out, Beth. Where is all of this coming from?"

I see a movement again out of the corner of my eye and jerk my head to see what it is, mainly out of frustration and distraction. The little girl is there again, and this time she is running toward the pond and then crouching underneath the dock. Beth turns to look at her this time and then back at me, as if to see my expression.

"Do you recognize her?"

I stare, afraid to say anything. I don't want Beth to say any more, but she continues to talk.

"Renee? Do you recognize her?"

I blindly turn back to Beth when I hear her call me by my middle name. "What?"

"Do you know who she is?"

I only answer by shaking my head back and forth distractedly.

"You do know, Renee. Look closer." Beth's voice seems to shift backward, her words sounding as if she is a little girl again.

"Why are you calling me Renee? You haven't called me that in years." I stare at the little girl curled up under the dock, rocking back and forth.

"Renee, look deeper." Beth's voice sounds just as it did when we were kids. "Do you remember why we were crouched under the dock? Look closer—we're both there."

"Why are you doing this, Beth?"

"Because the time is now. Your Gammie very much wanted you to remember this before her death, but time ran out. She feared that her death might trigger something in you. In fact, I think she knew it would. She wanted you to grow up before you faced the things of your past. She knew your gift, and she also knew that I was here, guiding you. I've been with you ever since we were eight years old. Ever since that day. Look at her, Renee. You know who she is. You just have to let yourself see."

I feel a single tear stream down my left cheek as more tears well up in my eyes, blurring my vision. As if on cue, a cloud slides over the sun, creating a dark shadow from tree line to tree line. Something inside me pushes my legs to walk toward the pond.

Now I see two little girls crouched under the dock, one with blond hair and the other with red. They crawl into the water up to their chins and stare across the pond, their eyes full of fear.

A tense mingling of dread and knowledge boils inside my mind. I know that something horrible is about to reveal itself. The act of closing my eyes changes nothing. With it comes the pounding of my heart in my chest, throat, and then ears as everything unfolds in my mind. The noise in my ears morphs into my father's voice, his heinous words stabbing deeper than any other words that ever came from his mouth.

I've wanted to get rid of you since the day you were born.

His words ring with clarity, and it is the last thing I hear him say to me—ever.

CHAPTER FORTY-THREE

Kevan
August 27, 1996

An unbearable ringing forms in Kevan's ears—a cacophony so loud that she can't hear anything else. Although she knows this man is a cruel human being, she still can't believe what she's seeing. She pinches her arm hard to make sure she isn't inside one of her nightmares. She feels the pinch, but she does it again to make sure.

Through disbelieving eyes, she stares at her father. The woman's stiff body draped over his shoulder still doesn't move, and as Kevan looks at the side of the woman's face, she now recognizes her as well. It's their neighbor Jackie—the woman she caught her father kissing. Jackie's face is a grotesque blue-gray and her lips are a faded, ugly purple. Her arm is twisted at an angle, bent in a way that only a contortionist could achieve.

Kevan's eyes dart back to Beth, who remains a perfect statue, only her eyes moving a little. Kevan wants to run to her, grab her hand, and race out of here as fast as she can, but her gut says she should stay put.

Kevan watches her father as he slings the woman forward, letting her body slam onto the ground. The dense thud resonates inside Kevan's ears and causes her whole body to shudder. Her frantic eyes dart back to Beth. She sees her begin to tiptoe through the tall grass toward the other edge of the pond. Toward the hidden side of the dock. Kevan crawls to the underside of the steps, placing her face between the boards, hoping Beth will see her.

Clyde stands and presses his fists into his back, leaning backward. As he stretches and grunts, he tilts from side to side. He turns to look toward the house, then toward the woods in the direction from which Kevan came, and then back down at the woman on the ground. He bends forward, grabbing the woman's contorted arm, lifts her stiff upper body from the ground, then squats to pull her body across his shoulders. With one arm wrapped around her neck and another hooked around one of her legs, he stands tall. Her rigid body stretches across his back like a distorted mannequin. He wades into the water of the pond, his legs disappearing as he goes deeper. Kevan's throat swells with panic as her hiding spot becomes visible and in full view for him. If he looks toward the dock, he will see her.

Panic-stricken, she duckwalks to the edge of the water, easing herself in, trying not to create ripples. Cool water moves up her body, chilling her warm skin as she submerges herself up to her neck. She buries her fingers in the slimy mud, readying herself to dive under at a second's notice if he looks her way. To calm her nerves, she moves her lips in a silent and familiar verse: *One, two, buckle my shoe. Three, four, shut the door.* The fear scurrying in her mind shifts the chant into different words. *One, two, he's coming for you. Three, four, hide some more. Five, six, do something quick. Seven, eight, it's too late. Nine, ten, the monster again.*

Seizing the opportunity as Clyde wades into the water with his back to her, Beth sprints to the dock and crawls underneath, then crouches. Kevan nods her head for Beth to join her in the water. The girls move themselves away from the bank to where the water level is just below their noses. Kevan turns wide eyes back to her father, who stops far enough into the pond for the water to reach just above his waist. He slings the woman's body off to the side, toward where the pond deepens.

A loud splash echoes off the trees and all around as the water ripples in large waves spreading outward, toward the girls. Kevan and Beth watch in horror as the woman's body sinks slowly out of view. The girls begin to bob up and down in the water as it pulls them away from land. They lean backward, trying to hold themselves in place, yet beyond their control, their heads submerge. The water quickly recedes and rises, again and again. Each time, they take in a mouthful of the muddy water and gasp, trying not to cough. Beth begins to choke. Kevan shushes her and looks to see if Clyde has noticed them.

He pauses, turns in their direction, scrunches his eyes, and leans forward. He focuses all of his attention toward them. Kevan's heart pounds against the wall of her chest so hard it hurts. She takes a deep breath and pulls her head underwater again. Beth follows her lead but is still struggling not to choke; she has to come back up for air, coughing uncontrollably.

"What the hell are you doing out here?" comes a hateful shout.

Kevan is trembling all over. Even with water plugging her ears, she can hear Beth's muffled coughs. Despite the blanket of water covering her, every noise seems intensified, rendering her unable to remain calm. Muffled cicadas scream and frogs yelp as if they are voicing their fear for her.

"I said, what the fuck are you doing out here?" Clyde yells. He begins to kick his way toward the dock, his strides tossing up large splashes of water. Beth panics and scrambles her way out from under the dock, a frantic crawl out of the water.

Stomping out of the pond, Clyde closes the ground between himself and Beth quickly, grabbing a handful of hair, yanking her backward. Beth screams. Gripping her upper arm, he jerks her around to face him and yells, "Where the hell did you come from? You here alone?" Droplets of spit cover Beth's face as he shouts the words at her. She is sobbing now, inhaling in short, quick breaths but unable to answer. Clyde stands and looks around in all directions once more and then barks again, "Anyone here with you?"

Beth jerks her head from side to side, continuing to sob. Clyde stands and looks around at every angle to make sure there's no one there. "You're in the wrong place at the wrong time, you little shit. You saw, didn't you?"

She continues to shake her head from side to side in short, quick movements, but she still can't say anything. She darts her eyes back toward the dock, searching for Kevan, but she can't see her. Clyde drags her back to the pond as she fights against him. It is useless. She tries to speak now, but her words are unrecognizable between her crying and coughing. She pleads with him to let her go. The only understandable words are, "I want my mommy."

Beth's white sundress sends streams of water down her legs as it clings to her small body. Clyde drags her by the arm, along with a fistful of her long hair, back into the water. Water flies up and out, filling Beth's face.

She screams, "Renee! Help! Please!"

These are the last words to echo across the air as Clyde shoves Beth's body down into the water, holding her under. She flails her arms and legs, scrambling to break free. Her arms move in wide, frantic swings, but she is no match for his strength. Bubbles rise all around her and her movements begin to slow, becoming weaker.

A hollow thud rings out just as Clyde feels it across his back. He releases Beth and stands to see what has hit him. Kevan is standing behind him with a thick tree limb in both hands. She swings again, hitting him on the side of the head. He stumbles, trying to catch himself, but fails and falls back into the water. She throws the piece of wood aside and attempts to wade in to Beth, but her father's hand grabs a fistful of her hair, yanking her sideways and down, forcing her to fight to stay above water. She punches him with all her might, trying to fight him off. It doesn't seem to faze him, even when she makes contact with his face. He picks her up, wrapping both arms around her, pinning her against his chest.

"What the hell are you doing out here, you little twat?"

Kevan turns to look at Beth, but Beth hasn't moved. Her body is facedown on the bottom of the pond a couple of feet below the surface of the water. Her white dress floats out away from her body.

"Beth!" Kevan screams. Then, to her father, "Let me go!" She jerks and kicks in all directions, but she might as well be tied up, because his grip prevents her from budging.

"How much did you see, you little shit?"

"Beth! Beth!" Kevan screams over and over, continuing to fight.

"Shut up, you little bitch. I'm not gonna let you go home after this." Clyde's words come out choppy under the strain of keeping Kevan contained as she wiggles to get free.

"Let me go!" Kevan screams in a high-pitched squeal.

Clyde looks around in all directions again and says, "Go ahead—scream. No one will hear you." He takes a few steps into the pond, past Beth's tiny, lifeless body. In a low, threatening tone, he says into Kevan's ear, "I've wanted to get rid of you since the day you were born." He bends forward and slams her face and upper body underwater, holding her there firmly with both hands.

She holds her breath and fights.

At first, Kevan's struggle against her father's grip is fierce as she swings her arms and kicks her legs, but then a voice inside her head tells her to calm down. The voice sounds like Beth's.

Instinct begins to take over, and she thinks about some of the things Gammie has taught her about swimming, especially about being able to stay underwater longer. She and Gammie have swum in this pond many times. Also, against Gammie's wishes, she and Beth have swum without Gammie's supervision when they've met up here. She's taught Beth all the things that Gammie has taught her. One of them is how to float both faceup and facedown.

When Gammie had taught Kevan how to float, she'd told her that the more calm and relaxed she was, the longer she could hold herself underwater without needing to come up for air. She and Beth had played this game where they floated facedown, pretending to be dead, and held their breath as long as they could. Kevan could always hold her breath longer. Beth could never hold it for very long.

Even though her father's grip is holding her down now, Kevan sends her mind to that game. She becomes motionless and sets her eyes in a half-open position. Just as she was taught. She relaxes her tongue slightly away from the roof of her mouth, lets her body go limp, and releases a slow, steady stream of air from her mouth and nose. Bubbles scatter around her, making their way to the surface.

Like a small whisper, she hears her brother Tommy say, *You won't drown*. His voice repeats it again, sweet and gentle, soothing her. *You won't drown*. She hears each word again, slow and calm.

Her body becomes like a rag doll, almost lifeless, as she feels Clyde's grip loosen. As his hands release her, she remains relaxed as she would when she and Beth would play their game. Everything goes quiet. Time seems to slow as she descends through the water like a feather drifting on a light breeze. Her mind is taking her somewhere else as she sinks farther and farther down. No longer scared, she begins to feel herself drifting into peaceful waters, somewhere else—away. She must be floating in a dream. She lets herself fall into it. Her body drifts, tilts, and rotates facedown and then face-up again. She sees Beth looking down at her, smiling gently. Sinking lower, she sees Jackie's dark hair floating out to all sides, her arms drifting outward as if she is reaching out for an embrace.

As Kevan's eyes begin to close, the light on the surface of the water moves on the ripples, back and forth, back and forth.

CHAPTER FORTY-FOUR

Kevan
August 27, 1996

Kevan's body bobs up and down in the water, yet she floats far below its surface. Something wraps around her shoulder and arm and then around her other arm. She imagines vines spreading and expanding, coiling themselves around her body. They pull at her. She wonders if she should fight against them or just let them have her. Maybe their embrace would be permanent—safe.

You won't drown, comes Tommy's whisper again.

She opens her eyes and searches for him. At least she thinks she does. Confusion makes its entrance, and she tries to understand why she is here. She has been holding her breath for so long. The vines tug at her harder as she feels her body being pulled upward.

It won't be long now, she hears someone whisper, but it isn't Tommy's voice this time. Still rising, she looks to her left through partially parted eyelids and sees Beth paddling alongside her. Beth waves for Kevan to follow and then points upward. The hold on one of Kevan's arms grips tighter—pulls at her harder. She feels her face break the surface of the water and immediately air gushes into her lungs, sending a tingling sensation all over her body as her limbs reap the rewards of oxygen.

Now, cradled in someone's embrace, she is being carried from the water. Splashing sounds echo in her ears as her body jars up and down, and then it feels as if the warm earth rises to meet her. She allows her head to rest on it, feeling tiny tickles brush her face, sliding back and forth along with a gentle breeze. After another gush of air into her lungs, Kevan coughs and feels her upper body being lifted and hugged close to someone's chest.

"Renee, you're going to be okay. You're going to be okay."

Kevan smells honeysuckle and realizes right away that Gammie is the one holding her. She hears another woman's voice and, for a moment, feels even more disoriented than before. As she is being rocked back and forth, she can feel water sloshing inside her ears, and it hinders her sense of hearing. The other voice sounds familiar, yet out of place. She tries to get her bearings, but dizziness takes over. Her ear is pressed firmly against Gammie's chest, and she can hear and feel her whispering something to the other person. The words sound like nothing more than a mumble, and she tries hard to understand, but she can't.

Then the familiar stranger responds, and Kevan can make out a few words: "We must get Kevan out of here."

Here? Where is here? Kevan tries to remember. She has no idea where she is. For some reason, she can't open her eyes no matter how hard she tries to convince her eyelids to do it. Gammie continues to whisper, and then Kevan hears another strange voice say, "You take Kevan home and we'll take care of the rest."

Take care of what? Wait. What's going on? Why am I here? Is Beth here? Maybe she didn't get to come today. Why did I go swimming by myself? Her mind swarms in a frenzy as she tries to stay alert. She is drowsy and dizzier than before, and for a moment she feels as if she's still floating in water. She can feel the movement of the water rippling up and down.

Again she questions why she went swimming. If her mother finds out, she'll be in trouble, especially for going out of hearing distance from her house. She has to say something to Gammie. Gammie can't take her home yet—not until she has time to dry. But Kevan is too exhausted to say so. She succumbs to the certainty that Gammie will take care of her and allows herself to fall asleep.

What seems like only moments later, Kevan opens her eyes to see pale yellow material covered in flowers. She feels something furry and soft tucked under her chin and realizes that it covers her whole body. Rolling over onto her back, she pushes the blanket down and looks toward the ceiling, fixing her eyes on the spinning blades of the fan. She knows where she is now.

"Well, hello, sleepyhead."

Kevan jerks her head around and sees Gammie seated in the chair in the corner of the room. Kevan sits up, kicking off the blanket. When she looks down, she sees she is dressed in her favorite nightgown, given to her by Gammie for sleepovers. She looks down at it for a hard few seconds, trying to determine when she came over to Gammie's.

"What's wrong, my dear?"

"I don't remember coming here, Gammie."

Gammie chuckles. "What do you mean, you don't remember?"

"I mean, I must have sleepwalked, because I don't remember coming to your house."

"Tell me what you do remember."

Kevan rolls her eyes upward and ponders for a moment. "The last thing I remember is going to bed, but I sneaked and stayed up with a flashlight, reading my book."

"You sure that's the last thing you remember?"

"Yep."

"Well, then, I guess you must have sleepwalked over here," Gammie says with a nervous chuckle. "You've been sleeping for quite a while. How about a snack, my girl?"

"I'm as hungry as a hippo," Kevan says and hops up from the couch. Gammie takes Kevan by the hand and leads her to the kitchen.

"I'll fix you whatever your little belly desires."

"I love you, Gammie."

"I love you too, my dear."

CHAPTER FORTY-FIVE

Kevan
Early Summer

This memory has been with me all along, but my mind kept it a secret. Our minds are equipped to store information better than any computer. However, a computer obeys and does what we tell it to. The brain often goes astray, and it will completely rewire itself so it can do its job under stress. Its goal is to protect its vessel at all costs.

Sometimes the mind will malfunction on purpose.

The trauma of witnessing my best friend being drowned by my own father compelled my mind to protect itself. When I couldn't cope with what had happened to Beth, it had no other choice but to initiate amnesia.

I've read about the ability to develop dissociative amnesia—to erase an event from one's mind as a safety mechanism. I always thought it was just a theory, or maybe even a cop-out for those who want to escape or hide from something—or someone. How many times have I done this in my life, either voluntarily or involuntarily? I certainly hope there aren't more hidden memories lurking in my head.

The loud *jug-o-rum* of a bullfrog brings me back to myself. I feel my breath laboring against nausea as I realize I am kneeling on the ground next to the pond. I have no idea how long I've been sitting here. Beth is kneeling next to me. I stare at her, dumbfounded, as the realization sinks in.

She isn't real.

My friend Beth actually died, right here, twenty-six years ago.

I force myself to swallow several times in an attempt to produce enough saliva to speak. "Why didn't you tell me?"

"I couldn't. I was here to protect you."

"But—" I stutter, searching through my list of questions for the one that I need to ask first. There are so many. How can I ever understand any of this? "But how did you know you were supposed to do that? How were you able to do *anything* after what happened to you?"

"I didn't remember what had happened to me—I mean, not like a person does when they're alive. My only goal was to keep you safe. I had to make sure you made it out that day, even though I didn't. And then I stayed, because you still needed me."

I bury my face in my hands and shake my head as I mumble, "This doesn't make any sense."

"Like I told you before, you're special. Your Gammie knew it all along. She knew it from the day you were born."

"Am I the only person who can see you?"

"Yes."

"How do you seem so real? Like . . . alive?"

"I'm whatever you need. I'm all the things you want to see, as well as the things you wish to see in yourself. Bold. Confident. Maybe a bit of an extrovert, which is the complete opposite of you. I'm who you need me to be whenever you need it. You needed me so much that you never even realized I only existed inside your private world. I was never with you in public. Never outside of your personal bubble."

I search Beth's face, eyes, and the outline of her head, looking for some sort of glowing light or maybe even a halo. The sort of thing one would see in a Hollywood film. There is nothing—just the same Beth I've seen for years.

"Did Gammie know about you?" I ask.

"She knew I existed only because you still talked about me. She didn't think you were crazy or that I was just some imaginary friend. Her belief was that spirits would accompany you throughout your life —and they have. Not just me."

Apprehensive, I ask, "Tommy?"

"Yes. There have been others as well—you just didn't realize it. Spirits are everywhere in this world, but only a select few get to interact with the living. You're one of the lucky ones who can. I wasn't the first one to be by your side, nor will I be the last one."

"But you grew up. I still see Tommy as a little boy."

"That's how you wanted it."

I stare into the water of the pond and fix my eyes on a swirl of minnows, zigzagging in one direction, then the next—much like the pattern my mind is moving in.

"Are you the one who pulled me out of the water?"

"I gave you the courage to survive until you could be pulled from the water. I was there to help you relax and hold your breath as long as you needed to. To keep you from drowning."

"Who pulled me from the water?"

Beth smiles. "A woman who has loved you all of your life."

I feel my lips curl into a half smile. Gammie saved me more than once from metaphorically drowning in the chaotic world I grew up in. Now I know she saved me from actually drowning too. I know she had a reason for keeping this a secret, but a small part of me is angry with her for doing so.

As if Beth can read my thoughts, she explains, "Your Gammie knew that the time for you to know all this was not right after it happened, and not even after you were grown. She felt she needed to wait until you were ready."

"I'm not so sure that I'm ready now."

"You are."

I divert my eyes from Beth and inhale as I take in my surroundings. My gaze moves upward, taking in the patterns of clouds and the blue sky in between. It seems I've spent most of my life looking down, avoiding the world around me. I've locked myself inside a protective bubble so that nothing and no one can hurt me. Now it feels as if I'm seeing my surroundings for the first time and through clearer eyes. Not just my immediate surroundings, but my entire world. I have been walking in the dark. Now, suddenly, it's as if someone has turned on all the lights and opened all the window shades.

"What happened to my father?"

This time it's Beth who turns to look away. "Gammie believed in the rule of karma: Whatever you put into this universe will come back to you. Let's just say it did for your father. This place is where his trail of hurt and heartbreak began and where it ended—for everyone."

I focus on a new swirl of minnows that are tinier and swim in a frenzy much faster than the others. I watch them scurry, often moving head-on toward one another but somehow always avoiding a collision. For years now, I've been on a collision course with this significant event of my past, but I've managed to dodge it until now. I'm just finding it all out, but Gammie had to live with it most of her life. Each piece of art that I saw in Gammie's studio reenters my thoughts as I realize that her art was her way of telling a secret she couldn't speak out loud. I'm still not sure I want to know the details of what she had to do that day, but I can only assume that she is why my father disappeared. She had the horrific burden of eradicating her own son. How awful that must have been for her.

I stare at the minnows until my eyes begin to bounce and it makes me dizzy.

"What else would you like to know?" Beth interrupts my thoughts.

Without looking up, I answer, "I don't think I want to know any more about that day—at least for now—but tell me this: Are you the little girl who disappeared all those years ago? Are you Gracie?"

"I was, yes. If you remember, we decided to call each other by our middle names. You said Elizabeth was too long to write, so you called me Beth."

"Yeah, I think I remember now. I also remember when we would play on the dock, drawing and such—you drew your family once. You drew your annoying older brother and your mother. I think I remember you drawing a grandmother?"

"It was my godmother—and yes, I had an annoying older brother, and there was my mother."

"Haven't you missed them over the years?"

"It isn't like that. I remember them, but not in the way a living person would. It's like—I know of them, but all I really know is my purpose for being now. I don't miss them or anything like that. I don't think I'm supposed to. I'm here to help take care of you. That day, I gained a new purpose. Does that make sense?"

I nod but say nothing.

"I'm not sure how to explain it. We all come back as something. This is what I came back as."

I press my lips together and take a long breath. "I believe I met your brother. The tall guy with the gorgeous eyes that I told you about? It was him."

"I know."

I raise both eyebrows and smile. Beth and I sit in silence for what seems like an eternity. The silence stretches time like a rubber band, but it quickly bounces back to reality.

"I think I need to tell him what happened to you, but I'm not sure how," I say.

"You won't have to do it alone. She will help you." Beth nods her head to the left and looks past me. I turn and see an elderly woman walking toward me—and Nathan is with her. My eyes grow wide, and I swallow hard.

"Looks like it's time," Beth whispers.

I stand, brush off my legs with my hands, and face the woman. To my relief, she speaks first.

"You must be Kevan. I'm Dorothy, and I was your Gammie's best friend." She reaches out her hand and I take it and then look at Nathan, who is standing behind her. He smiles and nods.

"I think we have lots to talk about," Dorothy says. "All three of us."

"All *four* of us," I correct her, and I turn to Beth, but she has vanished. Somehow I know that I will never see her again. I am filled with sadness but also a sense of peace: Both of us are now where we are meant to be.

I take a deep breath, blink tears from my eyes, and turn back to Dorothy and Nathan.

"Okay," I say. "I'm ready."

CHAPTER FORTY-SIX

———

Kevan
End of Summer

I slip off my black high heels once I step through the squeaky screen door and ease it closed behind me. The smell of stale cigarette smoke looms in the air, carrying with it the image of my mother staring out the kitchen window. I move my eyes across the stained walls and furniture—everything scarred with discoloration. Scarred like the lives that have been lived here. Every inch is a testament to the trauma endured inside these walls. Like a dead plant deprived of light and water, this house, its contents, and its people were never nourished as they should have been.

I force myself to take a few more steps into the house and breathe in the house's wounds—and my own. The hollow feeling I get when I visit this place is not different from before. The only difference is that the dread of coming here has shifted into something else. No confrontation, just a longing, lonely quiet.

There is something about funerals and burials that has a way of draining every ounce of emotion and energy from your body, leaving behind a hull of empty space. It doesn't matter whether you're close to the person you've laid to rest or not. Something about the entire process takes away your own existence for a short while and robs you of all feeling—replacing it with a numb existence. I exhale and look around the small house, trying to figure out where I should begin with cleaning out my mother's things. Following my mother's death, my brother Matthew told me she had actually left behind a last will and testament and that I was in it. I found it hard to believe that she had left me anything. Truth be told, there isn't anything of emotional value that I wish to take with me. But she included me, after all.

Going through the belongings of this house is not a task I am prepared for, but it was one of my mother's wishes. I'm not sure why. Maybe she knew that if she left it to my brothers, they would never part with any of it. My goal today is to pack up whatever I can and give it to those in need. I've already given my brothers a couple of days to take what they wished to have. They stuck around all these years, so it's only right.

Stepping down the narrow hallway to my mother's room, I don't avoid looking in the mirror. I'm not afraid anymore of what I might see there. I realize now that my fear of looking into the mirror was solely because of my troubled childhood and overactive dreams. Both of which no longer plague me. Something tells me that the mean ghosts of my past are gone from my life for good—at least, the latent ones that lurked around before.

I step my bare foot onto the old, shaggy carpet that has been sham-pooed so many times that the shag is threadbare, showing the rough, brown layer underneath. It's obvious as I look around my mother's room that my brothers haven't touched this part of the house. I'm not sure if it's too painful for them or if it's just the old-fashioned belief that a man shouldn't go through a woman's private things. A little golden rule Gammie taught them. My mother had her own rule, which was that we shouldn't touch anything in her room. In fact, our parents' room was off-limits altogether. She was more serious about this rule after my father left. I always wondered what was in here that she wanted to keep a secret.

Feeling overwhelmed as the numbness wears off, I pull the snug lower half of my dress up slightly and sit down on the edge of her bed. This room smells similar to the rest of the house, but combined with her favorite perfume. I feel a sense of loss as I look around the room, but nothing like I did when I lost Gammie. The connection and bond that should exist between a mother and daughter were never there for my mother and me.

I scan the tops of the bedroom furniture, which have collected a layer of dust. Sitting on top of my mother's dresser is a small, standing jewelry box that resembles a miniature curio cabinet. The front is made of glass, and inside are hooks and tiny shelves. Its interior lost the ability to light up long ago. I stand and look at the pieces that rest inside. My mother owned little jewelry of any worth. My father hocked most of what she had inherited from her own mother. He believed that what was hers was his, but it wasn't the other way around.

Lying on the top shelf is a vintage silver hair comb that I saw her wear many Sundays to church. She had convinced my father that it was fake and worthless. He must have believed her, because she still had it after all these years. I remember her telling me she had told him a little white lie and that it wasn't wrong because it was part of her "go to worship the Lord" attire. She claimed God would forgive the lie because it was for Him. I had forgotten that until now. It's funny the little things you remember about a person when you know they've left you for good. It's almost as if someone wipes off a dirty window inside your mind and you can see things you couldn't see before. I have done that a lot over the past couple of days.

I open one of the top drawers on the dresser and finger the items inside. The drawer contains mostly worn-out bras and panties and a couple of handkerchiefs that belonged to my mother's father. Sliding the drawer closed, I open another and find stacks of old letters from my father's military days as well as old Christmas cards from a distant branch of the family. There are a few drawings from my brothers, with only a couple from me. Giving my parents drawings with hearts and the words *I love you* wasn't something I felt the urge to do as a child.

I go through the rest of the drawers and then move to the side of the bed and open the drawer on the nightstand. I find things you might expect to find in a bedside table, like chap stick and lotion. In the far back is a small cigar box, the old kind that has a flip-top lid. Its lid is taped shut with a single piece of tape. I maneuver the box out of the drawer and use my thumbnail to cut the piece of tape. Inside the box, I find a heart-shaped locket without a chain. My father had found the chain, no doubt, but somehow my mother had kept the locket. Though the memory is very vague, I remember seeing her wear it to church on Sunday mornings. It hung on a thin gold chain that was long enough for it to rest just at her cleavage line. She didn't show her cleavage very often, and I remember my father telling her she looked like a hooker and accusing her of lying about heading to church.

Using my fingernail to snap the locket open, I find a tiny, faded photograph of my brothers and me.

I close the locket and lay it back in the box. Then I pick up an antique watch, its hands long stalled in place. It, too, is made of silver, and engraved on the back are my mother's initials. I have never seen it before, but I assume it was a gift from her parents. Another piece that my father didn't know about. I guess my mother had her share of secrets after all.

The last item in the box is a small key—much like one that would unlock a safe deposit box. I remember seeing one just like this as a kid. It went to a black metal box that my parents kept money in from their small business. I think for a moment and try to determine if I have seen the box anywhere today. Dismissing the thought, I put everything back in the drawer and leave the box where I found it.

I begin the task I came here for, sifting through my mother's things, my motions like those of a robot—not thinking, just working. After sorting and packing for several hours, I finally finish and stack all the boxes near the front door. I contact the pastor of my mother's church and arrange a time for him to come by and collect everything.

Just for old times' sake, I step into my old room, which remains void of my existence. The walls are still bare, and the smell is the same as the rest of the house. I walk to the bed and slide it from the wall, wanting to check out my old hiding spot one more time. There's nothing inside, but I go through the ritual of doing it anyway. I lift the loose carpet and board and peer into the hole. To my surprise, it isn't empty after all. I see something white. Puzzled, I reach in and grab it. It is a small, white envelope, and written on the outside are the words *I found your hiding spot.*

My heart skips a beat. Stunned, I stand and stare at the writing. I recognize my mother's penmanship. I smile. I flop back on the bed, and it creaks from age and lack of use. The sealed envelope has a letter from my mother inside. I immediately note that there is no *Dear* or *Dearest* in the salutation. Just my name.

Kevan,

I didn't find your hiding spot, actually, because I always knew it was here. Every girl should have one. Especially one that she can hide from the prying eyes of a man. However, your spot is very clever. Let's see if you can find mine.

I look up, wide-eyed, and grin slightly. Puzzled by her words, I feel a hint of excitement and shock.

You are welcome to look for it and if you can find it, then you will find the rest of this letter. If you can't find it, then I guess it will remain my secret forever. We didn't always see eye to eye, and I know you believed that I always put your father first, but I can tell you I really didn't. The sacrifices I made were for your brothers and you. I made mistakes like every parent, but in the end, I chose you. I hope in time you will know just how much I did. Whether or not you believe it, I love you very much. That never changed. Take care, my girl.

Love, Mom

I read it a second time and a third. Without moving anything back into place, I dart from my room back to hers. She said that my spot was clever, so I guess hers will be too. The first place I check is at the head of her bed, just like mine, but I find nothing. Next I check her closet, around the walls and the floor, and still find nothing.

I feel as if my mother is playing a game with me like she used to do when I was very little—back before our lives turned to complete shit. These play times didn't happen often, because my mother was always too busy pacifying my father or trying to earn a dollar to support our family. I vaguely remember her playing hide-and-go-seek with me and my brothers. Her favorite hiding spot was always in the hall closet.

I step back into the hall and flip on the light switch on the wall outside the closet door. Inside the closet, I find an ancient Electrolux vacuum cleaner, a broom, and some old coats that have been hanging here since I was a child. I pull the vacuum and other items out into the hall and kneel to see if there are any hidden spaces in the floor. Again, I find nothing. After rubbing my hands along the walls and coming up empty, I go to the kitchen to retrieve a chair so that I can search up higher in the closet.

I climb onto the chair. On the back wall above the top shelf, I find that the wall is covered in cheap contact paper, whereas the rest of the closet is not. The contact paper is something I don't remember—not that I would have been able to see it anyway. I still find it odd, though. I debate for a moment and think, *Screw it.* To peel the contact paper away from the wall, I use my finger to pick at the corner. The paper seems as if it has been peeled back before and then put back into place. Once I've peeled half the paper from the wall, I see an opening behind it. I remove the rest and find a hole cut out of the drywall, about the width and height of a sheet of paper.

"Clever spot, Mother," I say aloud.

Someone has wedged a piece of wood across the space, to keep whatever items were placed inside from sliding all the way down the wall. Standing on my tiptoes, I peer in and see, propped up against the back wall, the black metal lockbox. I twist it out of the space and step down from the chair. Remembering the key, I walk back to the bedroom, sit on the bed next to the nightstand, and take it from the cigar box. It fits, just as I'd suspected it would. When I open the lid, my breath catches, and I drop the box. It hits the floor with a clanging thud, and the single item inside falls free, making a pinging sound along with another light thud.

I stare at it, holding my breath, and then actually say aloud, "How the hell did she get this?"

Not able to move just yet, I see that wedged inside the lid of the black box is another envelope. On the outside I see my name, written once more in my mother's handwriting. This time she has written my whole name: *Kevan Renee Mays*.

CHAPTER FORTY-SEVEN

Frances and Dorothy
August 27, 1996

The glare of the sun does nothing to block the scene Frances and Dorothy see unfolding in front of them as they step out of the woods. They glance at each other, bewildered for a millisecond, and then run toward the pond.

A thick lump forms and wedges itself in Frances's throat, and she can't swallow it away. Dorothy runs alongside her. Desperate to understand what is happening, Frances feels as if they are running in slow motion, yet everything seems to happen at fast-forward speed.

Frances fixes her eyes ahead, seeing the man hunched over, holding something down in the water. As she nears the pond, though, her attention is drawn by something below the surface, a misshapen bubble that resembles a white pillowcase—but something tells her it is much more than that, and terror clamps her throat. When she and Dorothy get closer, they see slithers of blond hair swaying and swirling in the water like webs, and then they see the small, pale face obscured by that drifting hair. Frances hears Dorothy gasp. Both of them know

—even looking at her through the murky water, even in their panic, somehow they know for certain—that this child is past any help they can give.

Then something else in the water catches Frances's eye, and there is no mistaking that it is human too. She resists the urge to retch. For a moment, everything before them seems like a bad dream.

Confused more than ever, they spot a woman running into the water, gripping something large in her hands. She swings it hard at the man's head, bashing it against his skull. His bent-over body falls to the side, splashing into the water, leaving a swirl of red streaks through the waves as he flails his arms and legs. The woman rushes forward and scoops up what he was holding underwater. Dorothy and Frances watch in horror as they realize she is carrying a small child. Frances immediately recognizes the child when she sees the long red hair matted to her face and the tiny arms that hang toward the ground. Then she looks up and recognizes the woman too. Frances can't believe what she's seeing.

Edith looks up and sees Frances and Dorothy. Screaming to them for help, she lays the small body on the ground and turns to run back into the pond. Her feet stomp and kick their way toward the other small body in the water. Before she can reach it, Clyde grabs her by the neck, yanking her backward. She yelps but shows no fear as she forms a fist, hurling herself free, leaving a wad of her hair in his hand. She hits him square in the nose, then swings again. Not backing down, she punches and shoves over and over, until he loses his balance, falls backward, and drags her with him. They both disappear underwater for only a moment, and then Edith flings herself up and away from his grip. She finds the hunk of wood again, and as he rises out of the water, she swings it at his head. He blocks the blow with his arm, so she tries again, but he is too quick for her.

On the bank, Frances is checking for Kevan's pulse and finds a faint, slow beat. Kevan's chest rises and falls in the smallest of movements, but she remains unconscious. Frances hugs her to her chest and turns to see Dorothy charging into the water.

Just as Dorothy reaches them, Clyde shoves Edith backward and swings at Dorothy. She tries to dodge, but his fist makes contact with the side of her head, forcing her to fall. He reaches and wraps an arm around her throat. Edith pauses with the hunk of wood held high, trying to aim so that she can strike a solid blow to Clyde without harming Dorothy.

Frances lays Kevan gently on the ground and stands to charge in.

A loud crack rips through the air, echoing off the trees. Clyde, startled, releases Dorothy as they all look up in shock and confusion.

Sheriff Kenny is walking toward them, his gun aimed straight at Clyde.

As Clyde staggers in place, looking at the sheriff, a different crack sounds as the jagged piece of wood makes contact with the back of Clyde's skull. His eyes bulge wide and he stares straight ahead as if he is no longer seeing anything. Blood seeps down his wet, greasy hair, and his body falls forward.

Edith drops the piece of wood and follows his body. She bends down and places both knees on top of his back, holding him underwater. The sheriff reaches the pond and he, Frances, and Dorothy watch as Edith holds the monster down. None of them move to stop her. Bubbles rise to the surface, first in rapid succession but quickly slowing to the tiniest plopping sounds, and then they stop. Out of breath, the woman steps one foot, then the other onto the bottom of the pond and rises to look everyone in the eye. They all stare back at her, silent.

Frances steps deeper into the pond and scoops up the blond girl, bringing her to rest beside Kevan, who remains as if she is asleep. They all recognize the pale, still face: Grace Hill. Sheriff Kenny removes his hat, his face collapsing in sadness. Dorothy begins to sob as she kneels down and scoops up her goddaughter, cradling the little girl in her arms, rocking back and forth.

Frances kneels next to her, picks Kevan up, and cradles her as well. She reaches out to place a hand on Dorothy's back. Once Dorothy's crying slows to where she can speak, she looks at Frances and asks, "What do we do now?"

Sheriff Kenny answers her question. "This is something we're going to take care of ourselves."

Frances hugs Kevan in close to her chest and says, "Renee, you're going to be okay. You're going to be okay."

Frances and Dorothy hold the girls for a while longer and Edith squats down between them. Frances looks at her and says, "We must get Kevan out of here." They stare at each other in complete silence, their eyes solemn and understanding. Frances hands Kevan over to her mother, who embraces her little body tightly, stroking her hair.

Sheriff Kenny helps Edith to stand and says, "You take Kevan home and we'll take care of the rest."

Edith nods in silence. Then she walks toward the woods, carrying Kevan in her arms. They all watch until she disappears from sight.

"Unless we want to explain everything that happened here today, we're going to have to make it all disappear," Sheriff Kenny tells them. "You ladies think you can stomach this? If not, I'll take care of it myself."

Frances and Dorothy look at each other and nod.

"We've handled much worse in our days, Sheriff," Frances replies.

Out of habit, Sheriff Kenny hooks his thumbs behind his red suspenders and stretches them toward the center of his chest, interlacing his fingers. He lets out a small chuckle as he says, "I can't say I'm surprised to hear that." His face takes on a pondering look for a moment, and then he asks, "So, Frances, do you still have the deed to this property in your possession?"

Frances nods.

"Good. Keep it that way. This land must stay in your possession from now on. You can't sell it, and you can't ever file the deed at the courthouse. I'm guessing there's a reason you never put it in your name or filed it to begin with. I don't want to know, but it'll have to stay that way. Understand?"

"I understand."

Sheriff Kenny releases his suspenders and pulls at his pants before he wades into the water. He hooks his fingers into Clyde's belt and drags his body out of the water. Next, he unhooks the chain from Clyde's belt loop and pulls the black wallet from his pocket. Kenny stands and pushes both of his hands into his lower back, arching it slightly while sticking out the beginnings of a potbelly. He takes a moment to catch his breath, then steps forward and hands the wallet to Frances. She takes it without a word.

"You two go get a few things. Clothes, blankets, whatever you think we need—so that we can give the girl and the woman a proper burial. Frances, I'll leave it up to you on what we're going to do with him," he says as he points to Clyde's body without turning his head to look.

Frances stares at the wallet in her hand and then at her son, no tears forming in her eyes. She lost him before he was even born. He came into this world doomed from the beginning by the genes passed down to him. He brought hell to everyone around him, and she firmly believes that the pain he's put into this world has now simply come back to him, like a boomerang.

Clearing her throat, she says, "He came into this world a ball of hellfire, and he needs to leave that way."

Frances and Dorothy glance at each other, eyebrows lifted, and then they both turn to look past the house and cellar. Sheriff Kenny follows their gaze to the old kiln. It has taken care of a monster for them before. This monster will leave in the same way.

CHAPTER FORTY-EIGHT

Nathan

Dorothy stops speaking, and I stare out ahead of me, not sure of what to say or how to feel. For a moment, I feel as if I'm outside myself—it's like a bad dream, or a horror story gone wrong. At first I'm angry—angrier than I have ever been in my life. Everything around me fades into a white haze, and I feel the urge to stomp away. I'm not sure if I need to get a grip on my anger to avoid saying or doing something I'll regret, or just to keep from running away from what I've just heard.

"Excuse me." I walk away, calmly, and stop when I reach the edge of the pond. I stare out across the green water so that I can hold my thoughts and feelings hostage until I've calmed them.

Dorothy has known all this time what happened to my sister. She let my mother and me believe Grace had been kidnapped, or worse, and she let us search for her aimlessly. The water in front of me blurs, and the soothing sounds of nature transform into chaotic noise ringing in my ears. I hadn't expected a happy ending, but this is beyond anything I could have imagined. I clench my teeth, forcing my jaw muscles to expand and contract. I can tell that my blood pressure has risen to an uncomfortable level, and I take a quick inhale and close my eyes for a moment.

My mind reasons with the rest of my body that Dorothy didn't have a choice, and I force my muscles to relax. Life is only a long series of choices. We have to make them, and often we choose the wrong option. Humanity should make a person choose the right one, but in this instance, there was no right or wrong; there was only what needed to be done, and Dorothy, Frances, Edith, and Sheriff Kenny did it. Would I have done the same thing? I turn the mirror on myself and realize I'm not sure I could have handled it any better, given the circumstances.

I force my thoughts to shift to Kevan and what she must have gone through that day. It was so traumatic that she completely blocked it from her memory. What kind of man kills innocent children? My anger shifts, and now it's directed at the fact that I couldn't be the one to hurt the man who took my sister's life. I also feel anger that because of Clyde's terrible actions, Dorothy had to make such a decision and then live with it for the rest of her life.

I spend some more time calming my thoughts by staring into the green water of the pond. As I sort through my thoughts to gain my composure, I feel the anger dissipate. I turn to look at the two women seated on the old porch, and my rage subsides as sympathy takes root. Instead of being selfishly distraught about what I believe was done wrong or what should have been done differently, I tell myself that having knowledge of it would not have changed what happened. Nothing would have brought my sister back.

Dorothy has moved closer to Kevan now and sits next to her with one arm draped around her shoulder, while Kevan rests her head in the curve of Dorothy's neck. Looking at the two of them, my anger melts away. How horrible it must be to remember after all these years that your own father tried to kill you and succeeded at killing your best friend.

Feeling guilty for allowing my emotions to get the best of me, I walk back to where they sit. Kevan raises her head and wipes her cheeks with her fingertips, attempting to appear put together. She gives me a half-hearted smile with a lot of obvious effort behind it.

Dorothy speaks first, preventing an awkward silence from settling in.

"Well, now, since I've managed to rain on everyone's parade today, what do you say we take a walk and I will show you where we laid Miss Grace Elizabeth to rest?"

"I think I might have a pretty good idea of where it is. I'm pretty sure I found it earlier—although I didn't know it at the time," Kevan says.

"I'd like that," I say. No other words come to mind, so I say nothing more. What does one say in this situation? Pointing fingers or making accusatory remarks would be as useless as dipping water from a boat full of massive holes.

We walk alongside one another, Dorothy being the only one speaking. "I'm not sure you could find their graves, my dear. At least I hope it wouldn't be that easy. We wanted them to be laid to rest properly. For years, Frances and I came to visit the graves. We couldn't make it known that we did, but we were here often. My old bones won't let me come like they used to."

We finish our walk across the back field in silence and head toward the cellar. Puzzled, I glance over at Kevan and see that her expression matches my own.

Dorothy descends the steps as if slightly unsteady by stepping one foot down, then the other. She repeats until she reaches the door. Kevan turns to look back across the field and then back to Dorothy, with even more confusion settling over her face. Once the door is open, Dorothy turns back to the two of us.

"We decided that this was the best place to bury them. Sort of their own personal mausoleum. We knew it would never be disturbed, even after Frances and I were gone. We dug the graves so they each would have their own personal space—the woman and your sister. It was very important to us that they receive a proper burial. Some time later, we laid the wooden floor to protect their graves. At the far end, some loose boards are wedged in. You'll find their names carved on the undersides of the boards. Nate—your sister's is on the left, the third board down from the end."

Dorothy climbs the steps and then moves aside. I turn on my

phone's flashlight, enter, and kneel on the wooden floor. I look for the board that she named. My hand brushes over the surface. Unless you were looking for it, you would never know that it was possible to move it. I retrieve my pocketknife from my pocket and pry the board loose from its spot. When I turn it over, I find, carved beautifully in cursive, my sister's name. *Grace Elizabeth Hill. Born Oct. 1, 1988. Died August 27, 1996.*

Seeing the last part hits me in the center of the chest. The tombstone I've been visiting all these years doesn't have the word *died*. She has always been missing. The finality of it isn't what I thought it would be. I thought I would feel an immediate sense of closure and peace, but instead, this knowledge feels heavy and pointless. I choke back the lump in my throat to keep from crying. Here it finally is, the end to a long search, and somehow I still feel lost.

I remain squatted on the floor for several minutes and then stand, giving my knees back their circulation. I turn to Kevan and see a mournful look in her eyes. As I hand the piece of wood to her, she takes in a deep breath and holds it. She doesn't look at the board for long before she hands it back to me. I give her a genuine smile and fight the urge to reach out and take her hand. I don't believe she would welcome it. We just stare at the piece of wood in my hand in unified silence.

This poor woman put behind her a childhood from hell and became the person I see standing in front of me. Knowing all of this only makes me want to get to know her more. In fact, I fear I may not get the opportunity after everything that's happened. I look into her face again and it dawns on me that the two of us have had a connection for a long time, though neither was aware. Is that why I was so drawn to her the first time I laid eyes on her? I shake the thought, feeling slightly stupid. I'm sure she will want to run as far away from me as possible after today.

CHAPTER FORTY-NINE

Kevan
Early Summer

I stand motionless for what seems like forever, not speaking. Then Dorothy steps beside me.

"I know you must be full of questions, so is there anything else you'd like to ask me—either of you?" Dorothy turns to look at Nathan as well.

Nathan shakes his head, even though his facial expression looks full of questions.

My eyes remain on the opening of the cellar. I clear my throat. "Earlier, I tripped over two rocks back there." I point just behind the house. "Do you know what those are for?"

"Yes. It's a pet cemetery. We have a few pets buried there. One of my cats, and if memory serves me correctly, a dog of yours. Frances told me about him. His stone is the one with the *B* on it."

As Dorothy answers, my eyes widen with revelation. "I had forgotten about that." I say the words, but they refuse to come out as much more than a whisper. "My father beat our dog to the edge of death. Gammie and I brought him out here and hoped he would get better, but he didn't, so she buried him."

I feel Nathan staring at me with the same facial expression a person might have while watching one of those ASPCA commercials to save the animals. He looks down at the ground.

"I know a lot has been thrown at you two today already, but I need to let you know something else. Would you walk with me a while longer? Maybe take a seat and let these old bones rest?" Dorothy asks.

Nathan gives me a questioning look, and when I don't answer, he does. "Sure, Miss Dorothy."

"Come, then." She takes me by the hand and leads me toward the rocks in the middle of the field. Nathan steps in line on her other side, and she reaches for his hand as well. So the three of us walk hand in hand, and I remain quiet and curious about what else she has to say.

"Kevan, I'm sure you know your grandmother loved and cherished you more than anything. The two of you are—well—were so much alike. Much more than you realize. She used to tell me stories about you during our daily talks, and most of the time, it was like she was talking about herself. You have her stubborn streak, for instance. She was the sort of person who, if she put her mind to something, she would do it. She said you were just like that. But that isn't the main thing. You see—" Dorothy pauses, no longer walking or talking. Nathan and I turn around in front of her, giving her our full attention. "Each of you has a special gift. Frances—you, Kevan—and you, Nate."

Nathan glances at me, and then we both look back at Dorothy.

"How so?" he asks.

Dorothy walks again, her pace short and slow, and we fall into step alongside her. "It's very rare for three people with your gifts to cross paths, and especially rare for two people in the same family to possess the same gift. And for Nate to have the same abilities is nothing short of a miracle. Better yet, it's astonishing."

"You mean my grandmother could see and talk to—" I trail off, getting tangled up in my own question. I swallow and ask, "Why wouldn't she tell me, if she believed I had the same gift?"

"I'm pretty sure she did, when you were very young, but she didn't make a big deal about it. I'm not sure she believed that there was anything to it until you came along. I think it's how she always knew when you needed her. Especially when you were a child. When you began to experience vivid dreams and she discovered your ability to continue to see and talk to your friend—Nate's sister, after she died—then she knew that the gift was real."

Nathan takes an involuntary step back and then asks me, his voice hesitant, "You could see my sister even after she was dead?"

"You could say that. In my eyes, I guess she never died. She grew up and has been with me all of my life. I realize now that's the only reason why I could cope with what happened to her." I pause and scan Nathan's face. "She said that she was here to protect me and help me. I think I saw her the way I wanted to see her, but she was very much there."

Dorothy cuts in. "You see, Nate, you were also born with this gift. There are many who never realize it, and then there are those who don't discover it until later in life. I think your mother knew you were special. She would talk about you dreaming of your sister all the time after she disappeared."

Nathan looks at the ground, his eyes darting to the side as if he is searching his mind for memories of weird phenomena. "I remember telling her about my dreams and that I sometimes heard my sister laughing. She would say that maybe I was just the sort of person who could sense or see things others couldn't. Or maybe that it was my sister's way of saying she was okay. My mother said a lot of things around that time that didn't make sense."

"Yes," Dorothy says sadly. "She was distraught. But I think she also saw that you were hearing things around that time for a reason. I think you're another of those people I was talking about. You didn't truly discover it until later on in life. But it goes farther back than you realize."

"I don't quite follow," Nathan says, sounding skeptical.

"Like Kevan's grandmother used to tell her, people with such gifts walk through this life able to see the spirits that accompany them. You can interact with them, converse with them, and see them when no one else can."

"You mean talk to the dead?" Nathan asks, taken aback.

"Well, I'm not sure it's quite like that. It's just that some people are born in such a unique way that they can still see the people they're close to, even after those people are gone. Like Kevan and your sister."

"I wasn't able to see my sister. I might have thought I heard her, but I didn't see her." Nathan's eyebrows furrow.

"No, but that doesn't mean you don't have the gift. You weren't *meant* to see her. However, you can see me—right?"

Nathan's eyes widen, and he shoots me a look. "Of course. What does that have to do with anything?"

"Come, you two. Let's go take a seat. I'll explain more."

CHAPTER FIFTY

Nathan

We walk back to the rickety porch to find shade. Dorothy takes a seat on the steps, with Kevan on her other side. I lean back against the old porch post, which is still sturdy, supporting the saggy roof. With one foot propped up on the porch, I rest my forearm on my knee and wait to hear what else Dorothy has to say. A million questions spin around in my head.

"Nate, I know I've already filled your mind with overwhelming news, but there is one more thing you should know. You needed me, and I've always been here. I became your godmother because you needed me. I gave you a job because it kept you close. I guess I needed you just the same. But when my time came, I stayed with you because it wasn't yet time to go. I knew this day would come."

"Stayed with me? I don't understand, Miss Dorothy." My eyes dart past Dorothy and I see Kevan looking down at the ground as if she already knows what Dorothy is going to say. I feel as if I've been kept in the dark once more.

"You remember when you worked on that job a few years ago in upstate New York? The one that kept you away for a year?"

"Yes."

"During that time, I started feeling sick and Frances forced me to see a doctor. She was persistent, even though I didn't want to. They diagnosed me with stage four cancer."

I drop my foot back to the ground and sit up. "Why didn't you tell me this?" I bark a little more harshly than I should.

Dorothy holds up her palm as if she is patting the air and says, "Let me finish, son. First, you needed to finish that job you were working on because it was a lot of money, and second, I hate being fussed over. You know that."

When I say nothing, Dorothy continues.

"And after I—well, after, I stayed around for you. You still needed me, because the day had to come when the truth about your sister needed to be revealed. Apparently, the universe felt that the time was now for the both of you."

I remain silent and feel orphaned worse than before. I can't help but wonder if my ears have deceived me, but when I look at both of the women sitting in front of me, I know they haven't. It appears that Kevan has accepted all of it, but it's taking much longer for my mind to catch up. I'm not sure it ever will. Kevan has been told all of her life that she has a gift. Whether she believed it or not, I think it still did a great deal to cushion the shock of it all.

"How was this kept a secret? I mean—" I hear myself stuttering and force myself to swallow and start again. "Was there a funeral? Burial?"

"Frances took care of everything. She did as I wished and kept it a secret. My ashes remain at Frances's house. Kevan can arrange to get them to you. Right, my dear?"

Kevan says, "I remember seeing a yellow urn on her bookshelf. I also remember her telling me years ago that she'd just lost a close friend. That was you?"

"Yes." Dorothy pauses. "I requested that Frances keep my ashes until it was time for Nathan to know. Her passing came sooner." Dorothy turns to Kevan and adds, "Your grandmother left her journals with me, and they remain at my house. I believe it is time for you to have them now." She turns back to me. "Nate? Could you make sure she gets them?"

"Yes."

With apprehension in her voice, Kevan asks, "Was Gammie able to see you after you—" Her voice trails off.

"No. But I think she knew I was still around. Taking care of things until this day came. I suppose she didn't need me, but she knew Nathan did."

"And now? Will you stay?"

She smiles sadly. "The only way it's possible for you to see the spirits that stay with you is because you don't know that we are spirits. Once you find out, we soon lose the ability to be seen." Dorothy turns to look at Kevan. "Because it usually means you don't need us anymore."

Everything I've just learned churns in my head. The fact that I must say goodbye to my sister and my godmother at the same time is almost more than this grown man can handle.

Dorothy stands up. As if she can read my thoughts, she says gently to us both, "I know that this day has been full of revelations and heartache, but it all has brought you two together, which is not a coincidence. It is fate."

I look from Dorothy to Kevan, whose eyes fill with compassion and warmth as she returns my gaze. I feel a sudden, deep connection with her, and even through the shock of it all, a hint of something new plants itself in place.

As if on cue, a thick puff of clouds moves away from the sun, spreading a wave of light across everything around us, and I give Kevan the warmest of smiles in return. I watch Kevan's gaze move across the porch wall of the old house until it stops at a thick cluster of leafy vines that have attached themselves to the house. They look as if they grew there just this morning, with creamy white blossoms spread across the vines. A soft breeze blows, spreading the sweet scent of honeysuckle gently across the air. I watch Kevan's eyes close as she breathes it in.

CHAPTER FIFTY-ONE

———

Kevan
End of Summer

My thoughts bounce around inside my head like a bird trapped in a room with closed windows. I bend forward and pick up the black leather square, and the chain pings as each link lifts from the floor. I hold out my other hand, lower the chain one link at a time into it, and examine the wallet on each side. The stiff crease squeaks as I open it and look at the pockets inside—all of which are empty.

A realization dawns on me. My mother knew! How else would she have gotten this? Did Gammie give it to her? Did she tell her? I stare blankly at the wall, waiting for the answers to reveal themselves, but they don't come. I look back down at what I hold in my hands and I instinctively toss it back down to the floor, as if it has burned me, my hands shaking. Finding out what happened that day, and recovering the memory of it, still causes unexpected reactions.

I take a second to gain my composure and bend forward to pick up the metal box, lay it on the bed, and detach the envelope taped to the inside of the lid. I slide my finger under the edge of the flap, ripping it open, and remove the piece of notebook paper.

My Dear Kevan,

My heart leaps at the kind words that I have never experienced before from my mother. I try to imagine what they would have sounded like if she had actually said them in her own voice, but the sound won't form in my mind.

I see you found my hiding spot. Wasn't it clever? I know you must have a whole swarm of questions now that you have found it. Here are some answers you may be looking for.

I know you believe I wrote you off years ago, but the truth is quite the opposite. Truth is, I am very proud of who you are. I have always been proud of you. Over the years, you looked so happy and mentally healthy without your brothers and me in your life. When you said you were getting married at seventeen, I knew he was not the one for you, but it was your ticket to a better life. I wanted you to get out of here and stay out of here, so I never insisted that you come home to visit more. Sure, I had to pretend to be mad that you didn't come, but being out there, away from the madness of this place, was the best life for you. Your brother Matthew understood my reasons, but James couldn't quite understand. Still, they too wanted the best for you. I knew you were better off getting away from here. Let's face it, girls around here aren't given the same chances as boys, so I knew I needed to give you that. I would have left too if it had been in God's plan, but it wasn't. Your Gammie always kept me up to date on what you were doing and made sure that I knew all about your successes. I had to love you from a distance, which is one of the hardest things to do as a mother.

There are so many things that you never realized about me. When you were a child, I knew you would sneak away to a secret place. I found out because I followed you one day. In fact, I watched you for a long time. I saw you playing with your little friend and it thrilled me that you had one. It is why I never stopped you from going. So between your Gammie and me, we always made sure you were safe going there, but let you go whenever you got the chance to sneak away. Even after your friend's death, I let you go because that is what you needed. I knew you still saw her, somehow, when you went there. Your Gammie always believed that it was part of your gift and that it happened because you still needed her. So we kept your secret and our secret as well.

. . .

I pause for a moment, feeling chill bumps rise on my arms, and look through the window at the cluttered backyard, not really seeing any of it. *Secret?* Confused, I read on.

By now, I know you have found your father's wallet and you have questions about how I got it. At first, I tried to scare you from pursuing answers about what happened that day. I didn't want you going back to that place again. I thought the note on your car would be enough to scare you. You always were stubborn.

I am going to assume that you know now, since you're reading this. Here is the truth. That awful morning, your Gammie came to see you, but you were already gone. She had a gut feeling that something bad was going to happen that day, and when she left, something told me I should follow you. I am so glad I did. I only wish I would have gotten there sooner to save your friend. When I came out of the woods, I made a choice then and there. I chose you. I don't feel that you need to know the details of that day, but just know that I always chose you. Don't get me wrong—I loved your father and I always will. Life with him was a curse more than a blessing, but it was the life that was chosen for me.

Let me end by saying that you have become the woman that I always wanted you to be. Independent and strong. You are ten times the woman I could ever be, and I am so lucky to have been your mother. Please never forget that. Take care of yourself and keep living out my dream for you.

Love, Mom

A single tear drips from my cheek, and I feel my heart beating in an erratic rhythm as the realization sinks in. I can't seem to move or to look away from my mother's letter. Beth told me about what happened that day, but I just assumed it was Gammie who had killed my father. It wasn't. It was my mother!

I read the letter again. As I do, the past begins to rewrite itself. My mother was not the person I always thought she was. I spent my whole life trying not to become a carbon copy of her, but when I think about it, I suppose I am more like her than I realized. She had to be a strong woman to live a lie for so long, pushing her own child away so that child could have a better life than her mother did. In some ways, I have lived out a life of lies as well, only mine were for more selfish reasons. I feel a sense of guilt at knowing the truth now.

I fold the letter and put it in my bag and then return the metal box with the wallet back to its hiding place. There's no way my brothers will ever find it there, and it isn't something I wish to keep. Everything about my father has been left in the past now, and knowing that my mother was on my side the whole time gives me the final sense of peace that I have been searching for. I only wish I'd known before about her love and her sacrifice, but I suppose that peace and this place were never meant to mesh. My mother knew that. There were too many painful memories. Looking back, home was where the hurt was.

I press the contact paper back into place and return the items to the shelf, fold the stepladder and put it back into the hall closet. I shut the door and turn to look at the mirror at the end of the hallway. My heart kicks into warp speed as a man walks into view. Then I breathe a sigh of relief when I see it is my brother's reflection. James.

"How's it going in here?" he asks.

"You scared the living shit out of me." I pat my chest and let out a sharp exhale. "It's good, I guess. Our mother didn't let go of anything, though."

Two days ago, at our mother's viewing, James walked up to me without saying a word and gave me a long hug. When he let go, he looked me in the eye and whispered, "I'm sorry I've been such a dick." He squeezed my hand and walked to our mother's coffin.

Something about that one minor act erased years of silence and anger between us. Years of stubbornness between two people who just misunderstood each other.

There is something about death that can somehow renew life. Estranged siblings and relatives suddenly forget their stubbornness and pride and remember the lost love between them as if it had never been lost to begin with—just buried so deep for a while that it took a catastrophic event for it to uncover itself. Everything can begin anew.

I don't think I will ever tell my brothers the circumstances around our father's death. For me, finding out what happened gave me a different view of our mother—a positive one. I don't think them knowing would have the same effect. In fact, it might be quite the opposite.

I stack one last box in the living room and give James a sincere hug. He walks outside with me to find Matthew. I give Matthew a full hug as well, and I tell both my brothers that I will see them soon.

As I climb into my car, I hear a text come through on my phone. It's Nate, checking in on me to make sure I'm okay. Ever since that life-altering day for the both of us, we've been inseparable. We speak daily and have spent every weekend together.

Before Nate, I was like a cut flower. I had cut off my own roots years before while still trying to show strength and beauty. It was tiring and lonely. Nate is helping me with growing new roots and grounding me in a more settled life. Teaching me that I'm good enough just the way I am. Showing me how to let someone love me.

Gammie taught me that I could do anything that I wanted to do, all by myself. Nate is teaching me that it's okay to lean on someone too. He's teaching me how to live free of fear and, most of all, how to be happy. There's one thing I know for sure—you can't experience amazing kisses like Nate's when you try to do everything all on your own.

EPILOGUE

Frances June Hill

"Hurry up, Mommy!" five-year-old Frannie yells as she darts into the kitchen before stomping through the house and stopping in the open doorway that leads to the front porch. She stands there in the center of the doorframe, staring out across the front lawn as she runs her small fingertips over the raised carvings of the oak tree.

"Daddy?" she asks. "How come they didn't put all that green stuff hanging down on this tree?"

"What do you mean, honey?"

"I mean, like that green stuff hanging on all the trees out there." Frannie points out across the front drive. "You know—that stuff that looks like monsters and dinosaurs in the trees. How come they didn't put it on this door?"

Nathan walks up the front steps to stand in front of the massive door that he has admired since he was a boy himself. "Well, I think maybe this door was made before all of that green stuff grew on the trees. It's called Spanish moss. So, you can see monsters and dinosaurs out there?"

"Oh, yeah. They look huge!" Frannie hops out onto the porch and then hops several more times, stopping before she gets to the steps. "See," she says, pointing, "that one looks like Sulley from *Monsters Inc.*, and that one looks kinda like the Beast. You know? From *Beauty and the Beast?*"

"Oh, yeah," Nathan agrees. "I see it."

Kevan steps through the front door, closing it behind her, and asks, "You all ready for our picnic?"

"Yes!" Frannie squeals.

Kevan hands the picnic basket to Nathan and they descend the steps, Frannie hopping off of the last one. Nathan and Kevan each grab one of Frannie's hands, and they walk down the front drive, swinging her between them. Nathan stops in front of the familiar tree and asks Frannie, "What do you see in *this* tree?"

"Ummm, I see Rex from *Toy Story*. Only this one looks meaner."

Nathan gives Kevan a smile and then says, "I used to see a T. Rex there all the time when I was a little boy."

"Were you five, like me?" Frannie asks as she holds up five fingers.

"Well, maybe a little older. But I used to think the T. Rex was growling at the dinosaur in that tree. I always thought he looked like he had big, mean teeth. But now I can see Rex too."

Frannie leans her head way back to look up toward the top of the other tree. "That's the one I think looks like Littlefoot," she says.

"Why, yes, I can see Littlefoot too," Kevan agrees.

The three of them walk along together, stopping before each tree as they give the Spanish moss life by naming what they see. They take a detour from the driveway and walk toward one lonely tree that has been standing on the plantation longer than any other. Neither Nathan nor Kevan had ever looked at this tree closely before they discovered, as they walked together one day before Frannie was born, two old, deep carvings on the back side of its thick trunk. Carvings that had been there since the days of Dotty and Marge.

When Nathan and Kevan had found this treasure, they'd known instantly what they should do with Dorothy's and Frances's ashes. Now the two women who had raised, molded, and loved them rested beneath this tree together. Just as they would have liked it.

Sitting under the shade of the tree, Nathan and Kevan tell little Frannie stories about Dotty and Marge—and Dorothy and Frances. The censored, kid versions, of course. After they eat their picnic, Frannie jumps and skips back toward the drive, picking up rocks and flowers. Nathan and Kevan cuddle on the blanket as they look up through the branches of the tree. They lie there in silence, listening to birds, katydids, and the occasional chatter of Frannie in the distance.

Some time later, Frannie gallops back to the blanket with a bunch of wildflowers in one hand and something else cupped in the other.

"Here, Mommy," Frannie says, handing Kevan the small bouquet.

"Aww, thank you," Kevan says as she clutches them in her hand and sniffs them.

"Here, Daddy," Frannie says and opens her other hand to reveal three long stems of wildflowers, braided together, shaped in a circle, and tied together on the ends. "It's a bracelet."

Nathan's eyes shift into confusion, and his face flushes. He looks at Kevan and then back at the bracelet, taking it in his hands reluctantly. "Thank you, honey." He sits up and turns to look in the direction from which Frannie has just come. After searching in all directions, he turns back, eyebrows furrowed, and asks, "Did you make this?"

"Not by myself. The girl and the nice ladies helped me."

Kevan stands quickly and looks around. "What? Where did you see them?"

"Over there." Frannie points toward the far end of the lane. Both Nathan and Kevan take several swift steps in that direction. Frannie adds, "They said they couldn't stay because they were needed somewhere else."

"What did they look like, Frannie?" Nathan asks.

Frannie bends down to pick a small clover. "The little girl was bigger than me. Her hair was like mine, only blond. The two ladies were all wrinkly."

Nathan and Kevan look at each other, at a loss for words. Finally, Kevan whispers to Nathan, "Surely not. Is it possible?" Then she turns to Frannie. "Hey, Frannie? Why don't you try to find me some of those yellow flowers I like?"

Frannie skips away. When she's out of earshot, Kevan says to Nathan, "Do you think she really saw them? If it even was them?"

"I don't know. Had to be them. Do you think we passed our gift to her somehow?"

"I suppose it's possible. How else—" Kevan's words trail off and she looks over at Frannie and then off into the distance. She smiles.

Silent, lost in their thoughts, they both watch as Frannie skips through the grass. Then they walk back to their blanket. Lying back, they curl up together and look at the words carved in the tree.

Marge + Dotty, forever best friends, 1962.

ACKNOWLEDGMENTS

This book for me was like having a first child. I nourished, coddled and raised it with very little knowledge on what I was doing. It taught me numerous lessons while I loved it into maturity. I wouldn't have been able to achieve this without the following amazing people in my life.

Thank you Brooklin for being my first reader and biggest fan. You gave me courage and believed in me when I couldn't. Your support kept me moving forward with this life-long dream.

Thank you Ashley for always supporting me and shooting it to me straight. Most of all for making me laugh at the times when I didn't think I could.

Thank you Paul for being my rock through this and beyond. You believed in me when I didn't believe in myself. None of this would have been possible without you. I am forever grateful.

Thank you to my editor Sara Jane for working your magic and making the story so much better. You were the sweet spice to this recipe.

Thank you Clarissa for the outstanding book cover. Your artistic talent brought the story to life.

Thank you Sadie Mae for the production and narration of the audiobook. You brought each and every character in the story to life. Amazing job!

Last but certainly not least, thank you to my readers, supporters, and fans. Writers are nothing without readers. I couldn't do this without you! I hope you will stick with me for the next one.

ABOUT THE AUTHOR

I've always had the dream of becoming a writer, but like so many others, I put my dream on hold. I went on to complete two masters' degrees in education and have taught for over fourteen years. After raising two successful daughters and sending them on their way to college, I decided to scratch the itch and write my first novel, Where Secrets Stay. I live in Kentucky with my husband and two daughters.
Visit me online at www.cherannwright.com

Milton Keynes UK
Ingram Content Group UK Ltd.
UKHW011043231123
433129UK00005B/451